White Thirst

Surviving a New Life

Mike Anka

Cheers!

Contents

"They were young, beautiful and desperate for freedom. Only death could stop them. Some of them stopped, some of them didn't."

"A thirst I quench drinking this day
In small sips, painful and delayed."

Note From The Author

This is a true story. All timelines are approximately correct. All locations are authentic, as are the events. The names of all the people in the book have been altered in order to protect the privacy and security of some of the real characters found inside.

White Thirst

Chapter 1

Timisoara, Romania
August 1979

The dark back streets of the downtown core suddenly light up under the bouncing car headlights blasting through the streets, police sirens howling behind them. They are in a reckless, hot pursuit. Ahead of them, not more than around one hundred feet away, a black motorcycle with a black-leathered rider - nearly invisible with its headlights off - is racing ahead, looking for gradually narrower cobblestone streets. The rider is an expert at his job; he jumps, hurls and scrapes the big bike around corners, occasionally red-orange flames igniting under the frame as the chassis grinds into the pavement under the lean angles. Running out of streets, he quickly changes direction, blazing into a large public park. Sets of swings, jungle gyms, sand boxes and aged trees fly by. The park is deserted at this late hour of the night.

Suddenly, he has a plan.

The cops quickly second guess him however. Pistol rounds ring out, scraping the bike and chipping the trees nearby. The moving, zigzagging black target is hard to hit.

The second police cruiser cuts across the grass and heads full-speed towards the canal a few hundred feet away. From three different simultaneous angles, a mad race is developing for a passenger foot bridge crossing the river. The bike and the cruisers, both speeding, both nearly out of control, arrive at about the same time at the foot of the raised bridge.

Bastian, the rider, quickly shifts down a gear and accelerates the engine making his motorcycle raise up on one wheel, howling, just enough to clear the concrete barrier in front of the bridge entrance. Getting air, the bike and its rider fly over the barrier entering the four-foot narrow concrete and steel crossing bridge. The first cruiser crashes against the concrete posts of the bridge as both cops start shooting their pistols at the rider.

Bastian, adrenaline pumping high, laughs heartily and maintains his machine almost straight up on its rear wheel until landing it safely on the other side. A moment later, the black bike and its dark rider disappear in the city streets on the other side of the river.

Chapter 2

The old city is baking under the merciless early evening sun. The downtown core with its old, solid buildings touched by patina of time holds and protects a large numbers of people amidst thick brick and granite walls.

The colorful umbrellas and canopies of various sidewalk cafés perched in front of the gigantic store windows flutter gently in the light wind. A screeching streetcar winds by nearly empty, the driver ducked low under his transit-issue blue cap and large sunglasses.

A young man, about twenty-four, athletic, handsome features and with long curly hair, worn leather jacket, jeans and soft motorcycle-riding boots, exits one of the apartment buildings above the stores. He looks around wearily, expecting imminent danger. There is none in sight. He walks to a black sports motorcycle parked at the curb, kick-starts the large engine and the starts the machine up, blowing grey smoke into the street. Zipping up his leather jacket, he mounts the bike and rides away in a storm of smoke and burnt rubber. His name is Michael Agrafa and this is Timisoara, the town in which he was born and raised. Under pressing events coming up shortly, there is a reasonable chance that he won't see it again for many years to come.

He rides fast and furious displaying excellent skill, zigzagging in the street traffic. He rides for several minutes, occasionally looking behind him until he reaches the outskirts of the large city.

He slows his ride as the road narrows and the government-owned farms change the landscape of his route. He turns into an unpaved side-road where the motorcycle's tires stir up a large cloud of dust behind him. Noticing this, Michael slows down his bike, making the dust behind him disappear, thus masking his passage. He rides slow and cautiously, passing a couple of farms, one cattle, the other corn.

He pulls into a modest gravel driveway, no longer then eighty feet, ending up in front of a small red-brick bungalow. He rides around the house towards a large wooden barn built two hundred feet behind it. Parking the motorcycle, he descends and quickly looks around for followers. There are neither people nor vehicles in sight, except in the distance where a group of small children run barefoot on the road, laughing loud and stirring dust. A lonely horse on Michael's property raises its head toward the children's amusement.

Michael opens one side of the large barn door and pushes his motorcycle inside, immediately closing it. Through the loose boards of the barn wall, he takes another quick look at the road and the neighborhood. Releasing a sigh, he turns away, climbing up the steep stairs leading to a large and bohemian loft.

There is a sense of urgency and danger in his movements. His body is tense under the avalanche of thoughts rushing through his mind. So many important details, so little time... and this intense emotion tightening up his chest; mixed and powerful feelings wanting to burst and surface. Taking a deep breath, he reaches his sophisticated loft. Before turning the lights on, he closes the heavy curtains in front of the large windows facing the farmlands and the connecting roads below.

Once the curtains are sealing the windows, he walks to the wall switch and turns on the ceiling spotlights; the interior rushes into view. It's a very large loft with an open center which is protected by wood and brass banisters all around, surrounding a shining stainless-steel firefighter-style sliding pole. Posts and beams of rough stained wood and coarse metal bracings give the place authenticity and warmth.

Michael kneels beside a large wooden trunk resting on the wide-board hardwood floor. Unlocking it he starts retrieving various objects, his movements precise, knowing, rushed. Besides the open trunk he carefully places four different passports, a small wad of US dollars tightly rolled and held by a rubber band, certain one-page government sealed documents and a folding switchblade. He nervously checks his wristwatch: nine-twenty-two in the evening.

Walking over to one of the curtains, he peeks outside - it's already dark. Satisfied, he turns to the trunk when the ringing of a camouflaged telephone breaks the tense silence, making him jump. He walks to the wall, and lifting up the lead of a wooden box retrieves an old-style rotary receiver. He feels distracted:

"Yes...?"

He listens to the intense female voice on the other end: Marian, his friend: "It's me... I need to talk to you."

"Not now, it's not a good time, we discussed it earlier. I'll stop by your place when I'm finished with the apples. I should be there shortly after midnight... I need this line free now." Suddenly he hangs up and begins pacing the loft. A few moments later, the telephone rings again. Michael picks it up on the first ring.

"It's me. I need to talk to you tonight..." He listens to the other voice, then: "Yes... *Almost... Tonight is the night when the ghost horses go to the silver river.* Yes, as we planned..."

He laughs nervously at the other person's comments and gently hangs up the receiver, returning to his activity, preparing small pouches of plastic bags, rolling up the old documents, every so often checking the driveway for signs of movement. Placing the document he has in his hand on the floor, he stretches and starts looking through this place, so dear to him. He walks slowly touching objects, caressing a wooden beam, touching a poster on the wall...

He is saying goodbye to the place, knowing that he will never be back to see it again.

Suddenly, his alert eyes catch a passing beam of light in front of the barn. Quickly walking over to the curtains, he peeks outside and smiles, walking to the firefighter pole. He lowers himself to the main floor and immediately opens the large door allowing the other black motorcycle to roll in, engine still running. He quickly closely and locks the door while Bastian turns his engine off and dismounts his bike.

"Nobody followed me," Bastian says, answering Michael's mute question. "But I had a good run with the blue-boys," he continues, laughing and removing his helmet and leather shoulder bag, placing them on the floor. "They tailed me, but I lost them in the kids' park by riding across the river. That narrow foot passage we used to dive off from when we were kids - the bastards tried to shoot me again..."

Michael listens carefully, thinking and pacing. "I'm quite positive somebody spilled the beans on our plan. Good thing is that nobody knows the full details other then you and me." They quickly exchange a glance. "Not even Marian, I assure you."

"A few more short hours and we're on our way," Bastian says excitedly, checking some detail on his motorcycle. He is tall and slender, muscular and handsome. His very long black hair tightens into a pony tail dangling on his back.

"Yeah, a few more hours... I can't wait either. We meet as planned. Be there at three-thirty."

"No worries, I'll be there," he looks at his friend: "Have you gotten the goods?" Michael points to the loft.

"Upstairs."

He takes another quick glance to the road then climbs the steep ladder, followed by Bastian.

Michael starts showing Bastian the goods - documents, cash, small objects and gadgets only known to them.

"We have to make the packages as small as possible 'cos the bike chassis, it's not very wide," Bastian explains, rolling one of the bags with his fingers. "How's the cash situation?"

Michael points at the three tightly rolled plastic bags. "Six hundred and forty-eight US dollars and some other European mixed currency." Bastian shakes his heads, thinking. "Not much," he says picking up a roll of documents: "How about the paper work?"

"All done. Your diplomas and certifications - and mine - all here," Michael says, showing him his handy-work.

"Not bad. I think its bike-time."

"Yep."

They both use the pole to lower themselves back down to the main floor.

"This is what I need:" Bastian says walking to the black motorcycles. "Compressed air, no less than sixty-seventy pounds of air pressure, air and hand wrenches, good portable lights - two if possible, the two jack-pumps I know you have, electrical extension cords-"

"Got them all," Michael says, smiling. He knows that he himself is the 'diplomat', doing the bullshit talks, negotiations, planning and strategies - whereas Bastian is the action and techno guy of the two; a talented mechanical engineer with multi-disciplinary knowledge... *and* a hell of a good mechanic and road-racing warrior.

Michael shivers to a passing thought. "What...? Sorry, bud, coming right up," he shakes himself back to reality, looking at his friend setting up the motorcycles for the undertaking.

By this time, Bastian has removed his leather jacket and rolled up his sleeves, showing muscular bare arms whilst trying to place Michael's bike on a work-stand.

"I need some help here," he calls to Michael, who has just started the air-compressor in the back of the barn, carrying two large toolboxes.

"Coming."

He places the heavy boxes on the floor and helps Bastian raise the motorcycle on the stand.

"That's more like it," says Bastian expertly while opening up one of the tool boxes. "Not bad!"

"What can I help you with?"

"Just stand by for a while; I'll need your help shortly," Bastian says and starts work on the bike. Within minutes, he has removed the seat and all of the side covers.

"It looks so naked!" Michael comments.

"That's the whole point. Now, the fun begins." Bastian plugs in a drill and starts making a hole in the bike frame. After this he starts dismounting several mechanical components, carefully placing them on a piece of cardboard beside the bike.

"Pass me the money rolls first," he says, opening a small cavity inside the bike's framework. Michael passes him a couple of bags. "I want you to watch where I put everything, just in case something happens to me." Michael nods.

The documents follow the money, along with some more small gadgets and gizmos they both consider important.

**

It is late at night when Bastian finally turns off the light and wipes his greasy hands on a rag.

"That should do it," he concludes, glancing over both motorcycles which look 'normal' again.

"Not bad," Michael agrees. Bastian starts arranging his T-shirt, slips into his leather jacket and zips it up, pulling on his fine leather riding gloves.

"See you at three-thirty at the crossing," he says, getting to his motorcycle.

"I'll be there."

Michael opens the barn door and allows Bastian to ride out. A moment later, the black motorcycle, riding with the headlights off, disappears at the end of the dark driveway. Michael walks back in, places away the tools, turns off the loud air-compressor and tidies the place up a tad, hiding evidence of their earlier activity.

Walking back up to his loft, Michael glances at a couple of small travel bags already made up, resting on his bed. Putting his own seasoned leather jacket on along with riding gloves, he grabs the bags. Throwing them on his shoulders, he jumps on the pole and slides down to the main floor. He starts his motorcycle, rides it outside of the barn, comes back to lock the barn and re-mounts his machine. A second later he is driving fast along his driveway, turning into the road which heads back to the city.

***

As Michael rides his bike, his mind is working fast. Several thought patterns cross their paths, fueled by powerful emotions making him sweat under his helmet. This is the night when he will leave everything behind; everything he has worked for - all his achievements, friends, relatives, parents and plans - he releases a deep sigh - maybe, even his life.

"It's worth the risk," he concludes in his helmet as his motorcycle enters the poorly lit streets of the Timisoara suburbs.

He rides fast, his eyes recording everything all at once: small trees on the street, a lit window in a humble house with someone sitting alone at a table, a distant sound of a dog crying, the old and charming buildings of the city. As his motorcycle comes closer to the inner core, the streets become brighter; more lights are on in the tall apartment buildings lining the boulevard, although several trees shade the sidewalks. There is a frantic pulse in the air and Michael shivers under its intensity.

The city is alive, its heartbeat pounding in Michael's temples like a metronome of times past. He slows his ride as he approaches an old villa-style apartment building.

Chapter 3

The summer night is settling fast on the Polish landscape as the two black motorcycles blend into the highway traffic on their way to the Czech border crossing.

There is not much traffic on the highway at this time, so the riders open up the throttles and blast forward, checking out their 'new' bikes. The results are not disappointing; the razor sharp handling and the sudden acceleration sending the boys flying through the fast coming turns on the road.

They slow down a little when the first signs of Czechoslovakia begin to show up on the overhead panels. They cruise at the speed limit for a while, until the next border crossing sign indicates ten kilometers, upon which they start looking for a rest area. They find one a few kilometers ahead, and pulling in turn off the engines and look around. There is only one small car at the other end of the parking lot. They allow the steaming engines to cool off for a while as they dismount and Michael takes out his map. Unfolding it on top of a picnic table, Bastian helps by shining a small flashlight onto it.

"Thanks. Watch this." Michael points his finger on a line resembling the border between the Czech Republic and Austria. "We have to be very careful and quiet once we are in the zone. The Czech Army patrolling the borderline is very smart. They have vicious dogs which could sniff us out a mile away."

"What can we do about that?" Bastian asks, a little nervously. "I hate the border-mutt kind."

"So do I," Michael says and scrounges for something in his bag. He finds it. Removing a small pouch, he unzips it slightly, allowing a small whiff to escape.

"Ugh!" Bastian grimaces in disgust. "What the hell is that?"

"Bad stuff, man...brains and bones and guts all fermented together with some very vicious additives. Just imagine the dogs which have a sense of smell a thousand times more sensitive!" Bastian smiles. "Where the hell did you get that stuff from?"

"At the fair, yesterday" Michael answers casually.

"I wouldn't want to be a dog with this shit around," Bastian says, stepping a few paces away from the potent bag.

Michael laughs: "We're gonna be covered with it."

Bastian shakes his head in disgust. "What other yummy surprises like this you got up your sleeve, mister planner?" He looks at Michael suspiciously.

"That's about it. Now, listen." They turn back to the map, Michael hashing a certain area high in the mountains. "This is the basic area we are going to attempt, but we'll detail it when we get there. For now, we do the crossing. Let me do the talking, unless you feel like giving them a fat lip in Polish?"

Bastian thinks for a moment. "I'll do it."

"Good." Michael folds his map and places it back into his tank bag. "You ready?"

"Let's do it."

There are no more words exchanged between the two friends as they mount their gears and firing up the motorcycles ride out slowly from the rest area, heading for the crossing.

The ride is slow and intense, not because of the crossing to the Czech Republic, but because of the following tentative attempt to Austria. Each one of the riders is involved in their thoughts and emotions and before they realize they are now approaching the red flashing lights and the barricades of the border crossing ahead of them.

There are only three vehicles in front of them; two transport trucks licensed in Denmark and a small vehicle with the license plate issued in the Czech Republic.

The international carrier trucks have their papers cleared in minutes and the small car glides right through, itself of course going back home.

They are the next up.

Gliding slowly to the customs officer who is accompanied by a single armed soldier, they stop and remove their helmets providing a mandatory 'clear look' for him.

He asks them for their passports, which they provide, and Bastian addresses the officer in Polish: "Just heading back to school. We had a reunion with our Polish friends in Wroclaw. We're beat."

The officer looks them both over and disappears into the customs house, checking the passports. He reappears a few moments later and hands them back to Bastian: "Have a safe trip, guys," he says in plain English. The boys give him a big smile and an okay sign, mounting their machines.

Within minutes they are riding through Czech territory, relieved and energetic.

Chapter 4

The next several kilometers sees them riding in silence. Yet another hour later and the road starts climbing as the mountains begin to show in the distance. It is sunset and the landscape looks pretty; hilly with forest on both sides of the highway. At the next rest area they pull in and come close to a picnic table. The rest area is deserted.

Michael dismounts and lights up a cigarette, taking in a couple of thirsty drags.

"We're getting closer now. How do you feel?" he asks, looking at Bastian who seems contained, a little pale.

"I'm good," he replies without enthusiasm.

"We can pitch a tent and try it tomorrow night if you want," Michael says.

"I'd rather try it tonight," Bastian replies in a calm voice.

"Me too. Okay, then. Let's grab a bite from the sacks and get down to our plan. We have to move fairly quickly in order to find the right spot."

"Let's get to it," Bastian agrees. "Is there anything I can help you with?"

"There is. Take a close look at both bikes and make sure they're gonna take the drop into the water. We need them to start after that."

"I'll do that."

Michael offers Bastian a sandwich he's been saving in his saddle bag and resumes his careful planning.

After a few minutes, Bastian returns to his side. "We're all good. The bikes are as ready as they can be."

"Good stuff. Let go to the drop zone then."

They silently gear up, mount their bikes and slowly ride out from the rest area, Michael in the lead.

By the time they reach the higher elevations, it is getting dark. They ride for a while until pulling over into a small clearing beside the road. There is no traffic right now. Michael has been taking notice of visual markers for a while now and when he unfolds his map and lays it open atop of his bike, he manages to locate their whereabouts on the woody landscape. Bastian again, assists with his flashlight. Michael points to a spot on the map with his pen: "We're here. The creek is on the other side. That means we have to drop on that side, obviously."

"We need to find a deep spot in the stream and that's not going to be easy."

"No, but we'll find one."

"It's not only for the safety of the drop. We also have to make sure that we don't break our limbs, make any noise, damage or flood the bikes, hook some trip wires or wrestle with wild patrol dogs!"

"Details..." Michael says sarcastically and Bastian knows that his friend is dead serious, acknowledging the warning. "We start watching the stream about two miles from here - without headlights."

"It won't be the first time," remarks Bastian.

Michael packs up the map, and once again they mount their bikes and start riding, Michael as always in the lead. After two miles of riding uphill on the mountain road, Michael turns his headlights off. Bastian immediately follows.

Guided by the dim moonlight, their night-riding trained eyes follow small marks on the roadside and in the landscape. They can now both hear the louder roar of the fast-running brook to their left. They start slowing to a crawl now, closely watching the deep drop and the stream below.

Michael pulls over to the side of the road and stops. Bastian pulls up beside him a second later and his look follows his friend's outstretched hand.

"The water here looks deep enough to cushion our drop," Bastian says, in a low voice charged with nervous overtones.

"This is the spot indeed. See the shape of that large rock over there?" Michael points to a distorted granite rock on the Austrian side of the creek. "That's the rock Marin told me about on the phone." They both look at the dark landscape, counting, measuring and estimating space and time and their boiling emotions.

Michael breaks the silence after a while. "What you figure?"

"Let's do it before somebody shows up," Bastian says thinking logically. "By the looks of it, we need a good fifty or sixty kilometers per hour to gain some distance." Michael watches an imaginary launching ramp in front of them: "Yep. About right... I go first. Just make sure you don't land on top of me."

"Better yet - let's ride and drop at the same time, together."

"Before we do that, I almost forgot, here - cover yourself with your favorite dog repellent!" Michael says, passing him a handful of the disgusting stuff. Both cringe and gag, but smear it on their bodies and hands. "It's water resistant." Michael explains.

"Great, now you tell me!" grumbles Bastian. "Will we live with it for the rest of our lives?" He looks at Michael who laughs nervously.

"Only a few years - five tops!"

Michael positions his motorcycle on the opposite side of the road, establishing a short launch way. Bastian follows him. The two young men look at each other for a long second. They nod to one another and in the same instant accelerate and cross the mountain highway flying over the ridge.

With a subtle splash, the heavy motorcycles and their riders hit the water, disappearing beneath it.

A few moments later they both surface. Breathing hard and holding on to their motorcycles with all their might, they manage to push the machines to the other shore, and with great physical effort they reach the first bushes on the Austrian land. Dropping the bikes, they blow into their frozen hands, both remaining motionless. They can hear and see the Czech border patrol soldiers on the other side scouring the land with powerful searchlights.

The two runaways noiselessly ease themselves into the small bushes, trembling with cold, their teeth chattering, and their fear of being caught or shot dead, insurmountable.

As the soldiers' voices become louder, in spite of the danger, Michael falls asleep. He starts snoring lightly. Bastian shakes his head in wonder...they could be killed any minute or shredded by crazy patrol dogs! He pokes him lightly in the ribs and Michael stops making the noise. But in spite of the imminent danger - or perhaps because of it - Bastian starts yawning too. This is the way it's going to play itself out - they either die or they don't - a simple equation.

Pulling himself all the way inside the bush, he closes his eyes. A moment later heavy rain drops starts pounding the bushes and the grass around him.

He can hear loud cursing in Czech as angry voices call their dogs off, walking away toward shelter.

"Oh, well," Bastian sighs with relief and a second later he too is sound asleep.

Chapter 5

A sliver of sunshine penetrating through the dense bushes lands on Michael's face. Feeling a small heat source, Michael opens his eyes and moves them around in confusion. "What the hell-"

"Shhh!" Bastian hushes him down, wide awake too, much more aware than his buddy. "Stay quiet. We're hiding in the bush on the Austrian side, remember?"

"Oh, shit! You mean we made it through?"

"Not yet. Keep your voice down. We still haven't crossed the no-man's-land strip yet."

"You mean we are on the other side of the creek but still on the Czech side?"

"That's exactly what I mean, and the soldiers and their shitty, efficient dogs could be back any minute," Bastian whispers, all his senses alert.

In the same instant, both young men hear the distant barking of vicious border-patrol German Shepherds.

"Shit!" releases Michael. "Go, grab the bikes and run," he says suddenly wide awake, jumping out from the bush and finding his motorcycle covered in mud in neighboring shrubbery. Picking it up with visible effort, he pushes it away from the river, inland, toward Austria. Bastian follows close behind. Their wet clothes are steaming under the morning sun. The motorcycles leave obvious tire tracks behind them.

Adrenaline charged they both set running, pushing the motorcycles through muddy fields, tall wet grass and weeds making the advance difficult. Michael, breathing hard and sweating, is almost out of breath. He stops and stands his motorcycle up and opening its safety valves he releases the fuel line and kick starts hard. Nothing happens. With fury driven by high adrenaline he jams the level down so hard again that the engine, chocking and coughing fumes, catches on. Throttling it with feeling he manages to fire up all cylinders.

A moment later, taking a quick glimpse at his friend who nods fervently, he jumps on the machine and zigzags away, slipping and sliding on the wet terrain, barely keeping it in an upright position.

A moment later, Bastian fires up his engine also and jumping on the saddle takes off on one wheel as angry barking dogs can be heard behind him. A rattle of automatic rifle bullets whistle by his ears, burying themselves in the tall grass.

A couple of small explosions erupt immediately behind them as the motorcycle tires activate trip-wires buried in the grass. Michael hears them as well, and a high-caliber AK-47 slug buries itself in his rear suspension shock, barely missing his leg.

The old daredevil energy is suddenly awake in both of them. Ignoring death and mutilation, they roar their motorcycles into high gear and fly through the fields and low bushes. Laughing nervously and defiantly they storm away on the solid ground of the free world.

They ride hard continuously until they merge onto a well-kept country road. Engines howling, they follow it, riding harder still, driven by wild energies, away from the Czech borderline.

They ride fast for several miles, passing a few small and tidy Austrian villages until Michael figures they are far enough from the Iron Curtain's invisible and potent pull.

Coming to a halt on the side of the road at a small empty patch, they shut down the engines and remove their helmets, loudly slapping several hi-fives with both hands.

"Son of a bitch, we did it! We really did it!" Bastian screams out excitedly.

"Everything went according to plan" Michael tries a serious approach. "...and a shitload of luck! Cheers!" Again they slap hi-fives and Bastian checks the fuel gauges on both motorcycles.

"We have to tank up in within a hundred k from here. Beware."

Michael nods and digs out his map. "Next big city is Linz, about one-eighty from here. Can we make it on the existing gas?" Michael asks his buddy.

"Maybe, but we'll have to cut back the throttles a tad to make it last that long."

"Okay. One another thing, what the hell were the Czech soldiers doing back there shooting inland in a foreign country? They were breaking international laws."

"Of course they were. They are not allowed, of course, but on the other hand, the Austrians look the other way - pretending they never see anything... as long as every refugee is caught or shot."

"Nice arrangement," Michael says sarcastically, gnashing his teeth.

"We made it, man. That's all that matters."

"Yes. It's all that matters."

They mount their motorcycles and ride away, following the country road.

After a few miles they come to an intersection which merges with an international highway, indicating Linz as the next major city. They jump on the highway and ride along, breathing in the air of freedom.

Their excitement is short-lived however as after a few miles of highway driving, the sign of a toll booth is warning them to slow to ten kilometers per hour. As they do, taking the next bend on the hilly highway, they run into a toll booth setup blocking the road. Barely having any foreign cash left, they reluctantly approach one of several booths. The charge is high, indicating a private highway and the problem is that the system either takes a credit card or a highway token. They have neither.

Looking around for help, they realize that the toll booths are fully automated with no attendants on site.

"Shit, man. We're out of luck on this one," Michael grumbles unhappily reading the instructions on the wall.

"I've got an idea," Bastian says. "It might work. Come. We go back on the highway. See that sign?" he points to a small sign indicating a lane which returns the vehicle to the opposite site of the highway, built for people like them who can't - or don't want to pay the toll.

Mounting their bikes, they follow the lane back onto the highway in the direction they came from.

It is Bastian who leads the way this time, looking carefully to the side of the road. After about three kilometers he sees what he was looking for. Pulling the bikes to the side of the road they stop, Michael looking curiously at his friend.

"I thought I saw this area on our way through," Bastian says pointing to the side of the shoulder. "This is a service road for the highway maintenance crews."

"So what?" Michael asks still not getting it.

"We get on it and with some luck we might be able to jump onto the highway from the service road," Bastian explains, his eyes following the road winding toward the highway which has high concrete blocks on the side preventing any access or exit from it.

"*If* we don't run into an angry maintenance crew!" Michael finally gets it. Bastian nods and a minute later they are riding along the service road. Within minutes the road butts into the side of the highway, but there is a steel grill gate stopping the traffic. The two riders pull up in front of the steel gate. Bastian dismounts and kicks the gate furiously. It holds.

Michael dismounts and, approaching the gate, pulls it towards him with one finger. With a squeak the gate opens.

"It's not locked," Michael states and Bastion laughs nervously. Moments later they ride through and merge with the highway on their way to the city of Linz.

Chapter 6

They ride quietly for a while, each preoccupied with their own sense of perception of the free world. Everything so fresh, so touchable and real makes their heads dizzy.

Reality check kicks in eleven kilometers before the city of Linz. Michael's engine suddenly starts making guttural noises, coughing and choking black fumes, losing speed. Michael, a seasoned rider, immediately engages the clutch and coasts the engine to a stop on the shoulder of the highway.

Bastian pulls behind him, dismounts his bike and, leaning over, touches the oil trail Michael's bike developed in his wake with his index finger. He smells it and looks at his body. "Not good." Coming over to Michael's bike he examines it closely. "You blew an oil gasket," he states casually. "The engine is most likely almost toast already. Here; a bullet hole."

"Nice. I *really* needed this," Michael says furiously. "I think the engine *is* toast. I lost a lot of oil pressure."

"I can patch it up a bit but this is gonna be a Band-Aid I wouldn't rely much on. Gimme your lighter." Michael does and Bastian makeshifts something to temporarily seal the leak. "See if you can make it to Linz. It's not that far."

"Eleven kilometers," Michael answers, remembering the sign he saw earlier on the highway.

"Good luck," Bastian says mounting his bike. "You ride ahead of me so I'll be right behind you in case it blows. Keep your fingers close to the clutch."

"I always do," Michael says and fires up the engine which does not sound too good.

They ride along toward Linz, Michael handling his bike gingerly. In spite of his efforts, the engine coughs and spits fire on the dual exhaust pipes, jittering and fluctuating its speed, slowly dying.

Michael is working hard to keep the motorcycle straight on the highway. The dying engine is occasionally bucking the bike, nearly throwing Michael off the handles - but he holds it fast and manages every time.

In the next thirty minutes, they both start to see the glow across the landscape ahead of them. Michael in front, Bastian close behind him, they enter the outskirts of town following the street signs towards the downtown core. They find it shortly, and turning down narrow streets they reach a cobblestone-paved square where a farmers' market is being held.

This suits Michael just fine. He needs a busy place where they can blend in into the crowd and become invisible. He parks his motorcycle at the end of the large parking lot, wedging it between two market transport lorries. Bastian parks right behind him, masking Michael's ride even further.

With no further words spoken, Michael and Bastian dismount and immediately start working: Michael starts removing his license plate from the rear of the motorcycle while Bastian removes some of the documents and other objects hidden in the frame and accessories, transferring them over to his own bike.

"We need to leave some of your stuff behind," he tells Michael who nods and quickly goes through his bags, relocating some of the most important items to him.

"It will take some time until they figure out the identity of this bike," he says to Bastian who agrees. "The engine has gone now but it's been a good bike."

"You could say that bike has been in places no other bike's been before."

"Except yours."

"That's true. Let's move," Bastian says curtly looking around and feeling a little nervous about this whole incident. They are still just a pair of undeclared international refugees or runaways at this point in time and that makes them both highly alert to people, especially authorities, since they are illegally in the country.

Mounting Bastian's bike they roll away without a hurry, trying not to attract any attention. Within minutes they are back on a different highway again. This one is a public highway with no toll fees.

"I'm starving to death," Bastian announces and Michael suddenly realizes that they haven't eaten anything in days, the crossing being the only focus on their mind for the last forty-eight hours.

"We'll try to make it across to Italy and eat there, hopefully. We're flat broke now, by the way," Michael states - and they both know it.

"I got a few dollars left in my pocket but we need it for fuel," Bastian says and moments later he pulls the bike into a service station.

Dismounting the motorcycle, they check the fuel prices. "I've only got enough for about half a tank." Bastian counts his small change. "We are two on the bike; the consumption's going to be double too."

"Never mind the fact that we are heading uphill for the next two hours until we reach the summit in the Austrian Alps." Michael adds concerned.

"That's all we can do for now."

"Uh-huh."

Bastian pays and they mount the motorcycle and ride away.

Guided by Michael from behind, Bastian maneuvers the vehicle onto the highway leading to Bolzano, Italy - right through the European Alps.

They ride silently for a while, Michael checking the landscape and the signs, worrying about the motorcycle's ability and Bastian's physical condition. After a while, holding on tight to his friend, Michael falls asleep, exhausted by the last several hours events.

He sleeps deep and agitated for a while until he feels a small rumble and a sway in the bike's direction. As he awakes, immediately aware that he is on the motorcycle, he smoothly, with no sudden moves, looks around and realizes that Bastian, exhausted, has also fallen asleep. The bike starts slowing down a bit, as they are now riding on the sandy shoulder, easing over toward the concrete ditch.

Michael immediately realizes the imminent crash and holding Bastian gently by his shoulders, gradually shifts his weight to the left, making the motorcycle change direction back toward the pavement with a small rattle as tires pick up small rocks and debris.

Bastian suddenly awakes and his seasoned reflexes instantly kick in, allowing him to smoothly bring the bike back on the pavement, a moment later pulling it over to the shoulder, stopping it.

"Shit. I must've fallen asleep," he utters, getting off and stretching out.

"Yes, you did." agrees Michael casually. "How are you feeling?"

Bastian's face is livid, contorted in pain now, but toughens it out.

"I'm okay," he lies.

Michael checks his map using a pen light. "I'll take over from here so you can get some rest. We should hit the summit in about thirty-five minutes, roughly. How much fuel we got?"

"Not much. This climb is killing the gas, man. We might not make it to the summit," Bastian says, examining the fuel gauge.

"We've got no choice. We ride 'til it stops and if it does we deal with the situation then. Let's get moving," Michael says and prepares his gears for the drive.

They keep on riding, the highway becoming increasingly steeper as they near the summit. The bike is blowing out white smoke, overheating. The mountain fresh air helps it cool somewhat, and Michael expertly shifts gears balancing the power load. He feels his friend's grip loosening on his hips so he takes a quick glance at Bastian who is sound asleep behind him. Grabbing his friend's left thigh he holds him on the bike as he drives the motorcycle toward the ridge.

Huffing and puffing, the bike advances on the last drops of fuel in the carburetors.

With the engine is nearly dying, the road reaches a flat portion of pavement and the team touch the summit of the mountain ridge. Releasing a deep sigh of relief, Michael drives the bikes toward the deep descent which lasts nearly a hundred kilometers towards the picturesque Italian border town of Bolzano.

"Here we go," Michael calls out to nobody as he launches the motorcycle at the beginning of the downward slope and accelerating for the last time, he shuts the engine off saving the last drops of fuel for an emergency.

The heavy bike with its dual payload of people and packages starts rolling downwards, building up speed as Michael carefully steers and shifts gears as they descend toward Italy.

The road is winding downwards at a challenging rate keeping Michael on his toes, maneuvering the heavy bike through the turns. His only concern at the moment is to keep a good steady pace and allow downhill inertia to propel them toward the border crossing.

After several minutes of gliding - and even passing vehicles on the highway - Michael notices signs showing that they are approaching Italy.

He gently squeezes Bastian's thigh. "We are about three miles away from the border crossing," he informs his friend, who mumbles something unintelligible in his helmet. He lifts his visor and taps Michael on the shoulder: "What?!"

"Getting closer to the crossing for Italy. Wake up!" Michael replies and pulls the motorcycle over to the shoulder of the road, stopping. They both get off of the bike and stretch, looking around in the dark seeing nothing except for the headlights of the occasional passing vehicles.

"We are completely out of gas and money alike," Michael states.

"If there is a fee to be paid, we're out of luck."

"As far as I know, there are no fees here. I've been told that if there is nothing suspicious with either you or your vehicle, they let you roll right across the border without even stopping," Bastian explains.

"That's music to my ears," smiles Michael, looking at his good friend. "You don't look very well. How are you feeling?"

Bastian does not answer. His face is pallid, almost ashen in the moonlight and his whole posture curled forward, telling Michael that his friend is not well. "You need to eat something," Michael says. "We don't have any food or money left. We have to call our friends when we cross the border."

"Yeah. Let's go."

"Just one more thing - if they stop us, there is a lot of crap coming up fast, you realize that?" Michael informs his bud.

"We've got to bullshit our way through it, if it comes to that. If that's the case, let me do the talking this time. I'm more fluent in Italian then you are."

"Yeah. You got it."

Moments later they gear up and mounting the bike, Bastian takes control of the handlebars.

The next ride is short and fast. As the highway descends toward a valley flanked on both side by the tall Alp Mountains, the brightly-lit crossing assembly shows up in front of them. There is more traffic on the road again and the motorcycle, in line with the rest of the vehicles, follows the flow.

"Here we go," Michael announces nervously from behind him.

Bastian is sick but has it under control. "Stay cool."

Moment later he aligns the motorcycle in a single lane of cars heading for the officers' booth. When they reach it, Michael waves a cordial hello to the border officer. The young man waves back and moments later they are on Italian soil, heading for the city of Bolzano, perched at the foothills of the Dolomites. They start losing speed as the terrain levels now.

The bike slows down even further as they approach the city suburbs. They manage to roll for another half a mile and

Michael stops the machine in a small square not far from downtown.

Dismounting and stretching, both young men look in their bags and pockets for notes. They find what they're looking for.

"I'll try and find a public phone and call Angelo - let's see if he'll accept a reverse charge," Bastian states, looking toward the buildings surrounding the plaza.

"I got a couple of names too. Let's go. You don't look very well. You want to rest first?" Bastian shakes his head, pointing to a telephone booth on the sidewalk across the square. They start in that direction.

Moments later they reach the booth and Bastian enters it, leaning his body against the structure for support.

Michael, who watches him from a few paces behind lowers his eyes to the ground, saddened by Bastian's expression when he comes out a moment later. "He was happy to hear from me... until I told him I'm calling from Bolzano. He nearly shit his pants with panic! He told me to talk to the police first." Michael listens carefully.

"That's kind of bizarre. He's an old friend of yours from years ago."

"I'll try Cristiano next, and then you can have the phone after that," Bastian says and re-enters the booth, starting to dial digits. Michael watches him nervously and his anxiety increases just by watching his friend and reading his body language. Bastian slams the receiver down with frustration, kicks the door open and walks over to his motorcycle, starting to fiddle with the controls. Michael knows.

"I'll try with Sebastiano and Lucia," he calls to his buddy who does not turn but nods in acknowledgement.

Michael calls his contacts too but nobody wants to talk to them until they register with the police. Disappointed, he walks back to the bike and kneels beside Bastian, checking him out. "You're sick."

"And sick to my stomach, too."

"Let's ride as long as the little fuel left lasts and find a place to pitch the tent.

"Yes," is all Bastian says and the two of them silently gear up and riding the bike ride away slowly, look for a patch of grass to pitch their tent on.

Disappointed, hungry and exhausted, they ride in silence for a while, to their surprise the motorcycle still going on the little fuel left in the bottom of the tank. It is pitch dark by now and the city is busy with activity, but it suddenly looks and feels alien to them.

It has taken them years of planning, dangerous activities and close calls to get to this and now, for a short moment, they feel foreign to their own dreams.

They ride a little longer and now the engine starts misfiring, missing fuel. Michael notices a small patch of grass surrounded by a low concrete curb. He decides that will do for the night, so he rides the motorcycle over the small curb and pulling to a stop they dismount.

With robot-like movements, their minds miles away, their hearts in a vice but their spirit free like a bird, they set up the small tent quickly in the dark. Crawling inside, they almost immediately fall asleep. Michael, just before falling in oblivion, notices a couple of slices of light which appear and disappear moments later - from both directions.

Not paying any further attention to this small detail, he is fast asleep a moment later.

***

A loud car horn shakes Michael awake from his agitated sleep. Sitting up and stretching he takes a concerned glimpse at his friend; Bastian's drawn handsome face is white. His breathing is coarse and irregular and he is shivering. Michael wraps his side of the sleeping back on top of him and watches with compassion. This innocent, troubled-looking lifetime friend makes him smile in spite of the circumstances. An avalanche of crazy and wonderful flashbacks invade him, all at once.

A minute later, unzipping the tent he peeks outside and retorts and jumps up, hitting his head on the low canvas of the tent. More cautious this time, he drops down onto his knees and carefully peeks outside into the sunny morning. Shaking his head, he starts laughing and turns to his friend, who is now also awake.

"You gotta see this," he addresses Bastian, who pushes himself up on an elbow and peeks through the partially drawn tent opening.

"You gotta be kidding me!" Bastian says, crawling outside and immediately waving a hello to a beautiful young brunette driving by just inches away in a black convertible sports car. Michael joins him, the two rebels quite a sight for the Bolzano morning traffic - they are standing tall and wild-looking in the middle of a busy street intersection go-round grass island!

"How are you feeling?" Michael asks his buddy who is shivering in spite of the morning sunshine.

"Not too good this time. I've got no energy left."

"Because you're starving to death, you haven't eaten for days - that's a first for you, I'll bet. Get some fresh air whilst waving to pretty Italian chicks. I'll pack the tent and get us ready; I've got an idea," Michael tells his friend.

Bastian, zipping up his leather jacket, sits shivering on the grass beside his bike. Michael finishes packing and loading the bike. He starts it up.

"Get on. We'll ride it out from the go-round before the cops show up. We go back to downtown. It's a place I want to check out. We'll ride this beast to the very last drop." Michael pushes the bike off the island curb and they mount it, riding away.

The motorcycle runs a couple of short blocks then dies out. They dismount and park the bike beside the curb, locking it up. Bastian is wobbling, nearly falling down. Michael catches him and, supporting him on his shoulder, helps him walk away on the sunny street.

"I'm cold," Bastian states, shivering, and Michael takes off his own motorcycle jacket, wrapping it around Bastian's shoulders. "What about you?"

"Don't worry about me. It's August, the middle of summer - but you're sick." Michael looks around and spots what he is searching for.

"See that big Catholic church down there?" he points to a large granite Catholic church in the square. " We'll go in there and have you rest for a few minutes," he carries his friend to the front steps of the church and they enter through the large doors.

The soothing coolness is welcomed by Michael who helps Bastion settle into one of the dark pews. A second later, Bastian is sound asleep, shivering. Michael collects his thoughts for a moment. He can only sit there, taking in the silence, his eyes closed, his mind in a different realm, thinking of solutions for their present status-quo that is none too peachy.

A few moments later Michael gets up from the pew and walks toward the altar where he sees a Priest praying. He kneels beside him and casts a prayer.

"Padre," he addresses the Priest without moving his low-cast eyes. "We came a long and dangerous way to join the Holy Father's cherished world," he says in Italian.

His voice rises slightly, driven by passion. "We risked our lives to see the Holy Pope," he sits silently, eyes closed, his head bowed in prayer.

The Priest addresses him without opening his own eyes. "Where are you boys from?" he asks in a quiet voice.

Michael answers in his best Italian: "From the land that once was a proud Roman legion and now prohibits the Church and worshipping of the Holy Spirit. We escaped from Romania, signore."

"And what are your plans now, young man?" the Priest asks him in a soft voice.

"We want to go to Vatican and see the Pope. And pray," Michael answers with genuine conviction.

"That is a noble pursuit, but before you do that you have to register yourselves with the Italian Police. They'll take care of you."

"But Padre, they might throw us in prison. We didn't commit any crimes except that of escaping the communist regime. My friend is very sick. We haven't eaten in three days. He can't even walk."

There is a moment of silence then the Priest stands up, takes a quick glance at Bastion curled up pale in the pew.

"Come with me," he addresses Michael and gets up from his praying bench. Michael takes a glance at his friend who is pale, sound asleep.

"I don't want to leave him alone for long."

"Come," the Priest says in a warm voice.

They walk out from the main cathedral and into his office in the annex behind the altar. The Priest walks to a wall behind his desk and activates a code in a small safe, facing Michael.

"We don't have much money here but here's ten-thousand liras to cure your hunger."

Michael takes the money, his eyes and soul humble.

"Grazie, Padre. I'll never forget you."

"Go in peace."

Michael bows and leaves the office, once again joining his friend. He sits besides Bastian, his eyes closed, thinking of the Priest's words. After a few moments he wakes his friend up, supporting him as they walk out from the Church.

"Get on the bike. We'll go and buy something to eat."

"We're out of gas, remember?"

"Shit!"

"How? We're flat broke, the bike's empty." Michael nods and his mouth forms a small, passing smile.

They walk into the food market where the abundance of goods on display makes them dizzy. They find a small table with two wicker chairs painted white beside it. Bastian sits down, winded. Michael buys two loaves of fresh bread, sliced ham, a box of butter and two bottles of mineral water. He brings the plastic bag to Bastian.

"Let's go, good looking."

They walk outside and after a few steps sit on the red cobblestone curb beside their bike, wolfing down the food. "I'm almost sick again," mutters Bastian after a while wiping his mouth with the back of his gloved hand.

"Because now you've eaten too much, too fast. That's all. I'll make two more collect calls and then we have to make some decisions, buddy - fast." Bastian nods, pointing to a phone booth across the street from them. Michael walks over and makes his calls. The disappointed expression on his face, on his way back says it all.

"They're just too scared of the authorities."

"Frankly, I think they just don't give a damn about more hassle."

"You're probably right. Listen, we might as well follow the Priest's advice: check in with the police and do things the legal way. We've got nothing to fear."

"I'm not used to the legal way anymore," Bastian grumbles. "C'mon. We go for a walk and find the cop shop. This is not Romania."

They start walking the streets, seeing this new free world with different eyes now. Living so many years under the tyrannical communist regime made them feel suddenly fragile, as if they *were* criminals of some sort.

After a few blocks, they notice an old building with several police cars parked in front. The two exchange a quick glance and head straight towards it.

When they reach the impressive granite steps leading into the official building they stop for a moment, contemplating the possibilities.

"Let's do it. Only one thing, though - I am not going back to that fucked up communism, no matter what!" Bastian utters nervously.

"That makes two of us. Relax, let's go and talk to these people," Michael says and takes the first step toward the building. Bastian reluctantly follows.

Chapter 7

The Bolzano Casa Di Carabinieri is an impressive, beautiful building. The old police station which also serves as regional courthouse is gleaming under the patina of time when the two men step through the large wooden doors into the large open reception area.

A couple of young uniformed officers suddenly become nervous when the two rebellious-looking young men walk into the place. Bastian raises his hands and offers one of his charming smiles, making them relax a tad.

They approach the front desk and Bastian addresses the receptionist. "Bongiorno. We are two refugees and we are seeking political asylum," he whispers, watching her expression visibly change from friendly to a frightened as if they were some dangerous public enemy or carrying deadly diseases.

Michael and Bastian exchange a quick glance. The receptionist however recovers from the shock, and picking up the receiver speaks with a very low, controlled voice. Hanging it up a second later she looks at Bastian. "Captain Marinaro will talk to you in a minute. Please take a seat in the general waiting room," she says, pointing to the side where there is a small corner set up for the public. Bastian, followed by Michael, walks over to it and takes a seat as they watch a medium-built, athletic man in a worn two-piece suit walk towards them.

"I'm Captain Marinaro; please follow me to my office." As they walk back, they pass the two young officers to whom Marinaro makes a small gesture with his head. The young men jump to attention and discreetly follow the group. They enter the Captain's large and plush office where an expensive mahogany desk takes center place.

Several mug-shots of both local and national criminals are framed on the wall along with some fine modern Italian art prints. An eerie combination, Michael notes, as they are asked to sit in front of the desk on two very uncomfortable straight-backed chairs.

Michael is the one doing most of the talking now. There is genuine passion and drive in his voice when he speaks with the Captain who notices the open-faced directness of the young man.

"We are not runaways from the law, but something even worse - the filthy Communist Regime."

"There will be a criminal background check on you two before you leave this building," the Captain explains to them, referring to the political asylum protocol. "and also an Interpol checkup. But if you are as clean as you claim, you have nothing to worry about."

"We are," Michael responds casually.

Several more questions and signed statements follow while they are served pastries and good quality Italian espresso coffee.

Once the detailed meeting with Captain Marinaro is over, the two are placed in two different rooms where they are further questioned, fingerprinted and photographed. The process takes several hours and in the early afternoon, the two friends meet again and return to the public waiting room.

"I need a smoke," Michael tells to Bastian, who points at one of the police officers in the room:

"You'd better check with them first," Bastian replies and Michael is already on his way, talking to the Officer who nods and points to a certain area of the main entrance where he can keep an eye of him.

Michael thanks him and once outside lights up a cigarette, taking a thirsty drag.

A few minutes later he returns, thanks the officer and joins his friend in the waiting room.

"The Romanian butcher police could learn something from these guys," Michael says in Romanian.

"Maybe you want to take a course here in Bolzano and go back and teach the rednecks some manners!" Bastian suggests mockingly.

"No thanks. I'm happy that your uncanny sarcasm is returning. You must be starting to feel better by now," Michael says, happy to see his friend back to his old self.

They wait almost four more boring hours until Captain Marinaro shows up again calling them into his office. They settle into the same straight-backed chairs and look at the Captain.

"I'm happy to tell you that your criminal background check turned out clean," Captain Marinaro says.

"I could've told you that myself!" Bastian remarks, smiling at the police officer. "But now it is official, Signore."

"What happens next?" Michael asks, also in Italian.

"We follow our protocol as always," he twists his little mustache and looks at the young men. "I have two one-way train tickets for you to ride down to Trieste and register at our official refugee camp, *campo di profughi*."

The Captain catches Michael's silent question: "There is fifteen thousand Liras for each of you in this envelope, along with the train tickets. That should tide you over with food until you reach the *campo*."

"Thank you," Michael says simply and opens the envelope to check the content.

"A ride to the train station in a police car is also available if you want it," the Captain adds courteously.

"That's very nice, sir, but we need to take our bags and belongings from our motorcycle. By the way, where can we park it? Right now it is out of fuel and is not running," Bastian explains.

"You'll have to find a place out of the city parking areas so it won't be towed away," the Captain says. "Are you planning to come back and take it away later?"

"Yes," Bastian says immediately.

"In that case, you can park it in our yard. It will be safe here for a few weeks. On your way out, go to the garage and take some gas in a small canister so you can ride it back here."

"That's very kind. Thank you," Bastian says, relieved - he really likes his old motorcycle. "We'll do that."

The Captain rises and the two young men stand up too. He shakes their hand.

"Welcome to the free world. You are free to go," he says and invites them to leave his office.

"Thanks," Michael says, and leading the way exits his office and the police building, lighting up a cigarette on the sunny sidewalk.

"That wasn't so difficult," he concludes, looking at his friend.

"Nope. Just hang loose for a minute. I'm going to get some petrol," Bastian says, locating the police garage with his eyes.

"Fine. I'll have my smoke right here."

Bastian returns minutes later with a small jerry can and they leave the police headquarters. He and Michael walk without immediate purpose on the colorful streets of the mountain city, soaking in the sun and the light-heartedness of the moment. After a while, they end up in front of the motorcycle which Bastian, out of habit, checks out.

"We have to leave some stuff behind, on the bike," Bastian says, making sure that they have removed all of the important documents and qualification papers from the machine.

Michael has his tank bag which doubles as a shoulder back and Bastian's own tank bag which doubles as a modified backpack and they are now ready to go. Firing up the engine, they ride it back to the police station where a mechanic shows them where to park it. "Nice bike!" he comments.

"Thanks. I'll pick it up in a few weeks," Bastian responds and waves a small goodbye to him.

Walking the streets again, they find the ornate building of the Railway Station where they blend in with several tourists and locals. The train arrives a while later and they embark, saying a quick mental goodbye to Bolzano, not knowing yet that they are about to embark on the biggest adventure of their life.

***

The ride through Northern Italy is long and breathtakingly beautiful. They eat and sleep and watch people for a while, talking about the refugee camp, about which they know nothing. It will be many years later and in different parts of the world that they remember with both fond emotion and fear their time spent in Italy, a preamble to their current personal lives.

The long train pulls into Trieste station early the next morning and gradually comes to a halt.

A fair number of passengers of mixed ages spill onto the terminal, Michael and Bastian among them. They look around curiously and finding the exit in the beautiful city laying in front of them, they check it out.

"We have to flag a cab," Bastian says, watching a couple of taxis go by.

Michael does so, hailing an oncoming black taxi which immediately pulls up to the curb, the young Italian driver opening the passenger door. Michael leans in and looks at the him. "Do you take fares to the *campo di profughi*?" he asks in Italian, watching him flinch and look more closely at the two of them.

"Yes," he concludes after a brief analysis. "Hop in."

They jump in, Michael sitting up front with the driver who glances at him curiously.

"Have you taken people to the *campo* before?" Bastian asks him from his seat.

The driver shakes his head. "I'm new to the job," He explains. "Just summer work."

They ride silently for a while, the cabby tuning the radio to a rock station, trying to build a temporary shield between himself and his fare.

They ride along for a while. As Michael and Bastian watch the passing landscape of beautiful old-growth neighborhoods, the road ascends towards the hills looking down to the blue Adriatic Sea. Soon they arrive at a very large complex, perched on the hillside overlooking the Adriatic Sea. It was once an American military base and is comprised of several buildings and annexes surrounded by tall brick walls. It looks highly intimidating.

Michael pays the cabby, who drives away in a hurry. He and Bastian approach the huge gates leading into the camp. The sign on the wall reads *Caritas*. They are immediately approached by armed Italian Policemen.

"Stay cool," Michael whispers to his friend.

Michael hands them the official documents they received from the Bolzano police department and they are led into the large offices of the ex-military base.

The *Carabinieri* - military police officers - lead the two young men to a large reception office where they are immediately welcomed by a lady dressed in a grey three-piece suit. She introduces herself and the two boys look around curiously, interested.

"Bongiorno. My name is Patricia Verone and I'm the head of the camp administration, I'm in charge of new arrivals."

"Nice to meet you," Michael answers in her own language.

"You speak Italian, I see," she says, pleased.

"We both do," adds Bastian, also in Italian.

"That is very good indeed. It will help with the communication barriers we sometimes come across here. Please follow me to my office" she says with an efficient, professional tone and takes the lead. Michael and Bastian follow her, and once inside she asks them to close the door. Michael immediately notices two official-looking folders on top of her desk. He instantly realizes that Patricia already knows everything they said in Bolzano. Bastian also notices the folders, especially because the top folder has his first and last name printed on it.

This questioning session also lasts for several hours. They are served sandwiches and refreshments and visit the washroom but have to return and finalize Patricia's complicated interview. She writes several pages of notes in their binders, asking them numerous pointed and specific questions.

"The whole purpose of this meeting, gentlemen, is to assess and learn about your talents, level of education and people skills so I can facilitate your correct place in our organization," she explains to them. Bastian poorly conceals a yawn, which Patricia ignores. Through the screening process she learns that between them, the young men in front of her speak six languages fluently, are university educated and have high IQs which prove helpful for the camp's daily activities and chores. Their rebellious nature and instincts to defy authority could be a challenge though, she notes.

Verone closes the folders in front of her and looks at the two young men. "You should go and have something to eat now. We have a well-provisioned cafeteria. You might even be able to meet with some of your countrymen and women," she says, getting up from behind her desk and leading them to the main lobby. Here she stops in front of a female clerk. "Giovanna, take these two gentlemen to the cafeteria, please. They have just arrived at the *campo*."

"Si, signora," she replies.

Patricia turns to the boys: "I want you back in my office in an hour to finalize your file and to set you up with accommodation." They bow in agreement.

Giovanna takes a quick glance at the two new arrivals. "Follow me," she says in Italian, and silently they do.

The group walks down wide, solid brick hallways which with every step remind the men of the military origins of the building - solid, austere, functional. They encounter several people walking the hallways, men and women alike, their faces open, even smiling when they encounter the two runaways. It is nothing like the images Bastian and Michael had built up in their mind before entering. It was nothing like a concentration camp, quite the opposite. There are children running around the hallways, giggling happily. Two hot-looking young women look and smile at the newcomers.

"This beats Auschwitz by a long shot!" Bastian comments waving to the pretty girls.

"I agree," Michael says as they turn a corner onto yet another hallway, this one with a large double-door opening into the once-military cantina. As they approach it, the door swings open and a family - husband, wife and a small child, walks out carrying some sweets. Bastian holds the door open for them.

"Thank you," comments the middle-aged man in Polish.

"You're welcome!" Bastian answers back, also in the language.

Giovanna looks at her two companions. "All the people here are from Eastern Europe, the *Eastern Bloc*, as everybody calls it around here," she explains. "You guys are segregated by your own choices into national groups - Hungarians, Bulgarians, Romanians and so forth. You don't have to join the groups but if you merge with your countrymen, they might help you learn some information about the daily business in the camp," she explains.

"Sounds like a jump start," Michael says, his eyes scanning the large cafeteria and looking at the different groups of people there. Giovanna is ready to leave.

"Thank you for the intro, Giovanna," Bastian says politely.

"You are welcome. Be back in Patricia's office in an hour -don't be late! She's very punctual in everything she does," Giovanna says before leaving.

"I've noticed that," Michael agrees as she leaves.

The two turn their attention to the large cafeteria which has a capacity of around two hundred seats. They immediately notice the colorful groups of different nationalities seated separately - the Polish group on the right, the small Hungarian group further back to the left, the Russian group even smaller but intense looking, nested by the far corner against the back wall. They also recognize some Czechs and a small cluster of Albanians.

The groups don't carry flags or any other demarcations, but Bastian and Michael's life experience and previous travels in some of the countries allows them to recognize the signs fairly easily.

They don't look very hard for anybody however. Finding a vacant table they settle down, Bastian placing his shoulder bag on the chair. They both notice that their wild and rebellious looks have immediately attracted the attention of the various groups. They all know that the two are new arrivals and can't help but wonder about their origins, their story.

Every person here, man or woman or child, has a powerful story to tell, Michael will find out - sooner than he expects. But for now, walking to the serving station they take their plates and cutlery and the cook serves them lunch- soup and sandwiches at this time of the day.

"This is quite a crowd," Bastian says about the general gathering.

"We haven't seen it all yet, I'm sure," Michael responds occasionally glancing at the different groups.

They eat quietly, wondering what the next development will be in this new experience as international political refugees. But right now they don't have the luxury of dreaming about this new world because the current Hungarian group of six, including one particularly handsome man in his early thirties with long dark black hair flowing on his crafted shoulders, is watching Michael intensely. The flamboyant and expensive Channel long scarf wrapped daringly around his neck has class and finesse.

The two newcomers have almost finished their meal, and Michael checks his wristwatch. "We got twenty minutes to kill yet," Bastian states casually and looks up at the tall and slim

Hungarian fellow who was watching Michael earlier. He is approaching their table now, his eyes never leaving Michael who immediately diverts his look. He arrives at the table and the two seated men look at him curiously but amicably.

"You guys must be new around here," he addresses them both in English, his focus on Michael.

"We have been in the camp for almost seven hours already!" Bastian says, watching the visitor take the final steps towards their table. The Hungarian laughs delightedly and his movements are affectionate, quite feminine.

"I'm Jee-Jee," he explains. "We are Hungarian."

"I figured that much," Michael responds in fluent Hungarian, his tone sympathetic. "I like the scarf," he adds, nodding towards the flamboyant accessory.

"Thank you, dear," Jee-Jee says with affection in his tone, his right hand brushing over his face in a gesture reminiscent of a shy virgin. "You're such a big boy!"

Michael and Bastian barely conceal their smiles. "I'm Michael Agrafa and my friend here is Bastian Copacee and we come from Timisoara."

"That's a lovely city!" Jee-Jee explodes with enthusiasm. "The men there are very handsome and alive. I'm delighted!" he says, blushing charmingly. "Welcome to the Campo di Profughi where anything is possible!" he says, however Michael immediately catches deeply hidden fears and anxieties in his tone.

"Thank you," Michael says and checks his wristwatch. "It was very nice meeting you, Jee-Jee. Say hi to the group for us, but now we have to be moving - we have to meet Patricia Verone again."

"Miss efficiency personified! You'd better hurry because she hates latecomers. When you see her, just tell her that Jee-Jee sends his best regards!" the Hungarian says, adjusting a lock of hair on his forehead. The gesture is again gentle and feminine, Michael notices, recognizing an intelligent yet traumatized young man in front of him.

"How you do that?" Jee-Jee asks him perplexed.

"Do what?"

"Look into my soul like that," Jee-Jee reacts surprised.

Michael smiles, gets up from the table. "That's the way I am," he says, laughing as the two head for the door.

"Very nice meeting you, big boy," Jee-Jee calls after him as they exit the cafeteria.

"Looks like Jee-Jee has taken a shine to you," Bastian says laughing.

"He's very bright," Michael responds as they head down the hallway towards Patricia's office, thinking nothing further of it.

As expected, Patricia is already at her desk, going through various notes and official-looking documents. She looks up as the two enter. "You're a few minutes early," she addresses them, pleased. "Please take your seats. We have a lot of procedures to go through still."

"Jee-Jee sends you his best regards," Michael says with a small smile.

"Thank you, Michael. He is *quite* a character, that young man!" Patricia says, looking at him.

The two young men settle in front of her desk, reading and signing papers for hours, all the while learning the rules and regulations of the working camp.

***

It's almost dark outside by the time Patricia closes the folders and looks at the two men.

"Currently we hold over eight-hundred refugees and that takes a lot of management. I might call on some of your skills later, if the situation warrants it," she says, looking at them.

"We're happy to help if we can," Michael responds and Bastian nods in agreement.

"Very well, then. We are finished for now. Giovanna will lead you to your new sleeping quarters in the Romanian wing," she addresses them, picking up the telephone receiver and talking to Giovanna, who a moment later shows up at the door.

"Come with me," she says simply and the two young men follow her again, saying good night and thank you to Patricia on their way out.

They exit the main administration building into a small yard with concrete paths connecting several other buildings and annexes. The compound is huge and Michael makes a note of a full-size soccer field where a few men and women are kicking balls around. They walk past three other large buildings which were once military barracks, now converted into more accommodating dormitories.

They notice several armed officers patrolling the grounds, keeping order with their uniformed presence.

"The main gate is closed, but not locked," Giovanna tells them. "You can go in and out of the camp as you wish if you don't have emigration appointments to attend. The gate is locked at eleven o'clock at night and the only way to get back into the camp is by clearing your refugee ID with the Police at the gate."

She looks at her clients. "I strongly recommend that if you go out, be back before eleven o'clock because if you're late that will go on your record. Keep it simple and let them help you get wherever you want to go," she says as they approach another solid brick building with several steps and a stoop in front of the main entrance.

A young couple sits on the steps smoking and chatting as they pass by them. The couple looks curiously at the two; they know that Michael and Bastian are newcomers.

Giovanna enters the building and they climb a few stairs until they reach a wide hallway. They continue down it and stop in front of a door which has the number 212 stenciled on a silver plate. The building and the hallways are freshly painted and clean.

They enter the dorm and the three of them encounter seven or eight men sitting on their own beds, some reading, some writing letters, two in the corner playing a game of chess.

They all look at the newcomers; they all know Giovanna who brought most of themselves here.

"These are your new colleagues, Michael Agrafa and Bastian Copacee," she introduces the two who wave a small hello. Giovanna turns to the two and points to two military cots cleanly made up with gray blankets and white pillows. "These are your beds," she says and Bastian drops his shoulder bag on one of them, looking at Michael who nods and take the next one.

"Thank you, Giovanna," Michael says politely.

"If you have any questions in the future, just come and see me in my office," she says and waves a small goodbye to the rest of the group, exiting the dorm.

Michael and Bastian sit on their beds and turn to their country mates.

"This is our first day here." Bastian breaks the ice and some of the guys come closer, introducing themselves to the two. A few more join in and at the end of their game, the two chess players also come closer and participate. The ice is broken. They are all here for same reason - to better their lives and be free.

They listen to their stories and are amazed by the brevity of some. They mostly address Michael who they sense on an intuitive level really listens and feels for their drama. And he does, and he cares.

***

It's late at night and a small bedside lamp shines on the faces of about eight young men and three pretty women, all perched around Michael's cot. They are all Romanian except for Marya who is Polish, a friend of the group. They are in the middle of a heated discussion now. They are all speaking in English.

"...It all depends on a number of factors. But most importantly, I believe, is to summon up the guts to do it. Once you start the ball rolling, there's no looking back," Bastian finishes his sentence. Several heads nod in agreement.

"We all passed that difficult stage. How does the camp treat refugees?" Michael asks.

"The Organization is pretty decent, if you accept the Church in your life. The camp is run by the Roman Catholic Church with direct involvement and supervision of the Trieste Diocese - a very powerful organization," says Rodica, one of the Romanian girls. She's pretty, trendy, in her late twenties, very bright.

"How safe is it for the more radical Political dissidents?" Michael asks the group again.

"It's not quite a safe-haven here, there is no such thing... but as an alternative, if you're not the drug use and distribution and you cover your ass, it's pretty good," says one of the guys. He looks at the two newcomers and wants to comfort them. It's not exactly the way it comes out; "Nobody died in the camp in the last four days," he says casually. "That's pretty good, I think. No?"

The others, either verbally or through their body language, agree. Bastian exchanges a quick look with Marya. They like each other.

"The Russian and East German refugees are at the highest risk because of the KGB and STASI, the East-German Secret Police," says Peter, one of the guys.

"Once you are three or four months in, it's pretty safe. If they haven't got you by then or the camp hasn't expelled you - or passed you on to Interpol - you're doing pretty well," adds Florian, another of the Romanian boys, about twenty-eight, wild hair, penetrating blue eyes, thick glasses.

"The Criminal background check is quite thorough, as you noticed. They are linked with just about everybody. Sometimes it takes a while for the camp to receive confirmation on specific charges or suspect lists. Like Florian said earlier, if you're still here after three months, things look fairly good for you," explains Marya, focusing mostly on Bastian.

"What about the groups? Any particular one to watch out for?" Michael asks his new friends, knowing a thing or two about the *human element*.

"There is a bad apple in the camp. Watch out for the Albanians. It's only six of them, but they're dangerous. Just plain ruthless and vicious."

One of the guys from the far end of the dormitory raises his voice: "Wrap it up, guys. It's almost two o'clock in the morning and I've got to work tomorrow," he explains.

"Sorry, Adrian. We didn't see you there," Peter answers.

The group quickly dissipates; the girls leave the dorm whilst the guys head for their own cots. The dorm is dimly lit and Michael is wide awake in bed, thinking, processing all this new information. Being the intuitive, emotional type, he needs to get a *feel* of this new world and its baggage of risks and dangers.

***

It is another beautiful summer day in Trieste, Italy. There is a fervent drive of energy in people as they walk through the camp.

Michael is one of them, walking through the camp, exploring his boundaries, meeting new people. The early fall is charged like a high-voltage wire with hopes, dreams and hidden desires. Michael, all charged up himself within these new settings, wanders around, ending up in front of the administration office, where he had spent several hours a few days before.

He boldly walks into the office and runs into one of the Emigration clerks he met the other day.

"It's nice to see you again, Vanessa. How is life in the campo di profughi today?" he asks her casually.

"Hectic as usual, Michael. How about you?" she asks in fluent English. "Getting used to your temporary new home?"

"Yes. I'm all good with that," Michael says.

"Since you're here, I need you and your friend Bastian in my office later this morning, to sign some forms for me. Just protocol," Vanessa says.

"Will do." Waving a small hello he leaves the administration office and walks outside. It seems to be a good day - people are walking the alleys, talking, laughing, a group is playing volleyball on a court, another group is playing soccer in the field nearby, enclosed by the camp's tall brick walls.

A few days go by.

It's a fresh sunny morning and Michael leaves his building without a hurry. Lighting up a cigarette he wanders over to the soccer field and climbing on the bleachers enjoys the day and the game, thinking about the ways life has changed so rapidly under these new circumstances.

He enjoys this peaceful morning, watching the ad-hoc soccer game.

After a while, two handsome young men, stylish and 'dolled up' sit beside him, commenting on the game in low voices. The visitor is Jee-Jee and his escort, a powerful young man with broad shoulders and arms the size of fence posts.

"It's a lovely day. Too bad that some of us have to die today," Jee-Jee says in a low voice which doesn't escape Michael.

"We all die sooner or later," Michael replies casually watching the action on the soccer field. Jee-Jee giggles like a girl.

"I prefer it later... much later!" he says in a feminine voice.

On the soccer field one of the teams scores. The onlookers cheer and whistle in support. Jee-Jee leans over toward Michael. "Bastian's new friend, the Polish girl, Marya, will die today. I want you to warn Bastian," he whispers toward Michael who suddenly looks at him, but Jee-Jee's handsome face is impenetrable.

"How you know this? And secondly, why are you telling me?" Michael asks looking at him.

Jee-Jee giggles girlishly and taps Michael's shoulder. "First of all, I'm very well connected, and secondly, as you put it, I really like you and I don't want you to get hurt. Bastian is your friend. Isn't he?"

"I appreciate the concern, but thanks - I take care of myself. Since you're so well connected, can't you do something about Marya?"

"All I can do is warn people. The Polish Mob is after her. It's something to do with her past, that's all I can say... and you didn't hear it from me. I can't find her anywhere. I tried to warn her myself," Jee-Jee says with a tinge of nervousness in his voice.

"I might know where she is. Maybe I can help. Thanks for the warning," Michael says and gets up from the bleachers. Jee-Jee looks at him passionately:

"Anything for you, big boy. Look me up sometime!" Jee-Jee blushes and touches Michael's shoulder affectionately.

Michael reacts "No touching."

Jee-Jee and his silent companion get up and walk away. Turning to Michael, all smiles and google eyed he says "I'll see you around, handsome. Take care of that fine body of yours." Michael smiles and shakes his head silently, his mind busy now with Jee-Jee's words of warning. Moments later, he walks back to his dorm and grabbing his biker leather jacket and his wallet he walks out from the camp.

He walks along the sidewalks leading uphill toward his destination. Large estates and old-growth trees decorate the streets as he ascends the small mountainside a few streets above the camp. Occasionally he peeks at openings between the houses and glances at the Adriatic Sea down below. It is a serene night, but Michael can feel the dangers lurking under the surface.

Lighting up a cigarette he inhales deeply and releasing a whispered exhale he continues his walk toward *Antonio's*

Trattoria, a small and very cozy Italian bar tucked in the side of the mountain, a choice drinking hole for the locals and the politicos.

A few more minutes of walking and he approaches the Trattoria. Putting out his cigarette on a smoke dish by the door, he runs his hand through his rebellious long hair and enters the dimly-lit bar.

The place is cute. The indirect colored lighting makes the place appealing, safe and intimate. The Trattoria is a fine place for heart-to-heart discussions over a drink.

Michael adjusts his eyes to the lighting, waves a small hello to Antonio, the owner, who is behind the bar. He spots Marya and Bastian chatting casually at a small table in the corner. Bastian notices him too and waves him over.

"Campari on ice as usual?" Marya welcomes him. He nods and pulls a chair to their table while Antonio brings him a glass.

"Good to see you!" welcomes Antonio.

"You looking good, Antonio," Michael responds.

Antonio waves in disregard, "I'm an old man, *Michele*," he says and starts walking back to the bar.

"You don't show it though!" Michael calls after him, lifting his Campari glass in cheer.

"I don't want to interrupt you guys," Michael says gently, looking for the proper words, "but something came up and I have to talk to Bastian for *uno minuti*," *Michael says* slowly.

Bastian looks at him and immediately sees in Michael's eyes that he is concealing something serious. He knows his friend.

Getting up from the small table, Bastian looks at Marya. "We'll only be a minute," he says and Michael follows him outside.

Antonio knows his customers - many refugees for many years with many stories, dramatic and of all sorts. He just nods at Michael's gaze before they exit the bar.

"What's up?" Bastian immediately asks him as soon as they close the door.

"Jee-Jee came to see me tonight," Michael starts.

"That's not a surprise. He's got the hots for you! What else?"

"He is very well connected, you know that," Michael says gently.

"Yes. He knows things," Bastian agrees.

"He came over and warned me that Marya, you friend, is in great danger."

The two men look at one another. Their eyes meet for a second.

Bastian knows now that this is serious. "What? Who?" he asks.

"Jee-Jee says that there is a death warrant imposed on her by the Polish Mafia."

"Fuck! That's nasty news. They are just as bad as the Russians."

"Worse," Michael says in a soft voice. "My advice to you is to talk to her now and have her disguise herself and leave the camp tonight, before word gets out."

"Yeah. Your source is reliable, I should imagine."

"You know Jee-Jee. He knows his shit - and he likes Marya too."

Bastian bows his head a couple of times and turns to the bar door. "Thanks."

Michael nods and heads back to the camp, lighting up another cigarette.

***

It is late at night now and the camp is quiet. In the Romanian male dormitory a small reading light shines between Michael and Bastian's cots. Everyone else is asleep. They are facing each other, talking.

"She left for Spain this afternoon. Thanks for the warning," Bastian whispers. "She wasn't too surprised when I broke the news - as if she was expecting it to happen."

"She probably was," Michael says. "I hope she's changed her looks."

"Radically. She's disguised as a man with the papers to match - She came prepared."

"Good."

***

A week goes by and the emigration papers are processing from one stage to the next, from one country to the other. The efficient *Caritas* system is in full gear. The situation in the Eastern Bloc countries is very bad and the number of political refugees is much higher than in previous years. The sad fact is that the ratio of arrival-to-death is about three-to-one, meaning that for each successful escape, three others die in the attempt.

It is a sunny afternoon and Michael is alone in his dormitory, going through his notes, writing memos now and again in his pocket book. The door opens and Bastian walks in, dressed in shorts and a tank-top, his toned muscles gleaming with sweat.

Michael looks at him, "Good game?"

"Not bad. We lost but we had a lot of fun. Those Bulgarians sure know how to shoot a hoop."

"Having a good time's all it is about," Michael says, closing his pocket books.

"How are things with you?" Bastian asks his friend.

"Okay for now. Our papers are moving along just right. I just talked to Vanessa earlier today."

"Speaking of that... I mean the administration office stuff... the word on the grapevine is that Joseph is moving out to Latina next week, on his way to Toronto, Canada."

"I heard of that. Good for him. He's a good guy," Michael says.

"Word in the camp is that you would make the best candidate to replace him," Bastian says casually, getting his towel and preparing for a shower. Michael looks genuinely surprised, not believing it.

"What are you talking about?"

"You click with the folks in the office as if you belonged there. I saw that myself. Besides, you speak four languages, you type like a girl, know office paraphernalia... and the Archbishop of Trieste likes you."

"What the heck is going on, Bast? Talk to me, man. Straight talk. You're not high, are ya?"

Bastian is enjoying this.

"You know... rumors, grapevine, gossip, chit-chat... stuff like that."

"Get to the point."

"This *is* the point. I hope you consider the position if it comes up. I want to speed up the process of getting out of here and you will be able to do that."

"Just go and take a cold shower and cool your head a tad," Michael says light-heartedly. "You stink."

***

Michael, his bag on his shoulder, dressed in a white muscle-shirt with worn jeans and sneakers, heads toward the soccer field to watch a game and have some undisturbed lone-time. He mounts the bleachers and glances at the mix of casual players kicking the ball for fun. The soccer field is a popular hangout and activity center for the camp.

He is in the middle of writing a sentence in his notebook when he hears his name called on the P.A. system with speakers mounted everywhere - on poles, sides of buildings, even trees.

A female voice repeats the message: "Michael Agrafa, please report to the Administration Office as soon as possible!"

Startled, Michael looks at the speakers mounted on the light poles illuminating the soccer field.

Gathering his notes he quickly heads towards the administration office, several buildings away. He wonders why they have called him through the P.A. system. It looks urgent. Is something wrong with his emigration process? Is Australia raising questions about his background? A thousand other thoughts flash through his mind when he enters the building and is welcomed by Vanessa and her boss, a middle-aged, formal, professional and wearing an impeccable two-piece grey suit.

"Good morning, Michael. My name is Mateo Forzani and I am the chief coordinator of emigration processing. We checked out a number of people signed with this office."

Michael barely can conceal his boredom, *Get on with it, Forzani*! He thinks. It seems like the rumors he heard from Bastian might be coming true. "Si, Signore," he responds politely.

"We want you to work for our office, replacing Joseph, who you probably heard, is moving to Latina for his final stage of emigration."

Michael nods politely, looking directly at his face. "It would be our pleasure, *Michele*, to have you here in the office," Vanessa adds with empathy which immediately moves Michael.

He thinks for a brief second.

"Grazie, Vanessa. I would feel honored to work in this office," he says.

"With your writing and typing skills and your knowledge of languages, we are very pleased to extend the position to you," Mateo Forzani adds.

"Thank you for the offer and the kind words, Signore Forzani."

Forzani extends a soft, moist hand to Michael who squeezes it lightly.

"Very well, then ... I shall inform the archbishop that you have accepted the position. That will be all for now. We start at eight o'clock in the morning. That will be your desk," he points to one of the large office desks to the right. "Vanessa will initialize you with all the office codes and security procedures. Be here a few minutes before eight, tomorrow morning."

"Si, Signore," Michael thanks them again and leaves the offices, taking a stroll through the Camp, observing everything with new eyes now. Everything is happening so fast, something he really likes. There will be new responsibilities also, but that's just fine with him. He has and powerful and unclear emotion about things to come and events that will rock his world.

He doesn't mind that either but - like an angel's whisper - something in the back of his mind tries to come out to the foreground; however he can't put a finger on it in spite of his efforts.

"Time will tell," Michael mumbles, aiming back to the dorm to deposit his bag and get ready for the upcoming soccer game in which he and Bastian will eagerly participate.

Dressed in a pair of shorts, a loose tank-top shirt and sneakers, Michael walks out from the dorm heading towards the soccer field. Different groups and single people are sharing his path, enjoying some time outdoors in the summer day.

When he arrives at the soccer field, Bastian and a group of guys are already warming up for the game. He joins them but he is not that serious about the game.

They start play shortly afterwards. It is a fun mix of players from different countries blended smoothly together under the unifying powers of the sport. They enjoy the game and are cheered by the onlookers, adding even more zest and fun to their game.

When it is over, and with Michael's team losing, the two friends get together and head back to the showers.

"That was fun," Bastian concludes, his face and shirt glistening with sweat.

"Indeed."

They reach their dorm and both go for the shower stalls.

Back at the dorm, Bastian, dressed in a leisure suit, jumps on his bed with a motorcycle magazine in his hand. "I'll catch up a bit with the moto-world. What about you?" he asks Michael.

"I need to see somebody," Michal replies and puts his jeans on as well as a tank top.

"See you when I see you," Bastian says, getting into his magazine, while Michael runs his hand through his long damp hair and exits the dorm.

**

The early evening casts its long shadows on the ex-military buildings making them look austere, colorless and boring. Occasional refugees walk by him and their colorful outfits and young vitality balances the austere landscape - to a degree. Passing a number of barracks, he climbs a few stairs and enters the Hungarian compound which encompasses a number of adjacent buildings. Michael has entered the compound marked *B*.

Once in the clean, wide hallway he starts looking for different doors until he finds one with the Hungarian national colors painted across the whole door.

"That would be hard to miss!" Michael laughs out loud opening the patriotic steel door.

The dorm is similar to the Romanian one he is sharing with his co-nationals, but with two distinct differences. The first is that the dorm is considerably larger than his and the second, at the far end, is Jee-Jee's 'built in' private boudoir - nearly twenty feet of the back of the dorm is blocked off with expensive-looking drapes which fold richly on both sides of an imperial entrance, guarded by a large muscle-bound Hungarian boy reading a light porn magazine in a high back chair.

The 'guard' looks up and his stare stops Michael in his tracks.

"Can I help you?" he addresses Michael in heavily accented Italian.

"I'm looking for princess Jee-Jee," Michael says jokingly, in tune with the elaborate setup.

"Who is it, Janos?" comes the royal chirping from behind the heavy drapes.

"I don't know him, Jee-Jee. He seems new around here. You new?" he rudely switches to Michael who nods calmly. A moment later, Jee-Jee's appears behind the curtains, make-up on his face, his long black hair on curling rings.

"Oh, my! It's you, Michael... and you see me like this!" Jee-Jee says in a little panic, disappearing behind the drapes. "Just give me a couple of minutes; I'll be ready in a wink," he says in fluent English.

"You look fine." Michael comforts him in English and takes the waiting stance to relax the jumpy bodyguard.

"What a wonderful surprise! I didn't expect you in my quarters," Jee-Jee addresses Michael from behind the curtains. "I'm almost finished."

Michael smiles to himself and a minute later, Jee-Jee shows up once again, this time looking like a movie star.

"It's okay, Janos. He is a friend of mine," he addresses the bodyguard. "Please come in."

He waves Michael into the compound which is not short of a miracle in the way it is decorated. Colorful drapes of satin and cashmere - so light that if you breathe on them would they fly away - separate the bedroom area from the common living area. The bed is not the regular cot everybody has in the camp - it is a queen size, alcove bed suitable for *real* royalty. The living room has two small Italian fine leather couches, a coffee table and two end tables supporting freshly cut flowers, just like the coffee table. There is a teapot and a fancy Italian coffee machine in the corner along with some dry foods. The polished rock floor of the building is covered with new rugs, some of them hand-made; there is shelving with expensive clothes, shoes, designer bags and shades. There are a couple of lamps lit dimly in two corners. A small bar with assorted fine liquors and appetizers completes the decor.

"Wow! Nice place," Michael says, genuinely impressed. He looks again at his friend, "You look very nice too, Jee-Jee."

Jee-Jee laughs delightedly like a teenage girl. "You are such a gentleman," he says, eyeing Michael's tight muscles and proportional build.

"What a body!" Jee-Jee releases a light sigh making Michael laugh. "Please take a seat and talk to me," he says, sitting like a girl opposite him on the other couch. "Can I offer you a drink or a coffee?"

Michael glances at the shelves stocking all kinds of hard liquors.

"A straight Scotch would be perfect," he says.

"Now I know that is not only my good looks and fine liquor that brought you down to my quarters," he places a thick bottomed tumbler in front of him on a coaster. Michael takes it and has a quick sip, nodding with delight.

"The main office offered me Joseph's old position today," Michael says in a low voice, unheard by Janos, the bodyguard.

"Wow!" Jee-Jee exclaims excitedly. "That's wonderful! I knew they were considering you for a while but I didn't know they were moving so fast," Jee-Jee says seriously.

"I need some information from you," Michael says in the same low voice.

"Shoot," Jee-Jee says looking directly at him.

Michael takes another sip from his drink, leans forward towards Jee-Jee and twirls a flock of curly hair on his own forehead.

"I want to know more about the underground activities around here before I consider the position," Michael whispers and Jee-Jee's face turns even more serious.

"Give me just one minute," he says and getting up, walks over to the bodyguard and whispers something in his ear. The bodyguard nods, taps his hip to confirm a concealed handgun and walks closer to the main entrance of the dorm, on the other end of the room. Jee-Jee returns to Michael, pours himself a few fingers from the same Scotch bottle, and takes a nervous sip.

"We have a lot to talk about. You came to the right place," he says in a low voice, looking straight into Michael's face.

"Thanks in advance, Jee-Jee."

Chapter 8

Michael, cleanly shaven and dressed in dark blue business pants, white shirt and a loose tie, his bag dangling on his right shoulder, is walking and smoking, heading toward the administration building of the large camp. Correction: international political refugee camp.

He reaches the building in a few minutes and he feels he is ready for the challenge. Entering the main building, he finds his large office where Vanessa and three more Italian clerks are busily working on typewriters.

"Bongiorno, *Michele*," welcomes Vanessa. "Get familiarized with your desk and let me know when you're ready. It's your first day, so take your time."

"Bongiorno tutti," answers Michael, heading for his desk. "How many cases are waiting for me again, Vanessa?" he asks her.

"About two hundred and twenty," she says, watching his reaction. He tries to maintain his cool but his face suddenly turns pale. "You don't have to process them all in one day!" she adds comfortingly.

"Grazie," Michael responds and sits down behind his desk, starting familiarize himself with the folders, trays, *IN* and *OUT* batches, the typewriter and the keyboard.

About half an hour later he walks over to Vanessa's desk. "I think I'm ready to start," he says simply.

"Very well," Vanessa answers, getting up. "I will brink Mateo in. Just wait at your desk," she says exiting the office.

She returns moments later with Mateo Forzani who is carrying a thick bundle of folders under his arms. He laughs when he notices Michael staring uneasily at it.

"Hello, *Michele*. I don't expect you to process all these today," he jokes. "This is your workload for the next refugees up for the processing deck; the files are in different stages of development," he explains placing them on the corner top of Michael's desk. "We will go through them together a little later," he says and pulls up a chair beside Michael's. So does Vanessa.

"We will start by identifying the stages of development of each file," he opens the top folder on the pile. "On the first page you will see the photo ID of the applicant, along with the Caritas red seal of acceptance of the application. Not all files have a red seal."

***

The initiation goes on for several hours. It is late afternoon when Forzani finally gets up from his chair and places a fairly thick folder in front of Michael, opening it to the first page. A beautiful pale young woman with wild black hair and intense eyes looks back at them. She looks remotely familiar.

"You absorbed a lot of information, just like Joseph did," Mateo says, looking down at the picture of the girl in the file. "I would like you to start with this outstanding case of Klava Petrosima. She speaks many languages, including Italian and English. Joseph conducted the interrogation in English; it's all here in his transcripts."

Michael steals a look at the first page of his case and he is already intrigued, ready to sink his teeth into this first assignment. It shows on his face too. Mateo and Vanessa exchange a quick, knowing look.

"Don't forget, *Michele*, that Giovanna and I are always here to help if you need it. And Mister Forzani himself will help in difficult situations which will occasionally arise in some of these cases," Vanessa says.

"Thank you," Michael tells to both of them.

"Ci vediamo," they say goodbye and leave.

"Ci vediamo," Michael replies and sinks his eyes and mind into his first case...

Klava's Story

A slaughterhouse somewhere in Bulgaria

A young and beautiful girl comes through one of the doors of the slaughterhouse and walks over to the loading docks where three semi-transport trucks are preparing to leaves with their cargos of animal byproducts.

The girl has dark and curly long hair, a rebellious outfit and challenging, penetrating blue eyes. She approaches one of the truck drivers who she seems to know because he smiles to her immediately, calling her over to his truck cabin.

Klava reaches in her shoulder bag and hands the driver a thick brown bag. He counts a wad of US dollars. Satisfied, he looks at Klava.

"It's all here. Have you got your breathing paraphernalia?" he asks the pretty girl. Klava taps her shoulder bag which is made of a waterproof material.

"Get ready to climb into the tanker. I'm taking off in about ten minutes," the Norwegian trucker says, looking nervously around the place. "I'll stop and get you out of there shortly after we clear customs - if you're still alive."

Klava nods and extracts a short hose, about a foot long, with a tiny mouth mask attached to it. The Driver shakes his head, watching her simple setup.

"Don't worry about me. Just take me across and you'll get the other half," she says in a firm voice, her blue eyes stainless-steel sharp. The Driver shrugs and climbs on the top of the truck, closely followed by Klava. When he unlatches the hatch and shines a flashlight into the tanker, the girl notices that it is almost full to the brim with animal guts and fat. The driver turns to Klava who is very pale. She nods and placing her small mask on her face, sealing her shoulder bag shut, submerges in the disgusting cargo. The Driver latches the hatch shut, and getting into his cab drives away, still shaking his head, his nose wrinkled by the stench.

It is now night time at the border crossing between Bulgaria and Serbia. One armed military guard along with a customs officer climbs on the top of the tanker as the driver opens the hatch. A powerful stench hits the men's nostrils as the officer quickly acknowledges that the tanker is full to the top with the disgusting animal fat and guts.

"I wouldn't worry much about this place!" the officer says disgustedly as the soldier chokes, ready to vomit. The driver assertively agrees and retrieving his passport, salutes and waits for him to climb down from his truck. With a small toot he drives away into the western world.

Michael is sweating profusely as he closes the file and makes some notes on a legal pad. Vanessa who has watched him for a little while now, gets up from her desk and brings him a cup of espresso.

"You need this," she says.

"Yes, I do," responds Michael and his hand shakes when he picks up the coffee cup.

"I read many statements in this office but not too many are on a par with Klava's," Vanessa says in a soft voice.

"Did you read her transcript?" Michael asks her. She nods.

"She's a very gutsy girl. And smart too. Have you met her yet?" Michael shakes his head. "You will. Her background check cleared with Interpol and the Italian Intelligence agency. You have to start processing her emigration country of choice; I think she picked Canada."

"Yes, she did. Mister Forzani told Klava he scheduled her to meet with me first thing tomorrow morning," Michael says.

"Are you ready to handle it?"

"Not yet. But I will be prepared by tomorrow morning."

"Good. A quick word of advice - try to detach yourself emotionally from the cases. Just do your job."

"Sometime that's easier said than done, Vanessa," Michael says. Vanessa walks back to her desk with no reply.

It is lunchtime and as the Italian office staff leave for their meal, Michael gathers some of the newspapers and starts scanning them. After a short while a small article jumps to his attention. His face turns pale. He brings the page closer to his eyes: the photograph has a heading: *"EXECUTION STYLE MURDER, Identity unknown."*

The pretty young woman dressed as a man in the photograph is Marya, Bastian's friend. Michael pounds his fist hard on the desktop. "Fuck!"

He shivers with grief, slowly closes the newspaper, places it on the corner of the desk and returns to his stack of files. The next file in his hand reads Gunther Baumf, East Germany: *Status: Preliminary.*

East Berlin, 1979: night

Young Gunther, dressed all in black, with soft black runners and gloves, his face also painted black, is climbing the stairs of a low-rise apartment building. He opens the hatch and climbs on the roof, reaching for his pocket. He produces a small Morse code transmitter and sends a stream of beeping signals. Finishing the transmission, he leans over the edge and stares at the Berlin Wall, a couple of hundred feet away from the apartment building.

There is a tense silence broken by a small hiss and a bang. Gunther turns to the source of noise and finds what he was expecting: a stainless steel hook attached to a nearly invisible piano wire plunged solidly into the brick wall. He quickly attaches the hook to a special steel bracket installed on the building earlier for this very purpose. Taking a deep breath, he climbs over the ledge and clips a small bar with a roller attached to the taut wire.

A moment later and his black shadow starts to glide noiselessly across the empty space, coming rapidly towards the wall. A German soldier notices him for a moment and unleashes a few rounds of automatic fire towards him. The bullets miss, and seconds later Gunther crashes onto the West German soil, disappearing into a dark alley.

Michael closes the file and starts making notes on his legal pad. Finishing this, he checks some of the documents sealed in the file and he also reads Joseph's notes remarks of the preliminary meeting. It is Michael's job to learn and feel out all the lies and truths in the file and be prepared for the one-on-one legal interrogation he will conduct with Gunther in the next few days following Klava's interview.

Sipping from his coffee, he opens another case file and starts reading.

***

It's a peaceful evening in the Romanian male dormitory. There is idle chat going on in one corner while the other entertains the two chess players. Two guys are having a nap, Bastian is out somewhere and Michael is sitting on his bed, preparing for his case file with Klava.

Rodica, the young Romanian lady, storms into the dorm. She stops in the middle of the aisle, trembles, takes a few shaky steps then collapses.

Michael and Dimitr, his next bunk colleague, jump from their beds and rush to Rodica, immediately picking her up and carrying her onto Michael's bed.

She does not look good; her face is bruised and bleeding at the corner of her left eye, her hair and clothes torn and in a mess. As one, all the men in the room gather around her trying to help.

She comes to and looks at all those surrounding her.

"Hey guys," she addresses the group in a weak but firm voice. "I appreciate the concern, but I want to talk to Michael alone... please."

The men immediately give her the space she needs and return, apologizing, to their corners.

"What happened?" Michael asks, cleaning her face with a wet cloth.

"It happened about an hour ago. I was out with my friend Carlo and he dropped me back at the camp," she stops and has a sip of water from the glass Michael offers her. "They were waiting, watching us - I should have known better."

"Who are *they*?"

Rodica, under the sudden trauma, starts sobbing. Michael holds her hand in his, soothing her, waiting patiently.

"The Albanians. I told you they're trouble."

"What happened?"

She looks around, concerned, listening to the growling angry guys in the dorm who are just itching to find out who did this to their friend - and have him dug out from his burrow and dealt with accordingly.

"This *has* to stay between us," she whispers. "I don't need more bloodshed."

Michael nods reassuringly.

"Carlo picked me up from the camp to go out for dinner. Durak, the Albanian group leader saw us. Shit! I knew it was going to be trouble."

Michael raises his eyebrows.

"He has a crush on me and just won't take no for an answer," she continues, "I told him to stay away from me but... anyway, to cut to the chase, he and his goons were waiting for us in the shadows on the street. When we got out of his car they jumped on us. Carlo is in pretty bad shape too but somebody from the street must have called the camp police who came a minute later and the Albanians got away. So did Carlo and I... we don't need any more legal trouble."

Michael dabs her face and holds her hand for a minute, thinking fast.

"I'll take you to Jee-Jee's compound. He can help and he's pretty good at it."

"Yeah. He's pretty good, like a doctor. Thanks, Michael. I can find my way to him alone."

"You sure?"

"Pretty sure. The Albanians won't touch me on camp ground. They are not *that* stupid. I'll be fine... thanks."

"It's nothing. I wish I could do more for you," Michael says and he means it.

Rodica gets up. Michael helps her to the door and they leave the dorm.

"I'll be good from here. See you later," she says, her voice more energetic this time.

"You know where to find me... and don't hesitate."

"Thanks."

Taking a deep breath, she descends the six stairs of the stoop and heads toward the Hungarian compound. Michael watches her silently until she disappears around the buildings.

***

It is seven o'clock in the morning and Michael, dressed in a t-shirt and jeans, lets himself into the office; today he is the first in. The Italian policeman who guards the building waves to him; he waves back, asking if he wants a cup of coffee. The officer shakes his head.

Michael pours himself a strong dose and settles behind his desk, immersing into Klava's file and his side notes.

Klava Petrosima shows up a few minutes before nine o'clock and the two have a chance to get acquainted with one another before the official recorded interview.

For almost three hours, Michael takes her through the questioning procedure and records his findings required for the legal documents. They both look exhausted at the end of the second interrogation.

"I need a coffee," Klava says, looking around the office.

"Me too;" replies Michael getting up from behind his desk, "I'll get you one," he says and makes two cappuccinos on the fancy coffee machine of the office.

Returning with two cups, he offers one to Klava and settles back down behind his desk.

"You are free to go now. The meeting went very well. You were quite helpful," he tells her.

"So were you - I felt more comfortable on this second interrogation than the first one with Joseph."

"Joseph is excellent - and a good guy too. You were just too nervous about the procedures. That's all," Michael says.

"By the way, who did *your* first interrogation?" Klava asks him.

"Joseph. And I was a bit nervous too at the beginning!"

"So who's going to do your second interrogation?" Klava asks him, genuinely curious.

"It's already done - by me. I just had to sign a binding document stating that everything was true - which it was. That's all."

"Right on," Klava says, and finishing her coffee gets ready to leave.

"I will see you around... and... thanks," she says, getting up and preparing to leave.

"Yes. It was a pleasure meeting you," Michael says and walks her to the door.

After Klava leaves he returns to his desk and finishes work on her file, placing it onto the 'processed' pile. He reaches for the next one on the taller 'incoming' pile in front of him.

It is late in the afternoon when Michael grabs his shoulder bag and says goodbye to his colleagues and the new police officer on duty, heading back toward his dorm.

When he walks in and sees are a few visitors, some female, in the back of the dorm, he is exhausted. He finds Bastian ready to leave as he puts on some light work boots.

"I got an offer to try a late afternoon job in a garage," Bastian informs him.

"Good luck - and have some fun!" Michael replies, checking him over.

"You look like a pro."

"I am a pro!" Bastian answers and heads for the door.

"I know you are," Michael agrees watching him leave.

He stops and turns toward his friend. "By the way, there's a big game going on in a few minutes in the field - the Italians against the 'world'. It should be good," Bastian informs him.

"What are the odds?" Michael asks his friend.

"I call four-to-one for the world against the Italian team."

"I don't know, man. Those Italians are *real* good."

"Four-to-one. My final and only offer," Bastian says, laughing and getting ready to leave. "Have fun!"

Michael gives Bastian the thumb up as he leaves the room. In order to give more privacy to the group at the back of the dorm, he runs his fingers through his rebel hair and also leaves himself. Lighting up a cigarette he heads toward the soccer field where the high-adrenaline game is about to start.

He walks through the large camp and climbs onto the busy bleachers where several people, men and women alike, are making bets on the game.

"Five-to-one for the world. You wanna bet?" he hears a familiar female voice behind him. Startled, Michael turns and finds his Bulgarian friend, Klava, sitting behind him. Her rebellious long and black hair is kept under a bandana, and her leather pants and a dark T-shirt under her leather jacket make her look cool.

"You look hot, Klava. Some serious distraction for the soccer players!" Michael says light-heartedly. "I didn't see you sneak up on me. I don't bet, but *I* think the Italians are going to kick some serious butt."

Klava laughs: "We'll see about that. So how is the office work coming along?"

"I got some good news. Your papers are advancing nicely. I'll meet with the Canadian Consul tomorrow afternoon and I want to go through some information with you before I leave for the city."

"I'll be there first thing in the morning if you want me to."

"Make it nine - but don't be late. It only will take about five minutes."

"I'm never late. Birra?" Michael looks at her and she points at her shoulder bags where she has a few good Italian beer cans.

"Hit me."

They crack open the cans, and both smoking, watch the players getting ready for the game. There is a merry atmosphere on the bleachers which tries to memorize; this passing moment of carefree, unpretentious joy.

"I never had a chance to thank you for everything you have done for me in the office," Klava says.

"You did; besides, I am just doing my job."

"You should join me sometime when I visit my friends in the rock-n-roll suburbs of Trieste."

"Is it fun? What do they do?"

Klava laughs heartily. "They rock, you silly boy!"

They sip from their beers and shift their attention back to the now heated soccer game.

The two teams are very competitive, and equally matched. The Italian team is made of police officers, office clerks, maintenance personnel and suchlike, all related in one way or the other to the campo profughi. Mateo Forzani is one of the players.

The 'world' team is composed entirely from political refugees. The Eastern Bloc countries: tradesmen, teachers, engineers, students, adventurers. They all share the same passion for the game, and put on a good show.

The Italians lead 2-1 already and the world team is playing fast and furious trying to tie the score. There are two Russian players; Michael has met them both before. One is a university professor with democratic ideals, the other a mining engineer from Siberia. The Russians are the strikers and they currently attack the Italian half. They are moving quickly on the offensive when suddenly the professor trips and falls over. The game stops for a moment, players and referees alike waiting for him to get up.

He doesn't.

The referee approaches the Russian and turns him over from his face-down position. As the body rolls over onto its back, he jumps back in shock.

"*Madre de Dios!*" he mumbles. The referee is shocked. When the players gather around him, they all see the professor's face; he is dead, a tiny bloodless bullet hole showing in the center of his forehead.

The Referee immediately calls off the game while some of the Italian players become cops again; they hear an ambulance rushing toward the Campo.

Klava is frightened and curls up under Michael's protective arm, shivering. She is frightened.

"Let's get out of here. Come with me, Michael. I don't want to be alone," she says in a panic-stricken tone. "It could've been me," she utters. They get up from the bleachers. "It could've been any of us. Let's go," Michael says. They leave the sports park as camp officials and several refugees gather and watch the events unfold.

Klava leads the way through the camp until they reach her building. She turns toward Michael. "You ride motorcycles, right?"

Michael nods. "What has that gotta do with anything?"

She laughs mischievously. "More than you think. I'll be right back!" she says and disappears into the building compound housing the Bulgarian female refugees. She returns in under a minute carrying two full-face motorcycle helmets. She's wearing thin leather gloves and tosses Michael one of the helmets. He catches it and checks it out - it fits.

"Where's the motorcycle?" he asks curiously.

"Outside, by the main gate so the Police can keep an eye on it," she replies.

"Good place."

A few minutes later, they reach the main entrance and Klava waves to the Police Officer on duty. He waves back, happy to see her. The sports bike parked only a few feet away from the main entrance booth is an Italian-made Cagiva and is a beautiful machine. Michael whistles with admiration.

"It's Guido's. He lent it to me so I can zip up to his place on my own and save him time. He's a very busy man!"

"Cool."

They mount their helmets and zip up their leather jackets while Klava fires up the fast bike.

"I like the sound of it," Michael comments on the engine's performance.

Klava mounts the motorcycle. "Hop on," she says and Michael does; a moment later and they blast off from the compound heading toward the beautiful harbor on the shores of the Adriatic Sea.

They look good together.

Klava is a good rider and it shows when she leans the bike just a little to the right and accelerates and brakes fast with precision and agility. Michael is silent behind her, and appreciates every move she makes.

Within minutes they are downtown near the harbor and the picturesque *centre-ville* is charming at night. She parks the motorcycle by the curb, and they lock their helmets to the bike whilst both brushing their hair into something wild and nonconforming.

They light up cigarettes and start walking slowly along the busy and colorful downtown Trieste street.

"Guido lives up there." Klava points up to the ritzy hills where the well-heeled of Trieste live. "He has a very nice pad."

They walk silently for a while, with Klava showing Michael some of the hot spots on the promenade.

"Let's try this place, I think you will like it," she points to a quaint bar on the street. "Come. Tonight it's my treat."

Michael protests but she raises a hand. Michael shrugs.

"I need you with me tonight. C'mon," she says. She means it in friendly way - she feels comfortable in Michael's presence and the feeling is mutual.

"Okay."

They enter the sophisticated nightclub where the owners seem to know and respect Klava, because they come forward and talk to her politely, with respect.

The place is trendy; *the guys are cool and the babes are hot* figures Michael, looking around.

A British live band is playing good rock 'n roll on a small stage. The sound system is excellent.

It doesn't surprise Michael when his friend Jee-Jee shows up beside them with his escort, a distinguished looking rich Italian gentleman. Jee-Jee looks like a movie star: impeccable clothing of the latest trend, long styled hair, discreet makeup. He is really happy to see Klava and Michael.

"Michael, Klava... So good to see you!" he says, looking proudly at his escort. "Pietro told me there was an incident in the camp earlier tonight."

"KGB got Dimitr," Michael answers briefly.

"That's what Pietro said," Jee-Jee says in a feminine, affectionate tone. "It's terrible. One never knows when one's time is up," he looks at Pietro for everybody to see: "He's so well connected. He also insisted that you two join our table - *prego*."

Pietro nods and points toward their table; one of the best in the house.

A minute later they all settle down, ordering drinks. The owner of the place comes over and talks respectfully to Pietro and Klava. The two seem to know each other from before.

Seeing a discreet head signal of Pietro's, Jee-Jee gathers two beautiful Italian women from nearby, who take Michael to the dance floor. As soon as Michael and the girls are there, Klava, Pietro and the owner have an animated, intense conversation. Michael pretends he hasn't noticed anything unusual.

The night is a blast. It unfolds in a cheery way once the sudden briefing has been finalized and is not mentioned again.

It is two hours later when Pietro, Jee-Jee, Klava and Michael leave the nightclub and enter Pietro's waiting luxury black limousine.

***

A sleek sport motorcycle pulls up at the main guarded entrance of the camp. Michael, the rider, removes his helmet.

"Francesco, it's me. Sorry we are so late. Won't happen again," Michael says in Italian to the night guard. "It's my first time."

"It's okay, *Michele*. Just don't make a habit of it. I won't write you guys up this time. The gates lock at eleven PM when the head-count takes place. You know the routine. I will tell Luigi in admin to count you in. And who is that?" he says leaning forward while Klava removes her helmet on the back seat. "And Klava Petrosima as well..." The young officer looks at the two: "I hope you guys had a good time on the town!" he says. Michael and Klava nod and smile mischievously.

The gates open and Michael rides into the camp, dropping Klava off at her building and giving her back the keys and his helmet.

"It was an interesting night, thanks. See you later," Michael says.

"Grazie, bello. It was fun and I thank you too for spending the evening with me and my friends," she kisses him briefly on the lips and runs into the building. Michael waves goodbye and heads without hurry toward his quarter, thinking - not about Klava and he, since they are just good friends, but about Klava and her secret meeting behind his back at the night club. *Time will tell*, he figures and starts walking back toward his dorm.

***

It is early morning and Michael, mounted comfortably in a chair behind his desk, coffee cup beside him, has just finished reading a thick file with a Polish flag on the cover. Placing it besides him, he sets his sheet of paper in the typewriter, accessing some of the emigration forms for the United States. He works effectively for a while until Mateo Forzani, his boss, enters the room heading in his direction:

"What's the status on the dated Australian and American Consulate files?" he asks Michael.

"All processed, waiting for approval," Michael responds proudly and taps a stack of files on the right side of his desk. "I'm working on the last American 'app' for this month. It's not due until next week. I'll interview the young lady next Wednesday." Mateo Forzani is satisfied with his answers. "Very good, *Michele*. Get the files ready and prepare yourself too; the archbishop's limo is picking you up in an hour: Australian Consulate first, lunch, then the American Consul."

"Si, Signore. I'll be ready."

"Very good. I'll see you tomorrow morning."

Michael wants to inquire about the events of last night but Forzani makes himself deliberately unavailable. He exits the office as Michael organizes his papers, pretending that everything is normal.

Shortly afterwards he leaves the office, only to return minutes later - clean shaven, with a fresh white shirt and tie and clean jeans on. Placing his files in a fancy leather shoulder bag he steps outside and lights up a cigarette, waiting for the limo, another service provided by the Catholic Church's archdiocese to the international refugee camp.

Within minutes a large, black limousine shows up at the office entrance, the side of the vehicle emblazoned with the archbishop's coat-of-arms. The chauffeur, a young Italian with a fancy moustache, opens the door for him and a minute later they are on their way to the city's political quarter.

The fancy car pulls up slowly in front of the American Consulate building where Michael is immediately checked out on a US Marines' computer database. The marine returns Michael's papers and salutes. Michael salutes back as the gates open and the limo pulls up in front of the elaborate building; the driver, Tino, opens the door for Michael.

"I won't be long, Tino," Michael addresses the driver. "About two hours if you're lucky. Maybe more."

Tino says knowingly, "Is this your first time?"

"Yes. I'm Joseph's new replacement," Michael replies. Tino gives him the thumb-up and starts climbing the stairs, disappearing a moment later into the impressive building.

Inside, Michael identifies himself to the receptionist, also guarded by two more Marines who patrol the lobby.

Getting his second clearance Michael is led by a pretty legal secretary to the Consul's private office.

"Come in, Michael," welcomes him a distinguished-looking gentleman who extends a large, wrinkled hand. "Patrick Delaney, US Consul to Caritas emigration and external affairs."

"Michael Agrafa, emigration clerk for the campo di profughi," Michael says shaking his hand. "Nice to meet you, sir."

"Call me Patrick," the Consul says casually.

"Thank you. I have a few processed files for you, sir... Patrick."

The Consul walks over to his coffee table in the office, waving to Michael. "Let's get to it. I'm ready."

Michael sits down opposite him and opening his files presents the first case he has worked on for the Consulate. The two men get into the details of the business at hand, the Consul asking all sorts of thorny questions regarding the applicants, at the same time testing Michael's knowledge and training.

Just over two hours later the Consul is satisfied with the progress. "That's great, Michael. Good job. Talking to your office, I understand that you'll have another six cases ready for me soon," the Consul says.

"They'll be ready by next Friday."

"Excellent. I'll see you again then."

They both stand up and Michael places his files onto the desk as the Consul reaches out a hand to shake. "Until Friday."

"Until Friday," Michael responds and quietly leaves the inner office. He leaves the building and walks out to the waiting limo.

"Where to now?" Tino asks.

"The Australian Consulate. Busy day today."

The driver nods and places the car in gear. The limo drives through the beautiful streets of Trieste for a while until it pulls in front of the Australian Consul building, perched high on the green hills overlooking the Adriatic Sea.

"What do you know about Jackson Cole?" Michael asks his driver.

"Very smart person. Much younger than your buddy Delaney," Tino says. "He's a real nice man, easy to talk to," he adds.

"You just love to rub elbows with powerful people, don't you?" Michael asks, laughing.

"That's where it's at!" Tino says and putting on his super-cool sunglasses gives Michael 'the look.' They both burst into laughter. "It will take you about an hour and a half," Tino calls after Michael as he heads for the main entrance. He waves back in acknowledgement and enters the Australian Consulate, ready for business.

He goes through the same identification routine and after that is escorted to the inner office where he is met by Jackson Cole, the Consul.

"I've heard a few good things about you," Cole says, glancing at Michael's large stack of files sticking out from his shoulder bag.

"I'm still learning the ropes; there's a lot to be learnt," Michael says simple.

"Yes indeed. What have you gotten for me?"

Michael takes the files out from his bag and places them onto the coffee table in front of the Consul.

"Eight cases," Michael says, pointing at the files. "They have all been cleared for advancement."

The Consul starts leafing through them, checking the names. He looks at Michael curiously.

"I see that one of these files is yours," he says, looking at Michael.

"Mine and Bastian Copacee's, a good friend of mine. We have known each other since childhood."

"So you must've escaped together, I take it?"

"Yes."

"Very interesting. Before we get to you and your friend's file, let's take care of the rest of the caseload. Coffee?"

"Yes, thank you."

Cole picks up the telephone receiver on the coffee table and speaks into it: "Two coffees please, Isabel."

The coffees arrive shortly and the two start working on the cases, Jackson Cole asking a lot of questions, many of them relating to the element of the 'human factor', a subject in which Michael is well prepared for.

Nearly two hours go by until they reach Michael's own case. The Consul opens the file, looks at Michael and says, "There are a few options available..."

***

It is already dark outside when the archbishop's limousine pulls into the camp, Tino opening the door for Michael.

"It took longer than we both estimated," Michael tells Tino.

"You had a lot of cases and places to go today. I'm exhausted!" Tino answers.

"Go home and have a good rest. See you next time."

"That will be next Thursday, to be exact," Tino says with his usual efficiency.

"Yes, indeed. Good night, Tino."

"Good night."

The driver gets back into the car and slowly drives away. Michael, alone, lights up a cigarette releasing a small film of smoke and starts towards his dorm building.

The camp is quiet at this time of the night. Occasional laughter breaks the silence and loads it with a vibrating human presence. Reaching his building, he places the shoulder bag beside him and sits down on the top stair finishing his smoke, thinking about his conversation with Jackson Cole. A very pretty brunette dressed in stylish black leathers approaches him silently.

"It looks like it's been a long day for you," she says in a quiet voice behind him. Michael jumps with a start and turns around to face her.

"You startled me, Elisabeth; I didn't hear you coming. How are you?"

"Okay, all things considered," she says inhaling from her cigarette. She sits down on the top of the stairs and Michael sits beside her.

"I was waiting for you for most of the evening. How was the trip to the officials?" she asks in a gentle tone.

"Not bad. Learned a few things. But what's so important it couldn't wait until the morning?" Michael asks looking at her.

Elisabeth checks her stylish wristwatch: "My people, I mean the Hungarian boys, are planning to 'smoke out' the Albanians... tonight at midnight. It's going to be a bloodshed which I don't want to happen."

They look at each other and it is now that Michael notices that something is wrong with Elisabeth - she has heavy bruises on her pretty face which she tries to conceal.

"Show me that," he tells her to remove her hand from her face. She does. "Shit! Who did this to you? Let me guess; the Albanians?" Elisabeth bursts in sobbing tears: "They gang-raped me last night," she whimpers.

Michael takes her free hand and holds it tight between his hands, rubbing it gently. "Are you alright? Did you see the camp Doctor?"

Elisabeth shakes her head. "Lora and Rodica helped me get through with it. I can't sleep. If I close my eyes, the nightmares begin."

Michael wraps her arm around her shoulder with empathy.

"What do you want me to do? Call the Carabinieri to protect you from the Albanians? I can do that no problem - "

"Don't!" she interrupts him, even more worried now. "By all means no. That would totally ruin my friends' emigration progress status," she looks at Michael. "Since you're half Hungarian, you're also part of the group. I would like you to talk some sense into the guys. They would listen to you, I know that."

Michael chews on her words for a while. "This is very heavy stuff, Elisabeth. I will talk to them for sure, but this time they are not going to listen. The emotions will hit the roof and then there will be no room left for reasoning," he pauses and inhales deeply, turning to her "You know what? I feel like rushing over there and doing the 'smoking' myself... bastards!" Elisabeth starts crying again.

"I'm sorry, Elisabeth. They did a terrible thing to you," he cools down and stands up. "I'll go talk to them right now. There's not much time left. Where do I find them?"

"You will find Ishtvan and Gabriel having a drink at the Pastorelli Trattoria on the hillside," Elisabeth says in a low voice, lighting up another cigarette: "Do you want me to come along?"

Michael shakes his head.

"I'll drop my bag in the dorm and walk up there. Are the Albanians in their compound?"

"They have all come in by now, one-at-a-time. I watched them myself - from a hiding place, of course," she says, her voice sounding so fragile that Michael takes her in his arms and holds her fast, soothing her pain, caressing her long hair.

"You'd better stay with Rodica and the Romanians tonight. We don't know how it is going to turn out. It doesn't look good. And also, please, Elisabeth, find Jee-Jee. He is the best for finding resources under traumatic circumstances."

"He sure is. He's a Lawyer or something," Elisabeth agrees. "I will see him in his boudoir."

They both laugh a little and it feels good to release some of the tension.

"You be careful. We need you out here."

"Don't worry about me," Michael says, and giving her a small wave heads back toward the dorm to change, then back to the path leading to the main gate.

Changed now in casual clothes, he walks hurriedly towards the same Trattoria in which he met Bastian and Marya earlier. The thought of her being gone, murdered, makes him shiver, his tormented heart missing a beat.

The Pastorelli bar is busier than usual tonight. There are some local Italian customers mixed with the refugees, talking animatedly, the Italians laughing out loud often and with zest. Michael finds Gabriel and Ishtvan easily, sipping their drinks at a small table in the back of the bar. They look up surprised to see Michael here at this time of the night. They know him well because only a week ago Michael added some information to Gabriel's file making it progress a bit faster through the system. Ironic enough, that small addition to his file was about his generous time spent with the needy and the less fortunate.

"Double Campari on the rocks, *prego*," Michael says turning to Antonio. "You guys want another round?" he asks his buds who shake their heads.

Antonio places the drink on the bar as Michael stands between the two young men. The bartender leaves a moment later, called to another table.

"I just talked to Elisabeth," Michael drops the hammer to them. The two Hungarians quickly exchange a look.

"Let me guess... she told you about her 'misfortune' with the Albanians and she sent you up here to try to stop the bloodshed?" Ishtvan say looking at Michael.

"Something like that. It's not worth it for you to ruin your lives for *them*. There are other ways to deal with this."

"This is the best, the quickest way; burn them like rats and then kill the bastards," Gabriel butts in with anger.

"Cool it, Gabriel," Ishtvan says with a more leveled tone of voice. "They'll get what they deserve tonight and that's that. Finish your drink; we've got work to do," he addresses his friend then turns to Michael. "If you wanna help, keep Elisabeth out from harm's way for now."

"I already did that," Michael says quickly, realizing that he is running out of time and options. "But Ishtvan - "

Ishtvan gets up from his stool.

"That's all. Have another drink on me," he turns to the bartender pointing at Michael's drink. The Italian bartender nods and wordlessly prepares the drink while the two Hungarians exit the bar. Michael watches them helplessly; their minds are set.

***

The Albanian compound is partially lit. Occasionally, you can see silhouettes crossing the light through the large windows. It is a regular night in the campo di profughi - or so it seems. On the other hand, some of the insiders of the camp know differently - there is no such thing as 'regular night' in campo di profughi.

A group of young men, about a dozen, all dressed in black, stealthily approach the building, gathering in a dark corner - They carry a few heavy bags and baseball bats. Two of them begin to open the bags and remove their content: Molotov cocktails.

They are the young Hungarian men.

They all look at Ishtvan. He points to different windows; some on the main floor, some on the second floor. Two men light up the short gasoline-soaked rags and start tossing them through the windows. Within moments the windows light up in flames and you can hear the Albanians screaming, cursing voices reacting through the building. Gabriel dissipates his crew - two men with baseball bats on each side of the building - while Ishtvan and three of his countrymen post themselves at the main entrance.

Moments later the Albanians are jumping out through windows and doorways - and are welcomed by the Hungarians' wrath and revenge. Violent pockets of fights ignite everywhere. The Albanians are mean and dirty fighters but the Hungarians dominate the situation -- within minutes there are several bodies lying on the ground, bleeding and screaming in pain.

A gun shot echoes through the night coming from the inside of the burning building. One of the Hungarians collapses. Gabriel retrieves his own handgun and jumps inside the burning building. Five shots are heard and a minute later Gabriel reappears, his eyes bloodshot, bleeding from his head. In the distance, Police sirens are getting louder, closer. The young Hungarians gather around Ishtvan.

"This night never happened. Run and disappear... and stay quiet!" he utters in a commanding voice. Seconds later, the young men disappear in the large camp while Ishtvan and Gabriel carry their wounded friend through the dark back alleys back to their compound.

The building fully erupts into flames now as several personnel and refugees alike gather around at a safe distance making comments. Police, ambulance and fire trucks race into the compound with noises and lights as if a carnival was taking place on the hills of Trieste.

***

The sun is beaming down on the city as Michael walks slowly towards the administration building. It is the morning after the carnage and the whole camp is quiet, a somber atmosphere prevailing everywhere throughout the buildings and alleys alike.

Michael butts out his cigarette and enters the building heading for his office. He chats in low voice with Vanessa and Giovanna about last night's terrible events. Heavy-heartedly, Michael makes himself a large dose of coffee and finally settles behind his desk, immersing himself into his work.

Several hours go by when Michael finally closes another fat folder and stretches his arms, relaxing for a moment. His attention is triggered when he recognizes a voice and a particular laugh coming from across the office. He cranes his neck but he can't see the person talking.

Jee-Jee, all dolled up as usual, but in cashmere and satin this time, has just dropped a box of expensive chocolate on Vanessa's desktop.

"Grazie, *caro*. But I can't accept it. It's office policy," Vanessa explains. Jee-Jee waves evasively and smiling walks over to Michael's desk, taking a seat in the empty chair in front of the desk. Michael looks up from his file:

"How you doing, cutie?" Jee-Jee giggles and a moment later leans over the desk, looking at Michael.

"About last night..." he whispers to Michael. "Two of the Albanians are dead and the rest are burnt, wounded... in the hospital."

Michael releases a deep sigh of anguish.

"I couldn't stop them. I tried. How is Elisabeth?" "Shaken up, angry but otherwise recovering nicely," Jee-Jee answers.

"This is *very* serious stuff," Michael whispers looking around to check if there is anybody in their earshot. "The Italians started a thorough investigation this morning. There will be no stone unturned. They already interviewed me too. They have many suspicions but no clues. What I'm saying here is stay clean, all of you, and very quiet; your whole future is at stake. These Albanians are 'bad blood' and everybody knows that - but we are very concerned about the general public's perception, me included. The archbishop called me up this morning and wants me to join a televised panel of humane sciences delegates and economists along with reps of the Catholic Church, to talk about the violence in and around the camp. He wants me to represent and lobby for the refugees' interest."

Jee-Jee gets excited.

"That's wonderful, *Michele*. The whole camp and the city will watch it and cheer for you... and the Caritas. You're the right man for the job."

Michael waves down his enthusiasm.

"It's just an idea the archbishop came up with and it won't be for another week or so," Michael explains in a low voice. "It will be televised Nationwide... makes me nervous as hell."

"I've got the jitters already! You'll do fine though , I'm sure. Listen *Michele*; there's something else I came to see you about too - It's somebody new in the camp who really wants to meet you tonight. She claims that she knows you."

"Where is she from?"

"France."

Michael looks confused at Jee-Jee.

"She's not a refugee, she's only visiting. I can't say any more. Be in my dorm at eight o'clock tonight."

He gets up and leaves the office with class, making Vanessa and Michael exchange quick, friendly looks.

"I need a smoke," Michael tells Vanessa and walks outside, lighting up a cigarette. He is intrigued now... who could the woman be?

***

The working day is finally over for Michael. It's been long and stressful, with several official groups coming and talking to him, asking him questions, scrutinizing him and bouncing him around as if *he* was the offender.

At one point in time, talking to one of the officers from the Metro Police he had nearly lost his cool. He had snapped, "I'm not the offender here or anywhere else. I'm just doing a job here. Why has everybody come to me?"

"Because you know a lot of different groups and they confess to you either privately or for the emigration process," the officer had replied - and he had been right.

A lot of people liked Michael because, most importantly, he always listened. Having Empathy and caring, and being well informed, he was easy to talk to and dependable. He never took sides. Personal matters *stayed* personal, and privacy was never broken. Today though, some of the official questionings came pretty close to almost breaching that trust under the pressure of persuasion.

He stood his ground however, answered all of the questions he could and tried to help. And that was that. Now, on his walk back to the dorm at seven thirty in the evening, his mind is disconnecting and reconnecting to the mysterious visitor he is supposed to meet in a little while.

Reaching his building, he quickly takes a shower, brushes his teeth and puts on a fresh white shirt, clean jeans and white sneakers. He is good to go.

He walks slowly toward the Hungarian compound. He carries a leather shoulder bag, saluting a few people on his way before entering the building. Making his way down the hallway, he knocks on the door of the Hungarian dormitory, and then opens it gently.

Michael brushes his hand over his long hair and knocks at Jee-Jee's private room. Curiously enough, there is nobody in the dorm, not even Jee-Jee's ever-present body guard. A moment later, he sees Jee-Jee drawing his drapes a few inches and sneaking into the dorm to welcome Michael himself.

Jee-Jee is all dolled up and elegant, like an A-list movie star.

"C'mon in. *We* were expecting you."

He has a girly giggle which suits him fine. Michael follows him into his very private quarters which again take him aback. This time, everything is spotless and rearranged, fresh-cut flowers on the table, soft music in the background, an expensive, very sophisticated hint of a perfume in the air... remotely familiar. Michael's heartbeats accelerate a tad.

He hands over a fine wine bottle from his shoulder bag. Jee-Jee likes the brand and places it on the table. "This place is very nice," Michael says.

"*Grazie, caro mio,*" Jee-Jee says gallantly. "Take a seat and make yourself comfortable," he says, placing the wine in a chiller.

Michael's heart misses a beat. A beautiful, trendy brunette walks out from the small private bathroom and sends a kiss his way.

"Stephanie!" Michael whispers, out of breath. "What a surprise, *mon cher...*"

He meets the woman half-way and gives her a warm hug which they both hold in silence for a few long seconds. Jee-Jee watches them with delight.

"It's good to see you again. You haven't changed much," Stephanie says after they finally separate, and holding hands look at each other at arm's length.

"Just got older. How long has it been?" Michael says with a sad smile.

"Almost two years now," she answers.

"What are you doing in a place like this?" He quickly turns to his host: "Jee-Jee, I didn't mean your place... I meant the camp."

Jee-Jee waves him off evasively.

"I got word that you were here so I came to visit you. It's not that far from Lyon," she says, smiling charmingly. "But how did you know I was here?" he asks. Stephanie smiles mysteriously.

"I have my sources."

"It's good to see you."

"Same."

"You know Jee-Jee?"

Jee-Jee and Stephanie exchange friendly looks.

"Long before I met you."

"What do you know," Michael shrugs intrigued. Jee-Jee fills up some wine glasses for them.

"Why don't you guys step out and catch up a bit while I prepare some snacks?" he says gallantly.

Stephanie and Michael say "Okay." and taking their wine glasses walk out of the building, sitting down on the front step, Michael bringing a towel for Stephanie to sit on. They light up cigarettes.

"I missed you," Stephanie says in a low, soft voice loaded with melancholy. Michael takes her hand and holds it in his. They sit quietly and share the moment.

"How long are you staying?" he asks her after a while.

"I'm heading back to France tomorrow. I'm looking up an old friend in Trieste and then I hit the road. The business needs me in Paris," she says and her tone tells suggests that it is not what she wants to do.

"I would like to spend some time with you," Michael says.

"Me too... with you. We have all night if you want to stay with me at the Hotel Continentale."

"That's in the historic downtown? I'm game, but I have to talk to the camp about it. They have strict rules here."

"I understand," Stephanie says softly. She leans over and kisses him on the lips. Michael responds gently. They both sit there sharing silences for a while and it feels good.

"Thanks for coming down," Michael says after a while. "I have missed our time together."

A few Hungarian women come by heading to their dorm and wave small 'hellos' to them, mostly aimed at Michael, while checking out Stephanie - and she knows it. "You seem fairly popular around here," she says with a tinge of jealousy.

"It's not what you think. I do their emigration papers. It's all business."

Stephanie's sharp female instincts say otherwise. "Sure," she conciliates.

They enjoy the gentle night for a while until Jee-Jee comes out and calls them in. They get up, and holding hands, walk back into the building.

Nearly two hours later, it is almost curfew time when Michael and Stephanie walk to the main entrance booth. Michael talks to the Italian police officer who keeps staring at the beautiful French girl. He is not very cooperative until Stephanie leans over the small counter and offers him the Continentale Hotel's business card. "I'll bring him back safe and sound in the morning," she says in perfect Italian, laughing. The officer takes the card and nods jealously.

"He is a very lucky guy!" he grumbles. Stephanie laughs with delight.

"I think I am!" Michael agrees with the officer as the two leave the booth and enter in Stephanie's luxury black sports car which she drives away like a racer. She drives fast, laughing as Michael watches her delightedly.

"I just had to make an impression on the Italian police," she says mischievously looking at Michael.

"He will remember you for the rest of his life. I think he really, really likes you."

"Don't you?"

Instead of an answer he pinches one of her buttocks. "Drive carefully," he says casually.

Chapter 9

Stephanie's hot sports car pulls up in front of the main gate of the camp only minutes before eight in the morning. Michael kisses her on the lips as he pulls himself towards the car door.

"It was so good to be together again," Stephanie says, a grin lighting up her whole face.

"I want more," Michael responds.

"Me too. Listen... I'll drive to Paris and take care of the business for however long it takes and then I will be in touch. Now you know where to reach me if you need to."

"Same goes for you too," Michael replies.

"I've got to go. Ciao," she says, blowing him a kiss.

"Ciao."

He extracts himself from the low door and she drives away fast, tooting the horn once before blasting around the corner.

A familiar police officer watches him and shakes his head with a smile as he walks by.

"Stephanie says 'hi'" he tells the officer as he heads for his dorm to change for work.

***

The days fly by fast, turning into weeks. Michael is getting more and more involved with his work, becoming faster and more efficient. He has only managed to talk to Stephanie once in all this time when she had called him from London where she was closing an international clothing fashion deal.

It is almost eight o'clock in the evening when Michael leaves the administration building and walks back to his dorm. The room is empty with the exception of the two chess players going hard at the game. He finds a small note on the top of his bed and reads it:

Come join us:
Fireplace gathering and drinks
Behind the small warehouse.
Signed
Bastian

Michael crumples the note and tosses it into the garbage can. Taking a quick shower he puts on fresh clothes and leaves the dorm, heading toward the warehouses area close to the small park of the compound.

It is a great night and Michael's young blood is racing through his veins. Things are getting a little better now. The emigration papers are advancing well and his job is getting more intriguing and exciting by the moment, albeit shocking at times. And on top it all, he has reconnected with Stephanie, who he thought that he lost forever.

He reaches the warehouses area and he can see from the distance the gathering taking place around an open fire pit with a large but controlled fire taking center stage.

The group gathered around the fire chats casually, listening to the crackling flames. A teenage Czech girl is playing a classical guitar; she is very good at it, Michael immediately notices. He also recognizes some of his friends from the dorm, as well as Hungarian women and men among other nationalities. There is a silent harmony taking place here and Michael's sensitive heart feels it. He spots Bastian a few rows back, sipping from his beer and chatting with his neighbor, a cute Croatian girl.

Michael silently sits beside his friend who offers a bottle of beer to him. Michael nods and takes a sip, looking around and making small hello signs to people who recognized him.

"How's the night job going? Don't see much of you lately," Michael says after a while.

"It's okay. They pay me cash so it helps a little."

"Yep."

They sip their beers, watching the flames.

"Did you know about the downplay on the Albanians beforehand?" Bastian asks him in a low voice without looking at him.

"I'm not supposed to have known anything. Sorry, Bast," Michael replies in a low voice.

"But did you?"

"Yes, I did. And I tried to stop it," Michael whispers.

As if answering to a thought of his own, Bastian briefly looks at him. "I thought so. You told me the other day that we should switch to Canada. What's up?"

"It's the best country in which to start over and it's beautiful. Everybody tells me the same," Michael answers.

"Who's everybody?"

"Embassies, Consulates, camp heads, Caritas, etc," Michael says.

"How do you feel about it?"

"I think we should do it... soon."

"Do it."

"Good. Done. I need you to stop off at the office and sign some new papers, then," Michael finishes his beer and gets up.

"Thanks."

He points at the bottle.

"I'll drop by your office in the morning," Bastian says.

"Make it ten o'clock."

Bastian nods.

"Got to go," says Michael.

"See you tomorrow."

***

Next morning, as usual, Michael is diligently preparing his work cases for the day. When he reached his desk this morning he found another pile of fresh files on his desktop with a hand-written note from Mateo Forzani:

Michele:
Please process the top two
(#11 and #19)
I'm working on these cases this morning
Grazie
Signed
Mateo F.

Following his boss's advice, Michael opens case file #11 and nearly drops it on the desk, shocked and surprised at the same time. The picture of the handsome young man looking straight back at him triggers an immediate resonance in his mind. He moves his eyes to the name on the case file: Yuri Petrosima.

"I'll be damned," Michael whispers and after reading the details of the case there is no doubt in his mind: the young man in the picture is Klava's younger brother.

He checks his wrist watch: 6:23am. It's too early for any of the other staff members, who start at seven o'clock. Picking up the file, he starts work on it, making notes, typing data in the Caritas officially-formatted emigration papers.

By nine-thirty in the morning he shares the information about Klava's brother's successful attempt to reach the free world with Vanessa and Giovanna. The office girls are thrilled about the news. He had really wanted to talk to Klava first, to see if she knew about her baby brother's successful escape.

A few minutes before ten o'clock, Bastian shows up and chats with Vanessa for a few minutes before he comes and sees Michael who by this time has his case file ready in front of him.

"How goes the battle?" Bastian enquires, sitting down in a chair in front of the desk.

"Not bad. What's new with you lately?"

"Same old. What you got for me?" Bastian enquires.

"These are the new forms you have to sign, right by those 'X's. I'll transfer the rest of the information myself. This is just to state that you agree with the change," Michael explains.

"What about *your* papers?"

"Done already. Sign here." Michael tosses him the first document. Bastian signs it and Michael hands over him the next one. "Stephanie says hi."

"You mean *the* Stephanie, the French business woman?" Michael nods with a grin which spreads from ear to ear.

"You bum. So the rumor is true. She's in town."

"Not right now, but she was here earlier. She called me yesterday from London."

"Awesome. You still love that French girl," Bastian states casually.

"Nonsense."

"I know you, don't argue with me. Anyway, I'm getting a Ducati motorcycle tomorrow. You'll love it. Very fast! How's she doing?"

"Great. Her business is growing. I want to take it for a test ride."

"You will. I need to tune it up first."

They return their focus to the emigration papers, Michael asking some questions then typing them into the forms.

***

The long angular sun rays cast distorted shadows on a wooden picnic table located in the tiny green park in the middle of the camp. Michael and Rodica are perched there, folders open and writing pads spread on the table top.

They are working on something.

The silence of the day is suddenly broken up by wailing sirens of police cars and ambulances.

"Something's just happened again in the camp. They're coming this way," Rodica says, listening to the sirens getting louder.

"I bet you five bucks somebody was killed again," Michael states matter-of-factly.

Rodica is more positive, "Maybe not. I think it's a medical situation this time. Let's check it out."

"You do that. I'll see you here tomorrow at the same time; you need to catch up on your English."

"I'll be here, no worries; thanks." Michael gathers his papers and follows Rodica who joins a crowd watching the approaching emergency vehicles, asking questions.

"We're even, bro. You were right on your part - *Cosa Nostra* killed one of the Polish guys, Petrov. He was doing some shady things, that's what I hear." Rodica tells Michael the latest gossip.

"What's your part, sunshine?"

Rodica is a little excited, "A baby was born in the camp today, in the Czech building - a beautiful baby girl. By the way, we're invited for drinks and cake to celebrate the new arrival."

"Who are the parents?"

"Slava, the Czech translator, is the mom, and the lucky dad is Herzog, the East-German Mechanical Engineer. They're getting married here."

"Cool - life and death in the same day in the same place. *Vita di profughi*," Michael observes philosophically.

Rodica smiles at his words, "Corny as hell but true enough. You wanna come for a drink with them?"

"What time?"

"Seven thirty."

"I'll pick you up at seven twenty-five."

Rodica nods and gets involved in a conversation with her neighbor as Michael walks away, heading for his building.

Later on the same evening, Michael, Bastian and Rodica are walking the alleys towards the Czech quarters.

"I picked up something for the baby for the three of us," Rodica chirps jovially.

"That's thoughtful of you, thanks," Bastian says.

"Times two!" Michael enforces.

"Don't mention it."

They enter the building and meet the international community joining the celebration of life. There is a merry atmosphere in the place - they celebrate the birth of a new human being. Born free.

***

The next morning, Michael is busy with his work when Mateo Forzani, the office manager, walks into the office and approaches him. "Bongiorno, Michael. How is the day developing?" Mateo asks him in a good mood.

"Very good, Signore Forzani," Michael answers.

"Call me Mateo, *prego*. Remember?"

"Si, Mateo. *Grazie*. I have a new batch of files ready for the British Consul."

"Excellent. I'll contact the Consul and make arrangements for you to see him," he says, his mind elsewhere. "I've had some very good feedback regarding your work, bravo. Now, about that televised panel we talked about a few weeks ago; it will take place on Wednesday, two days from now. Get prepared and come to the office as usual. The archbishop's limo will pick you up at nine o'clock in the morning, precisely. You'll ride with the archbishop of Trieste himself!"

Michael is almost overwhelmed by the news.

"Thank you, Mateo. I will be prepared."

"Good. We're counting on you." Waving a small hello to Michael and Vanessa he leaves the office.

Michael gives a puzzled look to Vanessa who smiles, "No pressure..." he says.

"You'll do fine," she says with confidence.

It is about eight in the evening and the camp is quiet. Michael sits alone in the small dorm, writing notes in a journal. He reaches for a bottle of scotch and pours a couple of fingers into a tumbler. The dorm door opens and Jee-Jee walks in. "Make that two!" he calls.

Rodica and Klava follow him in, "Make that four!"

Michael smiles and draws out a few more glasses from the small stand he shares with Bastian.

"Yeah. I missed you too. What's up? Some sort of new conspiracy developing again?" Michael jokes, offering them the drinks.

"We have issues for you to address, buddy-boy," Rodica says casually but her tone of voice has an angle.

"Word must've leaked out about my trip tomorrow," Michael says smiling and looking at his friends.

"Only the whole camp and most of Italy knows about it about now. Caritas spent some serious coin on advertising this event," Klava explains.

"It's all about us, the beautiful political refugees!" Jee-Jee states flamboyantly.

"Cheers, cheers!" Michael says in good spirits raising his glass. His friends do the same:

"Cheers!"

A few moments later a heavy silence develops in the dorm. They are all preoccupied with their thoughts. It is Klava who breaks the silence. "Our national and international reputation is on very shaky ground lately. Too much violence, mischief and prostitution has reached the media," she says.

"It's not so much of it, as such, but of course, the bad news always grabs the public's attention the most," Rodica adds.

"I agree with Rodica. The population at large doesn't know anything about the *good* deeds we've done around here," Michael says.

"The archbishop and the whole Trieste diocese are trying to save face here," Rodica says in crystal clear Italian, for extra emphasis.

"It's all in your hands, Michael. You're our only hope," she says with pathos, then starts laughing.

"No pressure on the guy!" says Michael smiling and taking a sip from his glass. "There will be lots of questions fired at me, I'm sure. I *think* I'm prepared though."

"We'll be all watching. And we will be behaving for a day!" Jee-Jee says.

They all laugh. They sip from their drinks and Michael gives them a brief update on the progress of their personal emigration processes.

***

It is seven o'clock in the morning. The sun is shining brightly and indiscriminately on the shores of the Adriatic Sea and the refugee camp alike.

Michael approaches the main office building. He's early as usual. Lighting up a cigarette, he sits on the front stairs, enjoying the morning. His head is clear, he has prepared the best he knows how.

Before he finishes his cigarette, the large black limousine of the Trieste Diocese pulls silently up to the curb beside him. Michael steps on his cigarette butt and looks at the car. The rear door opens from inside and Michael meets the archbishop's round, distinguished face. "Good morning, *Michele*. Jump in."

Michael does. The limousine silently leaves the camp and heads toward the city, perched at the nearby shores.

The archbishop and Michael sip strong cappuccinos as the high-priest is talking:

"There have been many ups and downs over the years, but I believe that we do a wonderful job for these people," the Archbishop converses.

"I couldn't believe it more," Michael says. "Caritas is the only powerful and well-connected entity to support such a large number of people evading the communist regime, seeking a better life," Michael says carefully picking his words.

"We've been doing it for a long time, rather successfully," the Archbishop says in an even voice. "I want to do it for plenty more time to come," he gives a direct look to Michael.

"I will do my best, Signore. There is one thing you should know." The archbishop raises a set of bushy eyebrows.

"I will defend in earnest this camp - and the administration - because I believe in it." Michael sips from his cappuccino while the archbishop nods silently.

They ride quietly for a little while as the limo turns into the downtown core. It approaches a large engraved granite building with large marble steps leading to the main entrance. There is already a group of reporters and various TV Channel trucks parked in front of the building. As the transport approaches the main steps, the reporters rush toward it. Tino, the driver, opens the door for the archbishop and then walks around to do the same for Michael, who - just as the archbishop does - ignores the reporters' persistent questions.

The clergyman stops for a moment at the top of the stairs and turns to the media and says "The Catholic Church will make a statement shortly after the panel meeting. That is all for now."

He and Michael, surrounded by Italian police, walk into the building. The large studio is prepared for the controversial panel discussion which is to be televised nationwide. As Michael and the archbishop are ushered in, a dozen technicians are getting the set ready. Cameras and lights are also being prepared.

There is a large semi-circular table facing two armchairs. The large table holds six chairs, two of them presently occupied. The two armchairs in the middle are for the archbishop and Michael, with the questioning being addressed to Michael, but with certain policies and procedural points to be answered by the Church. There are several cameras and technical crew covering the discussion.

The anchor, a pretty young woman in her early thirties arrives at the scene, approaching the two men who now both stand beside their seats. "Are you ready for this, gentlemen?" she asks in a controlled, professional voice. They nod.

"Very well, then. Let's take our seats." The Archbishop and Michael sit whilst the anchor gestures to her technicians to fill the panel.

The professionals arrive one at a time and are guided to their seats. Once they are all seated, the anchorwoman glances to the floor director; everybody's ready. She makes a discreet sign and begins her on-air introduction. "Good evening, ladies and gentlemen. Today, the much anticipated panel is finally here and I am pleased to present to you the panel members:"

The professionals are introduced one at the time and they rise from their seats momentarily as they are introduced. Last, but not the least, Archbishop Monteverdi and Michael are introduced to the audience. They salute with discreet gestures and bow.

The panel discussions starts slowly but as the audience and the panel heat up, the questions - many of them difficult to answer - keep flowing in. Michael and the Archbishop perform a masterful job in keeping their perspective and focus unchanged.

The passion is flying high now and the focus is on Michael, who - not so much as an individual, but as a representative of a controversial group known as international political refugees - is place under scrutiny. Michael has come prepared however; he answers the questions diligently, displaying personal charm and triggering the audience's empathy for the cause he so passionately believes in.

After a while one can feel the anxiety dissipate from the audience. The open communication with a direct participant from the group starts paying dividends. Unnoticed by the audience (but caught by Michael) the anchorwoman breathes a deep sigh of relief; the difficult panel coverage has turned out better then she expected, making *her* also look good in the process!

The panel programming is finally over. It has lasted almost two hours and both the archbishop and Michael alike are extremely tired. They have fresh coffee waiting for them in the limousine. "Thank you, Tino. This was very thoughtful of you," the archbishop tells his driver. Now driving back to the camp, the he sips from his fresh cappuccino and glances at Michael, "You were very focused and eloquent back there, *Michele*."

"*Grazie*, Signore. I did the best I could. And that's the way I feel about it," Michael responds in earnestly.

"It will definitely help shape a more positive image of the profughi."

"I hope so, Signore. Thank you for trusting in me for this panel meeting."

"We are happy to have you here," replies the clergyman candidly.

By this time, the limousine is approaching the high gates of the refugee camp. They open and the car stops in front of the administration office. Michael spills out from the vehicle and waves a brief salute to the archbishop as the limo drives away.

Alone again, he releases a deep sigh - for better or for worse, it's all done now. Michael is walking slowly towards the building, his mind playing back vivid images from the heated panel discussions when a familiar female voice comes alive behind him:

"That was a fabulous debate, Mister!" Rodica says. Startled, Michael turns around and sees her, Klava, Jee-Jee and Bastian watching him.

"Where did you come from all of a sudden?" Michael asks them, surprised. "It's good to see you guys... it's good to be back," he says, lighting up a cigarette and inhaling deeply. "I sure could use a strong drink."

"We thought so," replies Jee-Jee. "C'mon, we'll zip down to the Trattoria - my treat."

"Sure, I'm game," says Michael in a tired but happy voice.

They leave the main gates and Bastian points to a Fiat sedan at the curb. "I just bought it yesterday. It's just to get me from A to B, but that's all I need for now. Hop in, I'll drive you," he says, unlocking the car. They all climb in and Bastian drives away, everyone chatting away like a happy family. There is a powerful closeness which Michael immediately senses and it makes him feel good, grounded again.

It's a quiet afternoon and the neighborhood is relaxed. The five enter the small café. When the patrons and Antonio see Michael, they all erupt in cheers. He blushes and waves a humble salute. A television set mounted above the small bar is tuned to the channel on which the discussion took place. They are showing feedback programs following the discussion.

The groups take seats on the 'reserved' bar stools and drinks are served by Antonio himself.

"Good job, *Michele*. I think you pulled at everyone's heartstrings," Bastian says to his old friend, sipping from his drink.

"Yes, you did," Klava adds passionately. "And shed some real light about the camp and us, the *profughi*."

"That was the whole idea. We're not that bad after all... well, not all of us," Michael says in a low, even voice.

"I liked it best when you told the Milan economist that we should sometimes be paid for our knowledge and expertise in certain services we provide. I have given them free consultations in business management for almost a year now," Rodica says.

"I know that. There are also many other experts like you in the camp," Michael says.

Now two Italian gentlemen dressed in business suits approach their table, "Another round on us. Please accept it," says the first man. "We all needed that sort of information. Thank you." Michael and his friends nod and salute the strangers.

As the excitement tapers off a little, the five get back to their own issues. "Sorry to bring it to you on a day like this but we have a problem in the camp." Klava breaks it to Michael as gently as she knows how.

Michael raises an eyebrow and looks at his other friends. They all support Klava's words.

"Can't it wait until tomorrow?" Michael asks in a small voice knowing already that this was a pointless question. "It could, but it might escalate more yet," Jee-Jee says in a whispered voice.

Michael is a little concerned now. "What are you talking about?"

The friends quickly look at one another then turn to Klava, as an unspoken chosen spokesperson. "There was a double-murder in cottage twenty-three today," Klava says in a clear whisper.

Michael is shocked. He raises his eyebrows inquiringly.

"The Bulgarians?"

They all nod.

"We have all tried to keep it under wraps for as long as we can," Klava explains.

"Who are the victims?" Michael asks them.

"Nicolay and Sophia. They were killed execution-style, shot in the face at close range," Bastian explains whilst Jee-Jee shivers, suddenly very pale.

"Shit," Michael utters. "We've got a serious problem here; that looks like a typical execution by the Italian mafia. This will be tough to handle."

"They both were doing business with the *familia* but they somehow crossed the mob - and that's a big mistake."

"I'd say outright fatal," Bastian adds.

Michael is thinking.

"This is not good. The timing totally sucks, I tell you that."

"One of my clients is part of the family," Jee-Jee says, playing with a lock of hair on his forehead. "I'll try and talk to him. It's definitely not a good time to go public with this."

Michael is thinking. They watch him silently.

"You try to get hold of him tonight, and tell him that I have a proposal for the family." Michael breaks the silence in a low voice.

Rodica and Bastian ask at the same time: "What proposal?"

"You can't be serious?" Jee-Jee says with a worried expression on his face. "These are guys you don't want to mess with."

"Keep your cool, Jee-Jee," Michael replies. "Let's have another round and I'll tell you what's on my mind."

The drinks arrive and they tuck their heads closer together, listening to Michael's proposal. A few minutes later, Bastian runs his left hand through his wild hair and addresses the group, "This is so crazy and dangerous it might even work... if we survive."

There is a moment of silence then the telephone goes off in the small bar. Antonio picks it up and calls Jee-Jee. "It's for you."

Jee-Jee jumps as if he's been burnt. "I'd better take this privately. It's probably Alfonso - the *crucifier!*" Michael shakes his head, smiling at Jee-Jee's reaction.

Jee-Jee hurriedly talks on the phone whilst walking around the small bar. The group have their heads down, thinking and smoking, waiting for Jee-Jee's return. After a few long minutes he walks back in, still looking like a movie star - elegant, stylish, aristocratic and confident. "That was indeed Alfonso. He would like to see you, Michael - tonight!"

Michael has an imperceptible smile. They didn't even have a chance to listen to his proposal. "You coming, gorgeous?" he asks calmly.

Jee-Jee blushes like a virgin, fluttering his long eyelashes. "But of course. Alfonso's driver is picking us up from here in about ten minutes. How do I look?"

"Ravishing," says Bastian.

"Beautiful," adds Klava.

"Elegant," comments Rodica.

"Desirable," says Michael smiling.

Jee-Jee is flattered.

"You guys are too much... but don't stop on my account!"

They all laugh in good humor.

***

The upper-class villa, surrounded by large trees, is in the best neighborhood of Trieste and is fully lit. The long driveway leading up to the mansion is occupied by a number of black sedans, some of them bullet-proof. A few armed guards are patrolling the estate which looks down at the beautiful Adriatic Sea.

A group of four men, in their late fifties and early sixties, all dressed in black suits, are gathered around a dining room table. Food is served. Alfonso is among the four. The host, the local mafia boss, addresses Klava's friend. "Alfonso. What's the lowdown on the campo di profughi?" Alfonso fidgets a little in his seat, rubbing his shoes against each other under the heavy table. "I hear that we had to clean up a couple of people there," continues the boss, "They are good help but I don't want any trouble with the Trieste archdiocese."

Alfonso turns red in the face. "These two profughi screwed up. We took them out quickly and quietly," he says in a nervous voice.

"You make sure that there are no visible or assumed connections to the Family" says the boss, his words weighing heavily on Alfonso's shoulders.

"I'll sweep our tracks clean tonight. No worries," he takes a deep breath and looks at the boss. "I should be leaving shortly. I'll meet with the second clean-up crew in an hour," he says in a low-key voice.

The host sips from his red wine. "Very well. You take care of it," he says and they move on to the next topic on their busy agenda.

***

A black, sleek limousine pulls silently in front of the closed gates, the driver reporting to the guard. Moments later the motorized iron gates swing open, allowing the vehicle in. The limo pulls up in front of the large estate and as Jee-Jee, Michael and Alfonso get out, two armed guards welcome them at the top of the stairs. The three enter the building, followed by the muscle.

A moment later Alfonso's butler shows up at the top of the stairs, awaiting them. They step inside and Alfonso waves his butler away. He fixes himself a drink from a well-assorted bar, "Something to drink?" he enquires casually.

"The usual for me," Jee-Jee says.

"I'll have what Jee-Jee's having," Michael adds cautiously. Alfonso prepares two single-malt scotches with water and brings them on a small tray to a low coffee table:

"Please, sit," he says.

They sit on the black leather couch, Alfonso opposite them on a leather recliner. He leans forward towards his guests. He is a tad nervous, but tries to conceal it. "I understand that you have a proposal for us?" he addresses the two, without any fuss.

"It's Michael's idea. Let him explain it," Jee-Jee says. Alfonso nods, turning in Michael's direction.

Michael takes a small sip from his drink, looks Alfonso straight into the eyes. "We all know what happened in the camp last night. A very sad and unfortunate incident which is very damaging to all sides." Alfonso nods approvingly whilst Michael continues, "I imagine you're aware of the archdiocese panel interview on TV last night?"

"I watched it myself. Very well spoken on your part," Alfonso replies.

"Thank you. The point here is that we tried so hard to better the campo's image in the public's eyes; I think they do a terrific job... Caritas, that is," he takes a short pause. "And then we had last night's incident. I think that was a big mistake on the Family's part. If those two individuals broke your rules, you should've dealt with them more diplomatically... elsewhere."

"That *was* a mistake," Alfonso says quickly. "What's your proposal?"

Michael takes a brief glance at Jee-Jee.

"For starters, use all your might and resources to stop the Media getting on to it," he says.

"Good point, but I'm working on that already," Alfonso replies.

"What I was thinking," Michael continues in an even tone, "is that there is a lot of great talent in this camp; much of it lost to violent death."

"That is sad and unfortunate, but that's life."

"What if your organization discreetly employs this talent and protects the whole camp as a token of good business. It would be a decent return on your investment, no doubt," Michael says, looking at him.

Alfonso thinks about it for a moment. "You mean 'protect our investment' kinda thing?" he emphasizes.

"Something like that," responds Michael.

"That has some merit. I'll think about it. Another drink?"

Michael and Jee-Jee nod.

***

It's late at night and the camp seems at peace for a change. Michael is in his dorm now and all his friends are sound asleep. His small reading lamp is on, he is wide awake, staring at the ceiling. Every now and again he leans over and writes some notes on his pad. He pours himself some whiskey and resumes his mental planning.

***

The strong Italian coffee tingles Michael's nostrils when he sips from the large cup at his office desk. It is early morning and he is alone.

Grabbing a thick folder from his pile, he starts reading it. He sets his form into the typewriter and starts making entries.

A while later, Vanessa walks into the office and brings him a cookie.

"It's home made," she says.

"*Grazie*, Vanessa."

"How is your day so far?" she enquires.

"Good, Vanessa. I'm swamped with these new files."

"That will be your last batch, *Michele*. Word has it that you are part of the next group moving to Latina for the final preparations," Vanessa says jovially.

Michael looks at her, surprised.

"That's good, I think. No?" Michael asks a little nervous.

"It's not good, it's excellent, *Michele*. That mean everything is on track with your file and Canada accepted your application," Vanessa explains.

"What about Bastian?"

Vanessa smiles. "He's on the list too, along with some other friends of yours."

"That's great. I'd better get back to work then. I don't want to leave any loose ends behind. When do I leave?"

"In about ten days. We need to find a replacement for you... and you have to train him or her," Vanessa says. "Do you have anybody in mind who could do this job?" Vanessa asks.

"Maybe. I will get back to you with this later."

Vanessa nods and walks back to her own desk.

Michael resumes his work, a small smile brightening up his face. "Latina!"

***

It is yet another rather uneventful day in the camp - but that is a good day here. Michael is busy with Rodica in the Romanian dorm, teaching her English. A couple of young men from the dorm also ask Michael politely if they can join. He looks at Rodica.

"Not a problem if it is okay with Michael," she says. Michael waves them to come closer.

They do this for about two hours until everyone is really tired.

"I didn't realize that learning a new language is this difficult," one of the boys says, exhausted. The other two students agree.

"Only the second language is difficult. Once you teach your mind how to learn a new language away from your mother tongue, the next one will be much easier," Michael says, smiling with empathy. He went through these same baby steps several years ago.

As the boys retract to their quarters, Rodica thanks Michael for his time and leaves the dorm.

Michael stretches, gives a small yawn and sits down on his bed when Bastian walks in. His face is full of grime and dirt mixed with motor oil. His coveralls look just as filthy but he carries a bright smile on his handsome face. Michael checks his wristwatch.

"Let me guess... you got a night job as a mechanic in town or you bought that heap of crap Ducati you were talking about a while back," Michael says in good spirits.

"As a matter of fact, both!" Bastian replies, removing his coveralls. "The real work is of course on the 'heap of crap Ducati' which I just finished tuning up now," he says, tired but proud.

"It sounds like it is almost time for a test run?" Michael says.

"Yep, I'll do that tomorrow myself just to make sure everything's holding together well. By the way," he says, looking directly at his friend, "I might have somebody to fit in those giant shoes of yours at the office," he says laughing.

Michael takes a quick glance at his own feet. "It's gonna be mighty difficult," he says, lifting his right foot and flexing his ankle. "Who've you got?"

"Her name is Hanna. She's very cute and very bright... and very Czech; she lives in the camp. You haven't processed her papers yet," Bastian says with a mysterious look on his face.

"How old is she?" Michael asks.

"Nineteen, twenty, something like that. I'll have to check with her older sister," Bastian says and Michael bursts in laughter.

"Now I figure... You're seeing the sister, no doubt."

"Something like that. We're just good friends..." Bastian says, a little too quickly.

"Of course," agrees Michael, letting it slide. "What did she study?"

"International economics and trade at Prague University. Wait until you talk to her," Bastian says with enthusiasm.

"Why don't you tell her to stop by in the admin office tomorrow and see me?" Michael says, interested. He knows that this is serious business and if Bastian recommends her, she must know some good stuff, worth investigating.

"I'll tell her tomorrow and let you know how it went," Bastian says heading for the shower.

"Thanks," Michael says and Bastian nods, exiting the room. "Shoot!" Michael exclaims; he has just remembered about the recent news of moving to Latina in ten days. He has to tell Bastian so he can finalize his numerous love affairs before the move. He can't help but smile when he thinks about his entrepreneurial and resourceful friend.

When Bastian returns from the shower clean and groomed he looks like a movie star. Michael watches him curiously as he gets dressed in an appealing, slightly provocative outfit. It is obvious to Michael that Bastian is seeing someone new and exciting.

"What's her name?" Michael asks him.

"What? Who?"

The two look at one another and Bastian knows his observant friend too. "Okay. She's totally fabulous and I think I am in love with her."

"Watching you doll up for her, I'd say yes, you are!" Michael says, laughing.

"I want you to meet her sometime. She's Hanna's older sister, Tatiana."

"You have a history of falling in love with beautiful Czech girls," Michael probes.

Bastian shrugs his shoulders in self-defense. "It's in my destiny. Yours is French girls," he says in a dramatic voice.

"Watch it!" Michael replies light-heartedly. "If Hanna is interested, tell her to come and see me tomorrow morning. By-the-way, I have some news for you, Casanova," Michael says.

"What?" Bastian looks at him inquiringly.

"Our papers are almost finished. It's all good. We're moving to Latina in ten days."

"Ten days?!" Bastian utters. "I've got so much on the go right now."

"That's why I warned you. You've got ten days to wrap things up. It will be a little more difficult with your *matters of the heart*. Tatiana won't be coming to Latina any time soon. You know that," Michael says.

"Yes," Bastian admits deflated, "It will be tough. Thanks for the news. I'll talk to Hanna tonight and I will let you know later or tomorrow morning."

"Okay. Have a good time and send my regards to the sisters."

"Will do," Bastian says, finishing his grooming and dressing. Michael gives him a thumb-up and Bastian leaves the dorm... nearly bumping into Jee-Jee who is on his way in to see Michael.

"Come on right in," Michael welcomes his friend. "Care for a drink?"

"Please," Jee-Jee replies and sits in one of the cheap chairs beside Michael's cot. "How can you keep abominations like this in your surrounding?" he asks Michael pointing at the crappy chair.

Michael shrugs.

"It's good enough for me. I'm low class."

"No. You're not!" Jee-Jee argues confidently.

Michael lets it go.

"To what do I owe this pleasure, cutie?" Michael asks him.

"A number of things, you beautiful devil," Jee-Jee says and makes a guttural lion sound. Michael laughs.

Squinting his nose, Jee-Jee reluctantly sits in the white plastic chair, fidgets for a few moments and finally looks Michael in the eyes. "We need to talk."

"Shoot."

Jee-Jee looks around the large room to see if anybody is in earshot. The dorm is empty. "Word in the camp is that you're advancing to Latina in a few days - congratulations," he says.

"Nobody knows about this except Bastian," Michael says.

"And me and a few reliable people in the camp. No need to worry about anything."

Michael looks at him inquisitively.

"Okay. I will be straight with you. There are two issues which need to be addressed and dealt with before you leave," he says in a low voice.

Michael looks at him expectantly.

"One:" Jee-Jee continues, "the Italian Family connection and new developments..." He stops, looking at Michael. This is serious stuff.

"This whole issue is out of my hands, Jee-Jee. You know that. I didn't even know about the connections until that dramatic incident with the Bulgarians. I jumped in in order to save face for the camp and us."

"Events have escalated since then," Jee-Jee says. "We need a permanent contact with the Family whilst we are here, to make sure we are protected *not* prosecuted," Jee-Jee says.

"You already know that because of my job in the camp I can't be that person," Michael says on the edge of caution.

"Of course I know that. I was thinking maybe you could assign somebody you trust for this delicate and diplomatic position?"

"You probably would be great for that, Jee-Jee, but you will advance shortly too."

"Thanks for the vote of confidence!" Jee-Jee says all flabbergasted. "We need somebody else then."

"How about that new Polish democratic writer. What's his name? I met him once; he is very bright and empathetic toward the people in the camp."

"Jarko. Indeed a very wise choice, Michael," Jee-Jee says, pleased.

"He's new here and is very eloquent in his words. Besides, he speaks Italian like one of theirs. I'll talk to him about this."

"That would be fabulous," Jee-Jee says with a sense of relief in his voice.

They both sip from their drinks.

"Two:" Jee-Jee continues casually, "this is a little more delicate..." he says in a very low voice, barely audible even to Michael. Michael leans forward to catch his words - then suddenly changes his mind:

"Before we get into that, I have a question for you too. What do you know about Hanna, one of the new Czech sisters?" Michael says inquiringly.

"Not much, but what I do is fairly relevant."

"Go on..."

***

The morning sun casts long shadows on the trees as Michael approaches the administration building for another day in the office. He is running out of time and things suddenly aren't so great. The random slices of information he received from Jee-Jee last night are not exactly the most reassuring about Hanna. He has to process her file before signing her on the job... and that could raise some issues with the authorities.

It is a delicate situation again and Michael's best judgment on this case is not enough. He has to rely once again on his intuition before he seals his last decision on the government papers. He closes his eyes and recalls his conversation with Bastian last night.

***

Bastian is on his way to meet Tatiana, feeling like a million bucks. He reaches the girls' building and ascending the stairs he approaches the dormitory door. A couple of young girls leave the dorm as he approaches and, instantly recognizing him, give him slanted eyes and the amorous smiles which he acknowledges but responds with a cool hello.

In the dorm he finds Tatiana in her corner, chatting casually with her younger sister, Hanna. They both look up and smile to Bastian as he approaches them. His penetrating eyes read on their faces that they were talking about some secrets he was not supposed to be a part of. His easy-going nature acknowledges the fact, files and stores it in memory for future use and switches back to the immediate reality and powerful presence of Tatiana.

"Good evening," he addresses the girls in Czech.

"Hey," replies Tatiana; she has a sudden and concealed shiver at the sight of Bastian. She is head-over-heels in love with him but she would never, ever, admit this fact to anybody.

Hanna says a passing hello and getting up from the cot walks out from the dorm, offering them the privacy they require.

"Just a moment, Hanna!" Bastian calls after her. Just before reaching the door, she stops, turns around and looks at him.

"I need to talk to you for a minute," he says and turns to Tatiana. "I need to speak with your sister for a minute. It's about that job in Michael's office I was telling you about."

"Okay, just don't make it too long. I want to spend some time with you."

"Me too," Bastian replies and the passion in his two little words makes Tatiana's world shake for a moment.

The two leave the dorm and hook up on the wide stoop.

"What's the matter?" Hanna asks him as soon as they close the door.

"I need to talk to you for a moment," Bastian says in his genuinely casual way.

"No better time than the present," Hanna says, and sitting down on the top step lights up a cigarette. Bastian sits beside her without smoking. They sit in silence for a few minutes, gathering their thoughts, adjusting their emotions.

"I'm ready," Hanna announces casually.

"Me too," replies Bastian. "About that event in Plzen..." Bastian's words trail away but their meaning sends shivers through Hanna's spine.

"How you know about Plzen?" Hanna asks, astonished.

"I know and that's that. How do you handle Plzen nowadays?"

"Differently."

"In a good sense, I hope?" Bastian asks.

"Yep."

"Michael is my best friend forever and I want to remind you of that. He also has his own powerful network of information. Don't hide anything from him. He is offering you a great position to redeem the past. Don't take it lightly."

"I won't."

They both sit in silence for a while, processing their thoughts.

"Be good with Tatiana," she says.

"I will. Be good with Michael," he replies.

"I will."

These brief words having been exchanged, they get up and walk in different directions, sealing a deal which could affect a number of lives in the next few months to come.

***

Michael starts climbing the stairs leading to the administration offices, his mind all wrapped up in thoughts which trigger anxieties and even remorse. He tries to shake them off but he quickly learns that this is easier said than done.

As usual, he is the first here. He salutes the night guard in the hallway and enters the large office. Activating the coffee machine, he sits down behind his desk and slowly clears his head of anxieties and worries.

When the steam whistle goes off on the machine, Michael is ready for another day. Bring it on!

***

By the time Vanessa brings him a second cup of coffee, Michael is already deeply involved in processing one of his cases.

"Good morning, Vanessa. Thank you for the coffee. I got so involved with this case that I didn't even notice you coming in," he says awkwardly.

"That's okay, *Michele*. I noticed you were totally absorbed in the case," Vanessa says. "Just remember, you're doing a job here. Try to keep yourself emotionally detached from your work."

"I'm trying!" Michael answers and resumes his work as Vanessa returns to her desk.

About an hour later, a young woman timidly shows up in front of his desk, looking at Michael. "I am Hanna," she says.

"Good morning, Hanna. Thanks for coming. Please, have a seat." Michael invites her to sit in front of him. At this time he already has her basic file open.

"Thank you for thinking about me for this possible position," she says in a shy voice.

"You are welcome. It was Bastian who recommended you to me," Michael says, looking at this very pretty girl. "I understand that you have some accounting and economics training?" he says.

"Yes. I was in the second year at the University of Prague when we escaped. My major was in international economics," Hanna says in a confident voice.

"That sounds good. How do you feel about people; do you like people?" Michael asks.

"I like people. I've been hurt by bad people in the past, but I'm over it now," she says in a low voice, casting her eyes downwards.

"That takes strength and character," Michael says, also in a low voice. "This position is not easy, Hanna. You have to detach yourself emotionally and keep your head clear under all circumstances," Michael explains.

"I understand," replies Hanna.

"About languages then. Which languages are you fluent in? English is definitely great and that's a big plus because all the legal documents are printed and written in English," Michael further explains.

"Not counting my English, of course there is Czech, Russian - which I hate but I'm fluent in - and I am also prolific in Polish," Hanna says in a casual tone.

"Not bad," he says. "Before we consider you for the position, we have to complete your case folder. It is incomplete at this point and I would like you to provide the information to the office."

Hanna does not feel comfortable with this proposal but she is very bright and knows that there is no way to get around it.

Michael watches her closely. "There are two ways to do this," he says, noticing her turmoil. "One is to write everything down in a chronological order, not missing anything essential, or two, we can talk it out, with me asking the questions and you providing the answers. This will be a recorded conversation because later I have to transfer it to the legal documents - the transcript," Michael says.

Hanna is still uncomfortable but after a short thinking time looks at Michael. "I'll opt for variation two, the recorded statement," she says.

"Fine. We will proceed in a few minutes. You can have a coffee if you wish, use the washroom, whatever. I'll be ready in about ten minutes."

"I'll grab a cup of coffee, please," she says.

"How do you take it?"

"Just black," she answers.

"I'll get you some," Michael replies, getting up and walking over to the machine where he makes two coffees, one for each of them.

Returning to his desk he starts setting up his recorder, his legal pad and pens...

Hanna's Story

It is the summer of 1979 in Prague, Czech Republic. Hanna Zarkov, a student top of the class in her high-school, arrives in Prague from a small town in the northern part of the country. She is ready and eager to enroll in the city's famed university. She has some money saved for the school and board, should she pass the super-difficult acceptance exams ahead.

The days prior to the exams she has studied everywhere; in parks, on street benches, in the street car, day and night.

The exam day arrives and she completes it with flying colors, ahead of most of her competitors.

She is immediately accepted and days later moves into the campus where she pays a fee for her dorm privileges.

The school year starts but shortly after her mother becomes very sick at home. She and Tatiana are the only kids; their father died years ago in a railway construction accident. Desperate, he turns to a particular shady agency which contacted her several times before asking her to work with them. Disgusted, she had turned them down every time. Being such a classy, smart and beautiful young woman, they want her to work for them as a high-class call girl.

Under the new financial pressure however, she finally accepts it.

In the next six months she will become famous as the most desirable call girl in the high political circles of the Prague government. This 'fame' instantly re-adjusts her financial situation. Her mother and Tatiana are well taken care of now, but to the detriment of her studies at this superior institution of learning. Her grades start plummeting and she is facing the risk of being expelled.

In a desperate effort, she gives up the call-girl assignments and dives neck-deep in her studies. Within weeks her marks rise to the top again - but now she is facing massive pressure from the agency to return; the politicians want her and they want her bad. It is during this time period that she and Tatiana are already planning to leave the country illegally and try to start a new life in the free world.

Their Mother is taken care of by a cousin of Tatiana and Hanna's who is paid by the sisters. Tatiana, through her job as a new railroad engineer, has made some interesting connections in her field. Through her repeated field trips on various trains and through many stations, learning their setup and communications systems, Tatiana became intimately knowledgeable about the inner workings of locomotives; cargo and passenger cars alike.

One dark, rainy night, she and Hanna, all dressed in black, each with one small bag containing a couple of sandwiches and some water, sneak into the train depot, into the train which Tatiana knows for certain is heading to Austria, then on to France and back through Switzerland. The two sisters sneak into one of the passenger carriages and with a small flashlight and some hand tools provided by Tatiana, they open up the panels above the passenger seats. Two little cavities show up between the network of steam pipes, hydraulic pipes and electrical harnesses.

"It's gonna be tight," Tatiana reminds her sister, helping her climb into the small cavity. "Once the train is in motion, stay put for several hours and tomorrow night when the train is stopped for a while, you kick off the panel and get out. There is a good chance we'll be somewhere in Austria by then," Tatiana explains.

"What about you?" Hanna asks.

"I will be in the next car and I will pull back up the panel by myself. I figured out how to do that when I was working here," she explained and starts placing the covers back on Hanna's cubicle.

"I love you and I will see you tomorrow night," Tatiana says, squeezing her sister's hand before driving in the first screw.

They kick out the panels just after midnight the next day, when the train has stopped for a technical check-up and refueling. They find themselves in the city of Kapfenberg, about one hundred and fifty kilometers south of Vienna.

Through hearsay they learned about the Austrian refugee camp but they did not like the rumored treatment of new refugees. They keep on going, by train first, then hitch-hiking until they reach Italy and immediately asked for political asylum status. They go through a very similar treatment to Michael and Bastian's, shortly afterwards ending up in the same camp in Trieste

Michael, who has listened carefully all this time, asking questions occasionally in order to clarify certain paragraphs, pushes the *stop* button on his recorder.

"Interesting story. Welcome to the Trieste refugee camp," he says - and he means it.

"What about the position?" Hanna asks.

"I have to process through your statement and I have to do some light editing in order to fit you in the standard mold of the emigration forms."

"This is a true statement and I signed my name on it," Hanna says with slightly damaged dignity which Michael is quick to notice.

"I honor your words, Hanna, and I truly admire you for this gutsy move. Let me do my part of the work; I would like you to come back tomorrow afternoon, to this office. About three o'clock would be fine if you could. And one more thing: I will not modify anything in your statement. I may just omit some minor parts," he says, softly closing her file for now.

"Thanks," she replies, a little nervous. "I will be here," Hanna says simply and, getting up, leaves the office.

Michael closes her file and walks toward the door, his face a mask of anxiety. Vanessa notices this. "Everything all right?" she calls.

He nods, "Just going for a smoke," he replies, leaving the office.

Once back behind his desk, Michael's day goes in a blink due to the enormous number of people and documents he tries to complete and process before he leaves for Latina.

It is late at night when he finally locks up the office, says good night to the patrolling officer and heads back towards his dorm. Walking and smoking, his mind is still on his cases when a soft female voice behind abruptly brings him back to the here and now. "You look tired," it says... and when Michael turns, he sees the shadow of a young woman with long hair standing behind him.

"I am. And who are you, if I may ask?" he says looking at her and trying to remember her face.

"Don't try so hard to recognize me because it won't work," she says in crystal clear Italian, with a slight southern accent. "I'm not a refugee."

Michael is intrigued, but keeps walking on, the stranger following him.

"Who *are* you?" Michael asks her in an easy tone.

"My name is Francesca and I live in Calabria."

"That's way south, almost in Sicily," Michael says, looking at her more curiously this time. "What are you doing in Trieste, and more so in this refugee camp?" he asks her.

She laughs with glee.

"Just visiting somebody from your office; I'm Vanessa's niece," she explains. "Do you want to grab a drink and chat for a while?" Francesca asks him.

"Where?"

"In the city. I will bring you back," she says.

"What about the curfew?"

She laughs delighted at the possibilities. "I'll take care of that. It almost feels like high school!"

Michael shrugs his shoulders. "Why not," he replies and they turn around, walking to the main entrance.

When they reach the gate, the officer in the booth jumps to attention when he sees Francesca. She leans over to his window. "I'm taking Michael to town for a few hours. Forget about the curfew; we'll be back before long," she says, laughing. The officer nods respectfully.

They climb in Francesca's sports car and disappear into the promising night where fears, desires and anxieties run hand in hand, charging it with wild and uncontrolled energies.

***

It is almost three o'clock in the morning when Francesca's sports car pulls back up in front of the main gate of the campo di profughi. Francesca reaches over, kissing Michael on the lip. He responds with ease, almost detachment but Francesca does not notice it.

"*Ci vediamo*," Michael says.

"*Domani pronto*," Francesca responds with a laugh and watches Michael get out of the car. He waves a small goodbye and walks slowly toward the main gate while Francesca floors the gas pedal making the car disappear around the corner.

Michael laughs, clearing the gate and starts walking toward his building.

* * *

The Next morning is a Sunday, Michael's day off. He wakes up at about ten-thirty and looks over to his left where he sees Bastian, fully dressed, sipping a coffee and leafing through one of his many Italian motorcycle magazines.

"Good morning, night owl," Bastian calls in good humor. "Who was that hot chick you peeled off with last night?" he asks.

Michael rubs his eyes and reaches for his cigarettes. "You mean Francesca?" he says, putting one between his lips but not lighting it. "She is a very interesting person. A very creative one," Michael says evasively.

"I bet she is!" Bastian pushes on. "Aren't you supposed to be at the office by now?" Bastian tests him gently.

"What time is it?" Michael asks a little agitated and checks his wristwatch.

"Shit! I'm four hours late!" he says and franticly jumps up.

Bastian fully enjoys this for a while. "What if I remind you that today is Sunday and the office is closed?" Bastian says, watching him curiously.

"Thanks! You're a great pal," Michael says, relieved. He has a sarcastic but friendly tone for his buddy.

"I know," Bastian says laughing. "You never ever sleep in - but today you did, till almost eleven o'clock. I must say that Francesca chic is a *very* creative person!" he says, knowingly.

"She studies modern art in Rome," Michael mentions. "I need a smoke," he says, walking out of the dorm. Bastian follows him and they both sit down on the stoop.

"The Ducati is ready and runs great," Bastian says casually.

"I wanna ride it!" replies Michael. "I sure could use a good speed run."

"It's all yours for the taking," Bastian replies. "I will show you a couple of tricks you should know on the controls I modified... it's fast."

"How about we have a coffee then we go see the machine?" Michael says, looking at his friend.

"Let's do that."

The two of them return to the dorm where Bastian grabs a helmet and a set of thin leather riding gloves while Michael fixes his messy wardrobe up a tad.

The wildly modified motorcycle is parked in the carpentry shop where Bastian has spent some of his spare time doing custom woodwork - and worked on the bike. He is very good with his hands. He opens the roll-up door and pushes the superbike outside, parking it in front of the shop. Michael follows him.

"You did a marvelous job to the heap of crap it was when you bought it. Is this really the same motorcycle?" Michael asks, astonished by Bastian's craftsmanship.

"Same one, and don't act so surprised. You know that I can make wonders out of these kind of old heaps," Bastian says in a casual voice. "Wait till you hear the sound of the engine and the pipes," he says proudly.

Michael watches him prepare the sports bike and is very proud of his friend. This passion for speed, danger and motorcycles will bring the two of them together again and again over the many years to come but they don't know it at this time.

Bastian finally fires up the engine and the twin cylinders roar to life with a sound which is music to Michael's and Bastian's ears alike.

"Come close," he calls, "I want to show you those modifications you'll have to remember for a smooth ride."

Michael approaches and watches him attentively. "Those are definitely good tricks to remember," Michael says after

Bastian finishes his demonstration. "Can I ride it now?" he asks eagerly.

"It's all yours for tonight. It's got fresh rubber so you can lean into it - and have some fun. This baby delivers!" Bastian says proudly; Michael has no doubt about his friend's statement - a tinge of caution is advised.

Securing his helmet and the fine Italian riding gloves Bastian hands over to him, Michael mounts the Ducati and revs up the engine a few times, getting the feeling of the response. He likes it so far. He looks at Bastian who watches him. "It's time to test these new rubbers," he says and a second later drops his helmet visor over his eyes. Opening the throttle wide, he sets the motorcycle in motion - a white-blue smoke covers Bastian and the front entrance of the carpentry shop, but before he has a chance to say anything, Michael releases the clutch and sends the motorcycle flying forward on the rear wheel, the front one reaching for the stars. He races on one wheel for a long stretch until he reaches the first intersection of aisles. He drops the front to ground and with a screeching sound, the motorcycle and its rider disappear around the corner.

Bastian laughs out loud and kicking pebbles starts walking back to the Romanian dorm. Half way there he runs into Tatiana and Hanna who have just stepped out for a stroll.

"Where's Michael?" the sisters ask in unison.

"Do I hear an echo here?" Bastian jokes, looking at the girls. "He just went for a test blast on my new motorcycle," he says casually. "If he doesn't kill himself he will be back in about an hour - that's all the gas I have in the tank and he doesn't have his wallet with him, I'm sure," he explains cheerily.

"We'll wait," says Hanna immediately; Tatiana agrees and looks at Bastian. "You want to hang with us? Please?" she says in a honey-coated voice.

"If you put it that way, I'll stick around. Hey, what do I hear about your country standing up against the Russian occupancy?" Bastian says and both sisters snap to attention.

"About that;" Hanna starts. "it is the beginning of a new era."

Bastian and the sisters sit down on one of the benches on the alley between buildings and listen to Hanna's informed presentation of the political turmoil and uprising against the Russian occupancy of her country.

On the other end of town, Michael is revving the Ducati high, making it fly through the charming streets of the coastal city. He is approaching the outskirts of town, fast. Within minutes he rides skillfully on the country road heading toward the city of Sgonico, toward the north.

He rides fast and furious and enjoys every minute of it. The wind blowing on his face and body, the sunshine on his side, the beautiful landscape makes for a perfect and ephemeral escape from life's current realities.

He returns the Ducati back to the camp about an hour later, exhausted but excited about his speedy escape. He finds Bastian on the bleachers of the soccer field still in the company of Hanna and Tatiana.

Michael salutes the group and hands the motorcycle key to Bastian: "I needed this," he says calmly, but his eyes still glitter with excitement. "There's not much gas in the tank. Sorry, I forgot my wallet," he says; the sisters and Bastian have a good laugh.

"I'm glad you enjoyed it. We thought you'd have been arrested for speeding by now!" Bastian says and Michael nods.

"I came close a few times," he admits. "How are you, ladies?" he addresses Hanna and Tatiana. They chirp back jovially. Michael looks at Hanna. "By the way, you've got the job in the office - if you are still interested?" Michael says casually and looks at Hanna whose face turns red with excitement.

"Thank you, Michael!" she says, handing him over a can of beer from her shoulder bag. He takes it happily.

"You are welcome," he opens his beer bottle and takes a swig. "We have a lot of work ahead of us," he says. "I would like you to start tomorrow morning if possible."

"I'll be there. What time?"

"Nine o'clock is fine. Lots to do and I have only a few days left to fill you in with all the details. You'll have to learn on the fly," he says, looking at her.

"Nothing new to that, I've done it all my life," she replies simply.

"Yeah, me too," responds Michael. They turn their focus to the soccer field where two female teams are going hard at it.

After the game Michael and Bastian walk the girls back to their dorm. "See you in the morning," Michael addresses Hanna.

"I'll be there at nine," she replies and Bastian and Tatiana make some arrangements of their own.

Minutes later, Michael and Bastian walk back through the camp, taking their time, with Michael having another cigarette as Bastian is kicking pebbles.

"So much has happened to us since that August day," Michael observes out loud.

"Yes. The first part of our main goal is achieved - to be free," Bastian says without looking at Michael. "Now since we've got that, the trick is to figure out what to do with it," he says.

"No worries. It will come to you," Michael says casually. "There will be lots to do once we are on our own, in Canada."

"Yeah, I guess. Just roll up the sleeves and go for it - hard," Bastian says, looking at his friend.

"Something like that. This will be the time to finally do whatever you always wanted to do and you couldn't. Just make sure it's a *good* thing," Michael says as they turn into another alley leading to their building.

Arriving there, they climb up a few steps and Michael sits down on the top landing.

"I don't feel like going into the dorm yet," Michael says.

"Me neither," Bastian says. "I'll go grab a beer. You want one?"

"Sure," Michael agrees.

Several months have passed now since Michael and Bastian landed in this camp; so much has happened - and so fast, sometimes making his head spin. And now, yet again, a new era is beginning for him and Bastian. They are one step closer now to their goal of total freedom.

Bastian arrives with the beers, handing one over to Michael.

"Cheers," Michael says.

"Cheers," dittos Bastian.

Bastian sits beside him on the stone step and the two of them fall silent for a while, each one preoccupied with their own thoughts.

The silence is suddenly broken by hurried sound of leather boots on the concrete pavement of the alley in front of them. They both look to see an agitated, worried Jee-Jee strutting with a kicked-dog look, trying to keep his composure. His expensive clothes are shred, covered with dust, and in places displaying blood stains.

Michael and Bastian jump up from the stool, leaping steps to descend in his direction.

"What happened?" Michael asks directly.

"We've been mugged and assaulted," Jee-Jee mutters between sobs.

"We?" asks Bastian.

"By whom?" asks Michael.

"They attacked us as we left Alfonso's limousine. Looks like they were waiting for us," he says sobbing.

"Let's go into the dorm and fix you up a little." Answering Michael and Jee-Jee's silent question Bastian says "There's nobody in. They are all at the gymnasium playing basketball."

They walk into the dorm and immediately place Jee-Jee on Bastian's cot. "I've done 'search and rescue' for years, no worries, Jee-Jee. We'll fix you up the best we can but you should still see the camp Doctor. She's pretty good," Bastian says, pulling out the elaborate first-aid kit from under his bed. He bought this kit here in Trieste and has used it several times already, mostly for sports injuries. Only one time had he had a bad case of severe bullet wounds - but nobody knew about that.

Helping Jee-Jee remove his jacket and shirt, Bastian carefully examines his face, his ribs. He has been kicked there several times.

"This is more serious than I thought," Bastian says, examining the blue bruises. "Does it hurt when you breathe?" Jee-Jee nods. "They must've cracked at least one of your ribs. Did they kick you while you were down?" he asks.

"They did," Jee-Jee says, grimacing with pain. Bastian takes a long flexible bandage roll and wraps it tight around Jee-Jee's chest.

"You have such powerful hands, Bastian," he says affectionately.

"No fancy ideas. I'm just doing a job I've done hundreds of times before. Relax," Bastian says, glad to see that his patient is in better spirits already.

"Where is Alfonso now?" Michael enquires.

"The attackers took him away in a black van," Jee-Jee says in tears. "I hope he is okay," he looks at the two friends: "I don't know what to do."

"Since you don't want to go public with this incident, probably the best thing would be to call the family and tell them about Alfonso," Michael says thinking. "Do you have any phone numbers for the capos?" he asks.

"Yes. Alfonso gave me a couple of secret numbers..."

"Good. Call them as soon as possible and let them take care of their own. They are very powerful and resourceful," Michael says.

"I'll do that from my room," Jee-Jee replies and turns to Bastian. "I didn't know you had those magical, healing hands!" he says, all glamorous again.

"Just *trained* hands, that's all," Bastian answers with a smile. "You should still see the camp Doctor. Tell them whatever and have her check you over for internal damage."

"I should be fine, I think. If it gets worse I will do that," Jee-Jee says, getting up and wobbling a little. "I need a hot, aromatic bubble bath now," he states like the queen of England. The boys laugh and walk her to the door.

"You want us to accompany you to the building?" Bastian asks him.

"I will be fine," Jee-Jee says with dignity and walks away from the dorm as some of the Romanian boys start arriving back from the basketball game.

Bastian and Michael, once again, walk outside and sit on the stoop.

"I'll get the beers," Michael says, getting up and disappearing in the building.

Bastian, all alone, thinks about the dramatic events Jee-Jee and his friend have just been through.

Michael returns with two Heineken cans and hands one over to Bastian. He sits on the stoop beside him, lighting up a cigarette.

"This is a very sticky situation, you realize that?" Michael says, referring to Jee-Jee's trauma.

"Yes. Once again, if word gets out to the public, all your hard work on the panel will have been in vain. The public are supportive but scared of the refugees. They support them and their cause because they want them to do well... and get the hell out of their country!" Bastian says and takes a swig out of the can.

"That's about it. I just hope Jee-Jee doesn't make it to the news. He likes exposure, but this is the wrong kind to have," Michael agrees.

The two old friends sit quietly, wrapped in their own thoughts.

"Did you hear any word from Stephanie?" Bastian asks after a while, breaking the silence.

"Nope. She's busy with her work," Michael says causally; but Bastian knows better. Michael had a passionate romance with Stephanie which lasted nearly one full year until he was forcefully conscripted by the Romanian Army. He was gone for nearly two years and in spite of their efforts the young hearts bled for a while before healing somewhat and moving on to their next throb of passion.

Stephanie's reappearance in the camp two years later was a shocking revelation to Bastian, reminding him yet again how unpredictable and untamed a young heart can be. He also knew that this brief, high-profile visit stirred up some deep, almost-forgotten emotions in his pal.

"You miss her," Bastian says in a low, friendly voice.

"And what's the big deal with that? I'll get over it," Michael says, a shade of poorly concealed bitterness in his voice.

"Fine."

"Fine."

"Can you discreetly follow up on Jee-Jee's condition tomorrow? I'll be busy all day in the office with Hanna," Michael says after a while.

"Of course, no problem."

They sit quietly for a while until another group of their friends return from the basketball court telling them the game's developments. Chatting casually, Michael and Bastian join the group and return to the dorm to continue their innocent banter for a while longer. It's good to disconnect from daily worries for a while.

**

The morning finds Michael bent over Vanessa's typewriter, watching her type. She follows a methodical sequence she has done thousands of times before.

"There is a certain pattern they have on these government forms," she explains, pointing at some paragraph headings. "You probably figured it out already but it's always good to go over them one more time with a different person, as you will do with Hanna shortly," Vanessa explains.

"I missed a few points myself; I think I will be good now. Thanks for your time," Michael says straightening his back.

"She's a smart young lady it seems. You should do fine."

"I believe so," confirms Michael and returns to his desk, preparing the documents he is supposed to go over with Hanna.

It is still early in the morning so he closes the last file he worked on, gets up from behind his desk and pouring himself a fresh cup of coffee, walks outside for a cigarette break.

Hanna arrives at a quarter to nine and she is dressed very conservatively. With a white shirt tucked into a pleated dark blue skirt, her long wild blonde hair contained neatly in a pony-tail, she looks like a high-school student when she enters the busy office.

Saying her polite morning greetings in impeccable Italian, she smiles to Mateo Forzani who smiles back from ear to ear.

She sits with her back straight in the chair in front of Michael's desk. "Good morning, Hanna. A well-crafted entrance!"

"There is only one chance for a first impression," she says casually and looks at her tutor. "I'm ready."

"Good. Let's get down to it. Before we go into the job details I want to start by reviewing your own file. It's a great way to learn the job, especially with you being the subject at hand. I've almost completed yours. Bring your chair around and join me on this side," he says and Hanna moves her chair, sitting beside Michael, watching his work attentively.

Michael and Hanna spend several hours working on the files, Hanna absorbing everything fast and efficiently. She is like a sponge.

"Learn it well and fast because I want you to continue Tatiana's case file too. I started all the preliminaries, including your escape, and is all laid out for you in her case file," Michael says and Hanna notices fatigue on his face.

"Sounds great. You look tired," she says.

"We've covered a lot of ground and you're holding up pretty well, I must say," Michael says with a smile. "I need a smoke," he says, getting up.

"Me too," Hanna agrees and they both walk out from the office, locking it. It is only the two of them in the office now. Michael glances at his wristwatch.

"It's almost eight o'clock at night. We'll have a smoke, I'll show you your sister's file and then we call it a day. We'll continue tomorrow," Michael says.

"Okay."

They smoke in silence for a while, each one processing all the information they traveled through during the day. Hanna has done great; a huge relief for Michael. It feels good to have found a talented successor like Hanna.

***

Around ten months have now passed since Michael and Bastian first arrived and registered with the international refugee camp at Trieste. The emigration papers for the two of them are nearly complete now.

Hanna, under the close guidance of Michael and Vanessa has become well acquainted with her duties and responsibilities. With Michael's discreet hints she has adjusted her flexible attitude to suit the working environment. In spite of her wild nature, Hanna has managed to maintain her working skills and her attendance is impeccable.

Bastian has managed to buy *another* damaged Italian motorcycle, an Aprilia this time, and after he has fixed it all up and made it look nearly new, he, Michael and occasionally Klava too, have had some great day trips through the Lazio region of Italy.

There have been a number of events in the last few months but they have managed to keep them out of the media and the public eye. The Family kept their end of the bargain and employed various high-skilled labor and intellect from the camp at legitimate firms owned or controlled by their network. For the services rendered, the camp talent has been well protected and provided for accordingly.

***

It is three thirty on a sunny afternoon when Michael, riding Bastian's Ducati, and Klava, riding Alfonso's Cagiva, pull into the camp after a great ride through the city.

"That was just a perfect ride," Michael says excitedly, tapping his motorcycle gas tank with satisfaction.

"A very enjoyable one, for sure," Klava admits. "I had a lot of fun."

She locks her motorcycle, unzips her leather jacket and ruffling up her already wild hair, she looks laughing at Michael.

"What's so funny, pretty girl?" Michael asks his friend.

"We got something cooking tonight..." she says in a mysterious tone.

"Who is 'we'?"

"You could find out yourself if you stop by at the Bulgarian female compound around seven o'clock tonight."

"I can do that. It'd better be good," Michael says genuinely, not detecting in any suspicious meanings.

"Great, then. I'll see you tonight at seven."

"Any hints?" Michael asks with a tinge of suspicion building up in his voice.

"See ya tonight!" Klava says laughing and heads towards her compound which is in the opposite direction of the Romanian quarters.

"Why is the..." Michael mutters.

His words trail off in the wind as Klava waves and turns into an alley, disappearing behind the destroyed Albanian building.

Lighting up another cigarette, Michael starts toward his own building.

To Michael's surprise, the dorm is empty at this hour. It is the in-between time when he would expect most of the people laying around, doing nothing until dinner time.

Shrugging his shoulders in careless acceptance he drops onto his cot, still fully dressed, and a minute later he is sound asleep.

Twisting and turning, he finally opens his eyes and looks at his wristwatch. He jumps as if he's been burnt. His watch shows 7:27pm.

"Shit!" he utters and starts looking frantically for something decent to wear. *"Wear something nice."* Klava's words resonate in his memory as he is putting on a cashmere shirt with the collar up, as always, and pulls on some clean, fresh jeans. Running his fingers through his long hair he exits the room and has a final face wash in the bathroom down the hall.

The Bulgarian pavilion is a medium size building in the shape of the letter L, locked between the small warehouse building and the fire hall of the camp. As Michael approaches the main entrance on the shorter wall, he suddenly has an eerie feeling that he is being watched. Not paying any attention to his intuitive hunch however, he climbs up the five stairs leading to the main entrance, puts his cigarette out in a self-standing ashtray and opens the door.

The hallway is dark and silent, with a dim light burning somewhere halfway down the hall.

Michael hesitates for a moment then advances along the hallway listening for sounds or voices.

Nothing.

He stops, trying to find his bearings. In all this time in the camp he never has been in this building. He knows several Bulgarians, including Klava, but he has never met them on their own turf.

A few more steps bring him closer to a large dorm door with a makeshift sign on it reading *This way, Michael.*

A sudden shiver runs through Michael's spine a second before he opens the door. The room is dark but it feels warm, as if heated up by several human bodies...

"Surprise!"

The single word thunders through the dark room amplified by the strength of several voices at unison. An instant later and the lights come on; Michael finds himself in the middle of a party room with at least two dozen men and women cheering for his arrival. Klava, Rodica, Bastian and Jee-Jee are some of those he immediately recognizes as they come close to him.

"What the hell...?" Michael mutters, aiming the comment at Bastian and Klava.

"It's your leaving party, Mister," Rodica explains and places a shot of good scotch in his hand. Michael shrugs humbly and raises the glass over his head.

"Cheers! And thank you; you'll follow me shortly too," he calls. Several glasses are raised and jovial voices light up the night with good vibrations.

When he looks around more closely he realizes that most of the people in the large group are Hungarian. He calls Klava to the side.

"You knew about this all along. Who organized this whole thing?"

"We all chipped in but the whole idea was Jee-Jee's, solidly backed up by his Hungarian group," Klava explains.

"You guys are too much!" Michael says with a smile.

"For a few hours, let's worry not and enjoy the party... have some fun," she says - and she means these words.

"I'll drink to that," agrees Michael and the two blend into the party crowd.

***

The following five days fly by fast for Michael and Bastian alike. While still busy in the office, helping Hanna hone her skills, a few fast trips to the Consulates with her, Michael takes care of his last few loose ends in and outside the office. He also misses Stephanie because he has not heard a peep from her for several weeks now.

For Bastian, things haven't been so easy. Matters of the heart take a lot of gentle handling and kids' gloves. He and Tatiana have been to the town many times, spending their last days together; wining and dining, watching movies, walking and talking. There is a good chance that they will never see each other again; Tatiana is immigrating to the United States.

It is a late sunny afternoon as Michael and Hanna are wrapping up their work in the office when Mateo Forzani walks in holding a telegram in his hand.

"I've just had word from the headquarters," he says, waving the little slip of paper. "The next group, which is yours, Michael, leaves for Latina tomorrow morning by train. You will be in charge of the group, *Michele*," Forzani says.

Michael isn't too surprised - except for the fact that this is such a short notice.

"I will be ready for that, Signore," he says.

"Very good. That's all for now," Replies Mateo and, turning around, heads for Vanessa's desk. He stops, turns back around and takes a few paces back toward the two. "We are also very pleased with *your* efforts, Hanna. Keep up the good work," he says.

Turning to Vanessa, he hands her a list he just withdrew from his pocket. "I want you to announce these people through the P.A. system about their departure to Latina, tomorrow morning: eight o'clock at the main gate. Be ready with all the gear they'll take with them on the train."

"Yes, Mateo. I will do that right away," she says and looks over the list, preparing her announcement.

***

The next morning is already here; it is April 14th, 1980. A group of around twenty people, young and middle age, male and female - and one baby - gather around the main gate and security booth, waiting for further instructions. Michael and Bastian are among them, accompanied by Tatiana and Hanna. Klava is there too, but is not one of the people who can leave.

Tatiana is sad to see Bastian go; he is not too happy either.

Shortly after eight o'clock the commander of the police comes out and gathers the travelers around him, calling out their names from a list, handing out Caritas envelopes containing a one-way-train-ticket to Latina, Italy. The envelope also contains fifteen-thousand liras allowance for food on their travel south towards Rome.

The Caritas bus arrives shortly and the group members, holding their envelopes in their hands, climb in to be taken down to the elaborate train station of the city.

***

The train ride is long and boring. Most of the refugees are quiet and withdrawn, a little anxious about the new place in which they will have to stay for an undetermined length of time. But this is the way it has to be, so they ride it out, sticking to the rules.

They arrive safely at Latina station where two police officers await them with serious faces. They escort the group to a waiting bus which they embark. The bus sets off, revealing to them a new city, quite beautiful, but an entirely different style to Trieste.

Chapter 10

Latina lies just inland from the infinite and immaculate sugar sand beaches of Latina Mare about a third of the way south of Rome towards Naples. Up until the 1920s this entire area was known as the Pontine Marshlands, a huge swamp area that was effectively uninhabitable due to the massive clouds of malaria-bearing mosquitoes which thrived in the hundreds of square miles of bog. The area was a scourge of Ancient Rome as it is just on the doorstep of the Seven Hills, and was considered for centuries a morass that could never be tamed or populated to any extent.

Nowadays this is an entirely modern city which is built on the former boggy swamps; Mussolini's historic project drained the Pontine Marshes and turned the entire region into arable farmland. The major city built on the marshland was Latina, a small metropolis built from scratch unlike all the other cities in Italy which boast centers that date back millennia. This 'carte blanche' form of development created a city that is almost American at first sight, with very un-European, wide, straight streets, logical traffic interchanges, flowing and immaculately maintained green spaces and massive ultramodern shopping centers.

Latina would be very much at home in California or Florida were it not for the very identifiable Fascist architecture which forms the core of the city. For the uninitiated, this particular form of building is an imposing form of purified art deco, which takes Roman shapes and forms and simplifies them to pure, smooth, sparse design, incorporating them into enormous, blocky, stone-fronted monumental edifices. It is truly an indescribable form of architecture that has to be seen to be understood, and nowhere in Italy is it more evident than Latina which was founded on that very type of building.

In a country where these elements are the exception rather than the rule, Latina can be said to be the perfect, clean, safe and modern Italian city. Latina is an amazing and completely off beat Italian urban environment. Although it is most certainly not the primary destination for the lover of ancient cathedrals or museums filled with precious antiquities, it does offer a considerable city center which features a wide variety of very Italian bars and cafes where the citizens gather to discuss soccer and politics over cups of fragrant espresso, or simply engage in the southern Italian's favorite pass time, *Dolce far niente* or 'how sweet it is to do absolutely nothing!'

***

The bus cruises along wide streets with monumental frontages making the refugees look in awe at this completely different landscape.

It is most definitely not what they were expecting. As the bus gains distance from the blue sea and climbs a small hill, they suddenly face a huge complex of buildings in front of them. Yet another ex-American military base with the whole nine yards of security, large buildings and a sports center, full accommodation for soldiers, military personnel and auxiliaries alike.

When the bus finally pulls up in front of the similarly large gates of the main entrance of the compound, the driver gets out of the bus and exchanges a few words with a police officer who seems to be aware and prepared for their arrival. Getting back into the bus he drives the vehicle close to one of the larger buildings in the compound.

The passengers watch curiously as the casually dressed people walk through the compound, many of them in tongue sandals and shorts.

When the bus finally stops, a few Latina refugees approach it, also watching the newly arrived batch curiously.

There is a friendly, almost jovial exchange of greetings as the new group, led by a uniformed policeman, enters the administration building where they are expected by office clerks who will identify each and every one of them, checking them off their lists and providing them with the details of their new dormitories and cafeteria locations.

***

Michael and Bastian settle in their corner of the new dorm and arrange things to suit their needs for the weeks to come. All done, they finally rest on their cots, Michael pulling out a bottle of whiskey from his bag. He pours it into a couple of plastic glasses he finds on the small night table supporting a reading lamp.

He hands one over to Bastian.

"We have come a fair way since August the twenty-third, nineteen seventy-nine, Mister," Bastian states philosophically.

"Oh, you're such a prophet, Bast," Michael says laughing. "Yeah, you could say that we have come a fair way," he says lifting his glass: "Let's drink to that."

They clink their plastic glasses and down them like shots.

As Michael starts pouring a refill in their glasses, a crackling voice comes through one the off-white ceiling:

... Michael Agrafa, please report to the Administration Office at once. You have a visitor waiting for you...

The message repeats twice and the crackling intensifies as the P.A. system finally dies off.

The two young men exchange curious looks.

"That was fast, whoever it is. You just came into the camp minutes ago," Bastian says intrigued.

"I'll keep you in the loop," Michael says, wondering himself and getting up from the cot. He smoothens his hair down with his fingers, steps into his white sneakers and leaves the dorm.

Michael steps out from the dorm, along the dark hallway, down the front stairs and onto the walkway between the buildings, heading without hurry towards the new administration building, which is almost adjacent from the main entrance's security booth.

His mind guesses - or rather hopes - that the only person who could find out his instant whereabouts is Stephanie with her endless network across Italy, Europe and onwards. The thought of her makes him feel a strong pang in his heart, so powerful that his breathing suddenly shallows, making him stumble on his feet.

A young couple, approaching from the opposite direction, reach out their hands trying to stop his fall. Michael stabilizes a moment later and thanks the young couple for their good intention.

"I got dizzy for a moment," he mumbles in perfect Italian and the couple waves a brief sympathetic hello and move on. Michael's preconceived mind makes him shiver and he tries to shake off the emotion of sudden excitement when he thinks about Stephanie. It's been so long since...

The words stuck solid as a log in his throat, he stares goggle-eyed at the gorgeous, absolutely ravishing, breathtakingly stylish and beautiful young woman looking at him casually from the office.

"I can't think of a more pleasant surprise!" stutters Michael, stepping towards her, the envious policemen watching them.

Stephanie, in a well-studied gesture for the police force, throws her long hair back with a wild swing and stepping forward leans over Michael, planting a juicy, never-ending kiss on his wanting lips. "It's been too long. I thought I lost you again," Michael says after they come up for air.

"I was much closer than you think," Stephanie laughs with self-confidence, but happy to be with him nevertheless. "I missed you too," she says and looks him over. "You look delicious."

"Stephanie," Michael says embarrassed, "what's the plan?"

"It's simple. I already talked to these fine officers about your release of duty until tomorrow morning. By the way, in case you don't know yet, you will be working in the Latina office for a while too," she says laughing when she sees his stunned face. "I'm connected, remember?"

Michael shrugs his shoulders. "I give up."

"Let's go," she says suddenly, eager to be alone with him.

Michael glances at the police officers who nod slightly.

They walk out from the Security building into her sports car, a red one this time, and blast away into the night. They ride quietly for a while, busy with their own thoughts. Michael looks out of the window for a while and notices that they are approaching the beautiful blue seashore.

Within the next few minutes, the car pulls into a public parking lot facing the sandy beach.

"Let's go for a walk," Stephanie says, throwing off her expensive shoes and stepping barefoot into the golden sands. Michael does the same with his worn sneakers and socks.

Locking hands they head towards the edge of the sea, they walk along the beach. "My company has good ties with the Trieste archdiocese; I always know what's going on," Stephanie breaks the silence.

"You certainly do," Michael says in a mellow voice. "It's a nice gesture of yours to come and look me up in Latina," he turns to face her, caresses her face; a gentle gesture: "We had some really good times together," he says, casually.

Stephanie smiles, vivid memories in her mind. "We sure did. Different times, different worlds. Will you call me from Canada?" she asks in a longing, almost fearful tone.

"Yes."

"There is also another reason I'm here today," she says in a cushioned, satin voice. Michael waits patiently. "Two reasons actually..." she says. Michael looks at her curiously, lighting up a cigarette. "One is business; I had a meeting yesterday with the Commonwealth Caritas reps, extending our ties in Asia and Latin America," she pauses, takes a deep breath then looks at Michael. "The second reason is you *and only you*." They look at each other. There is great chemistry flowing between them.

"Don't read too much into me - I'm just a homeless bum and a bad boy biker," he says and he means it this time. Stephanie smiles.

"That's the problem. I love bad boys."

Michael reaches out a hand which Stephanie takes. Holding hands now they walk silently for a while along the shoreline. "I'm opening a few boutiques in Montreal next spring," Stephanie says out of the blue. "How would you like to oversee the operation?"

Michael looks at her. They connect without words. Nice and easy, that is what Michael loves so much about Stephanie - amongst many other things.

"And if I do, you will come down periodically to check on business?" he asks coyly. "And on me?"

She nods smiling. Michael pulls her in his strong arms and they kiss passionately. Suddenly she breaks away from him and walks away fast, her tears streaming down her pretty face. Michael reaches a hand for her but stops; there is passion in his eyes. "I already miss you too. but Montreal is beautiful."

With a light sigh he kicks a loose pebble furiously and starts in the opposite direction. He knows Stephanie - she is complicated - she acted the way she did because something was really bothering her. Usually she came around once she had it all figured out and Michael knew that. It wouldn't be the first time. *The impossible French woman* he used to call her at the beginning, but now there was a much deeper understanding between the two of them.

More convenient? Heck, no. Just the opposite but at least by now he knew its nature so he could live with it. The good thing with Stephanie was that it never lasted too long and when she finally decided to come around, the French passion was in full bloom, worth all the frustration he encountered earlier.

His head lowers and staring into the ground he slowly walks along the peaceful beach. After a while he finds a large rock at the very edge of the water and climbs on it, his eyes cast over the open sea.

He sits on that rock for a fair amount of time, immersed in thoughts of today and tomorrow when a raw slice of bright light sweeps over him. When he turns his head, the light nearly blinds him but with considerate effort he makes out a female silhouette approaching. By now he knows who it is. He turns his gaze back to the open sea.

"I hate you, Michael."

The voice is soft and pregnant with passion when whispered in the back of his ears. He shivers vehemently but doesn't turn or move. "I hate you because you somehow managed to make me love you so much," Stephanie whispers in his ear with French passion and her beautiful accent. Michael shivers but does not move a muscle. He just sits there staring at the moving sea.

"We have to come to terms with the concept that we are happier together then being apart, whether we like it or not," he says in an even voice without taking his eyes off of the sea.

"I hate you," she utters again with passion and, grabbing his wide shoulders, turns him toward her, kissing him passionately. He immediately responds and their passion heats up the cool night.

She finally pulls away from him, weaker and trembling. "Let's go to the hotel. I... I... I..." She gives up.

"Say it," he retorts without mercy.

"I... I... I... love you," she finally utters the forbidden words.

"I love you," he responds and before she can say another word, his lips find hers and the night ignites yet again with their unleashed passion. When they part, again she is shivering.

"Let's go somewhere warm. I'm freezing to death," she says.

They hold hands they head back to her car and she drives it away furiously and impatiently, throwing large wakes of sand behind the rear tires as the machine struggles to lock a hold onto the pavement.

***

It is early morning and the sun has just started to send its angular rays to the streets of Latina as the red sports car pulls in front of the main gate of the refugee camp. Michael gets out of the car and glances over at Stephanie.

"I want more of this," he says. "How long you'll be in Latina for?" he asks.

"I'm not sure. It all depends on business developments. I had a great time too, bad boy. I'll stay in touch," she says and a moment later the car sets in motion and diminishes on the downhill street.

"Yeah..."

That is all Michael can say and he walks through the gate saying 'good morning' to the same police officer, who gives him a funny look.

***

The next morning, whilst having breakfast at the cafeteria with Bastian, Michael is paged again to go to the administration office. This time the announcer does not specify anything in particular however.

"I've got a hunch that you'll be doing some work in the office again," Bastian comments.

"I don't mind, but this could be something different," Michael says.

They finish their breakfast after which Michael goes to the office and presents himself to the staff.

He learns from the Latina office manager Leticia Bellacorte, a dynamic grey-haired lady with a powerful presence, that he has been offered a part-time job in their office, to help facilitate some of the slower cases. Michael thinks about it a little and accepts the position.

After the basic interview is over and Mrs. Bellacorte is satisfied with his knowledge of protocols and procedures, he is shown to his office and the caseloads awaiting further processing.

"When do I start?' he asks simply.

"Whenever you want, but the sooner the better for us," his new boss replies.

"I can start tomorrow morning then," Michael says in an even voice, his mind flashing occasionally to Stephanie and their time together.

"That will be excellent and much appreciated. Some of the office staff will initiate you in the immediate needs of the process." Mrs. Bellacorte concludes their meeting and Michael is released from the office.

Taking his time, he decides to explore a little the new compound. He heads toward the sports center which has two tennis courts, a basketball / volleyball field and a soccer pitch too.

He notices that various groups of people are enjoying the facility, playing different games. He approaches the volleyball team who, as it happens, are setting up players for two teams. He expresses his interest to play and he is elected into one of the teams.

Whatever it is that makes the sport a beautiful, international bridge between people manifests itself once again. His team contains guys and girls from various countries, cultures and backgrounds - but the common passion for the game makes the team play a wonderful experience.

They play three sets and end up losing the last game but everybody has a great time.

Thanking his colleagues for the game, all sweaty and tired, he walks back to his dorm and heads for the showers.

***

A few days fly by, Michael getting into the groove of the new office, still quietly waiting for a sign from Stephanie.

He misses her already. A lot.

Bastian meantime finds himself a part-time job on the auto-moto racetrack in town. With his thorough understanding of racing dynamics and techniques, easy-going attitude and sharp racing skills of his own, he has developed an elite entourage of Italian friends and acquaintances, having a lot of fun in the process. Being a business-minded individual has not hurt him a single bit either.

***

The warm spring sun casts twisted shadows on the dark pavement. The light breeze makes the trees sway gently on the wide sidewalks. As pedestrians walk by going about their daily business, a racy motorcycle takes a lean angle on one of the street corners, heading fast on the new tarmac.

The rider is highly skilled, a fact obvious from watching the way he slides deep into the turns on his fast machine.

The rider is Bastian on his rebuilt sports bike, heading toward the outskirts of town to the well-known local racing facility, Il Sagittario home to various motorsport activities, but currently mainly car and motorcycle racing.

He reaches the facility in minutes and saluting some of the drivers hovering around their machines on trailers and in the paddock, getting their bikes ready. It is not a racing day, just a practice day for motorcycle racers who wants to hone their skills or experiment with new mechanical setups on their machines. He pulls up to a small group of young men working around three prepped-up cycles.

Bastian removes his helmet and says hello to the group, who welcome him amicably.

Bastian has met these motorcycle enthusiasts through his connections with one of the young Italian police officers from the camp, himself a passionate rider as well. They had been out riding together and Bastian had fixed a couple of bothersome glitches on the cop's motorcycle.

Right now, Luigi, one of his mechanic-rider buddies approaches Bastian. Luigi is almost as tall as Bastian, something unusual among the Italians.

"You got some time today to go on the track for a few laps?" he addresses Bastian.

"Luigi, ciao," Bastian welcomes him. The two men shake hands firmly. "Absolutely. I need to burn off some frustration," Bastian says pointing to his heart.

"Bella ragazza?" Luigi asks, laughing and showing white, even teeth.

"Bellissima," answers Bastian looking at him. "You coming out on the track tonight?"

Luigi nods. "Remember those Giga-Motto gloved we were talking about?" he asks.

"Yes."

"I've got a few pairs here, along with some leather riding jackets you might be interested in," Luigi says, looking at his friend.

"Very much so. Show them to me. I would like to try some out on the track tonight," Bastian replies.

"Excellent," Luigi says and walks away to his trailer while Bastian completes the mandatory safety checks on his motorcycle, before entering the race track.

Luigi returns with some magnificent-looking soft leather riding garments. He hands them over to Bastian. "Try them on," he says. Bastian does and they fit perfectly - the studded gloves hold paddings and enforcements and so does the leather jacket which has double-padded elbows and shoulders. They look perfect on Bastian.

"I, of course, have the matching leather riding pants too," Luigi says. "I don't have them here but if you are interested, they are available."

"I am," responds Bastian zipping up the new jacket. "You coming?" he asks his friend jokingly. Luigi is already geared up in leather jacket and pants.

"Meet you at the grid in five minutes," he says, walking to his high-power superbike and getting himself ready. Bastian nods, and strapping on his helmet mounts his motorcycle, riding to the grid section for a technical checkup.

The safety check passed without a hitch, Bastian pulls aside, watching and enjoying the racy atmosphere of the track, checking out the pretty girls in the pits, coming out to watch this wild bunch of 'bad boys' in action.

Luigi arrives minutes later and he passes *his* safety check in minutes too. The two friends look at one another and they both smile - it is going to be a friendly challenge, a mini-race in its own right, as they always do.

"Right side up," Luigi says locking his visor on his face.

"Always," responds Bastian and a moment later the two fast machines pull away; one high priced, high performance racing motorcycle, the other just an old sports bike with a big bore - and some very secret and tricky modifications under the tank.

The first two laps they ride side-by-side, warming up their tires.

Two laps later, as they pass the grid area, their motorcycles start gaining speed. Their angles through the corners are becoming leaner, the engines being howling louder and louder as the boys turn the ride into a high-performance mini race.

Many riders and tech people from the track are watching them with delight - the two expert riders fly by each other with safe margins in place and their skills are a joy to watch.

After about a dozen laps, the two motorcycles pull into the pits and park in the same spot from which they left off.

Dismounting their machines, the two remove their helmets and slap a loud high-five, laughing. Joy and excitement is glistening in their eyes for a while after they return to assist other riders for their trip out to the track.

"That was fun out there," Luigi tells Bastian. "I don't know what you did to that old Benelli but it sure is fast."

"It's a fun bike to ride," agrees Bastian and points to Luigi's high-performance Aprilia. "That thing goes too."

Luigi laughs and pats his beloved high-speed action toy.

"So how you like the Giga gears?" Luigi asks.

"Excellent. Very smooth. I think I'm interested in your proposal. It might work out for both of us," Bastian says and looks at Luigi.

The Italian guesses his question. "Yes, you can keep them and wear them; show them around too," he laughs. "I have to load my gears because I've got to go soon."

The two men shake hands and Bastian starts gearing up for his ride back.

"We should do this again," Luigi says, loading his motorcycle to the trailer.

"We will. I have a good friend, a top rider. I would like him to try the track for a few laps," Bastian says.

"No sweat, bring him round," Luigi says and Bastian places his machine in gear.

"Thanks," Bastian says and slowly rolls out from the pit area heading for the open road.

***

It is early morning on the same day. Michael, dressed in light blue sleeveless coveralls rides an old-style bicycle down the busy streets of Latina. It is rush hour and his bicycle is the lowest priority to the busy morning commuters. He manages somehow to survive the cars and heads to a suburban industrial complex.

He finally parks his bicycle, the only one, in a large parking lot filled with small cars, a few motorcycles and mopeds.

It is his day off; somebody recommended him to this high-volume furniture factory and he accepted the invitation. The time for migrating to Canada is approaching and he sure could use some extra cash for his new beginning across the pond.

Walking to the front office he talks to the receptionist, who calls a name and tells him to wait in the lobby. Michael, without hurry, walks back noticing various award posters and framed pictures on the walls.

Moments later, a stocky man with bowed legs and a round face with a mustache trying to cover a big black wart under his nose, comes close to him and addresses him in Italian. "You must be Michele Agrafa," he tells Michael who nods briefly and shakes the Italian's strong, working hand. "Come with me. I will show you around."

The two men enter the production shop where Michael is introduced to various people who show him what he is supposed to do here - sanding, cutting and gluing various wooden parts under strict guidelines. And yes, cleaning and dusting is also part of the job. Michael does not mind. Work is work.

Within a few hours, Michael gets used to this new working environment which is a little different from his office clerk duties - but he likes it, the workers are great people, jovial and helpful and he likes them too. A couple of them recognize him from his earlier national broadcast interview in Trieste, something which makes things a little bit easier for him at the factory.

***

A fast week goes by in which Michael is working part-time at the office *and* part-time at the furniture factory, occasionally squeezing in a fast ride around the racetrack with Bastian's friends.

In his quietly intense way he is missing Stephanie. He has not heard a word from her for a couple of weeks now. That was quite customary between them before, but now something has shifted and he knows exactly why he misses her so much.

Bastian is also working at an automotive shop where, after hours, he can play and improve his motorcycle. With Luigi and his associates, he decided to pick up the Giga-Motto motorcycle accessory and clothing line for distribution in Canada. It is a prospect which excites him because the merchandise is of excellent quality and it will keep him in the field of motorcycles and racing circles he loved so much.

One evening, around nine o'clock, when Michael walks beat-tired into their dorm, Bastian offers him a glass of good scotch, smiling. Michael happily takes it and looks suspiciously at his friend. He knows Bastian too well.

"Good scotch but what's the real occasion for this?" he asks his bud.

"Can't I be just for once a spontaneous and nonchalant carefree dude just hanging out for the sake of hanging out and doing nothing?" Bastian asks him.

"No. It's not your type. Let's have it," Michael says, smiling and sitting down on his cot, facing his friend.

Bastian scratches his beard, pulls on his long locks, and glances at his friend. "Two things," he says, sipping from his drink, taking his time because he has some news which will make Michael pay very close attention.

Michael, on the other hand, knowing him, patiently waits him out. "One," Bastian says, "I have talked to a few places in Vancouver, Canada, and it seems that they might be interested in my motorcycle accessory lines."

"That is really wonderful news, Bast. You like this stuff and you know all about it. It is always good to have something to start things out with... congrats." Bastian thanks him and Michael, judging by his friend's extended silence, knows that the second item is related to him not to his friend. He patiently waits Bastian out.

"Two," he finally says slowly. Michael instinctively feels an emotion building up in his chest which Bastian does not miss, enjoying this. "Stephanie called. She is in Latina and she left a number to reach her on when you come in," he says. "She sounded very eager to see you."

"Give me the goddam number," Michael rushes him, his face a little red from the emotional turmoil.

"It's on your night stand," Bastian says, laughing and pointing to a slip of paper resting on the night stand between the cots.

"Thanks," Michael mutters with visible relief on his face. "I need to clean up first then I'll call her."

"Sure, tough guy," says Bastian, smiling, and opens up one of his high-performance motorcycle magazines.

A minute later, Michael disappears into the shower. When he returns, he looks like a different person - clean and handsome, fresh, a glow on his glittering skin which even Bastian notices.

"Don't overdo it," he tells his friend.

"What?!" Michael reacts. Does it show?" Bastian nods and goes back to his reading.

"You fell in love with her again, didn't you," Bastian says without moving his eyes from his magazine. There is a moment of extended silence then Michael turns to his friend, his face calmed somewhat under quick thinking. "I have never fallen *out* of love with her," he states calmly. "You know me. I just don't talk about it," he says casually.

"So now what?" Bastian asks, genuinely curious. Michael and Stephanie are going through a difficult transition stage right now and emotional distractions could be damaging and dangerous.

"I don't know," Michael answers with honesty. "This time I just have to go with my gut feeling, not with logic or the heart."

"Good call," Bastian agrees. "You'd better go call her. She sounded anxious to see you too," Bastian says.

Michael does not respond but Bastian's words sooth his tormented heart somewhat. He is almost dressed, now. Pulling on a pair of socks, he slips in his white sneakers and running his fingers through his long hair once, walks toward the door.

"You work tomorrow?" Bastian calls after him as a caring friend.

"Off from both jobs tomorrow," Michael replies and a moment later closes the dorm door behind him. Bastian, alone now, smiles at a private thought - he is also in love with Tatiana and she is not here.

Michael stops at a telephone booth close to the main gate and dials the number Bastian gave him. Stephanie answers in the middle of the second ring.

"Michael?" Her voice sounds emotional.

"It's me," he replies, himself barely keeping his emotions in check.

"You got some time?" she asks him in a guilty, small voice.

"Yes. You want to meet?"

"I'll be at the main gate in ten. Be there," she says and hangs up. Her soft voice still resonates in Michael's ear; he caught the nervous, longing emotion behind the words... or so he thinks.

Lighting up a cigarette, he walks to the main gate booth and looks in to see which police officer is on duty tonight. He sees Bastian's young biker friend and exhales with some relief.

"Eduardo, *bona sera*" he calls the young cop.

"*Michele*. Ciao. How is it going?" he asks in Italian.

"It's all good. Listen, Eduardo. I might have to stay out late tonight," he confesses to the young cop. "I don't know exactly how long..."

He stops his words in mid-sentence as both men turn their faces toward the fast approaching red sports car which stops with screeching tires inches away from the main door.

The officer, noticing the beautiful and stylish girl behind the wheel, quickly looks at Michael. He nods just barely visibly.

"Just be back before eight o'clock in the morning when my shift ends... and enjoy the night!" he tells him with a broad smile.

"Grazie," Michael replies and a moment later steps into the sports car where Stephanie is already holding the passenger door open for him, a wild look in her eyes. He steps in, the two make brief eye contact. A blink of a second later and the red car blasts off from the main entrance door, disappearing down the hill leading to the city.

As soon as the car has cleared the hillside, Stephanie who has been quiet all along, pulls the car to the curb, places it in park, and throwing her 'attitude' shades on the dashboard jumps on Michael kissing him passionately. Michael is more than ready to welcome this wild and beautiful girl who has played with his heart strings for almost three years now. They kiss passionately for a long time, and when they come up for air they just look at one another silently for a long time, breathing hard, feeling each other's presence and emotions.

"You found me again. I thought you'd dumped me," Michael finally breaks the silence without looking at her.

"I never lost sight of you... and dumping you? That's the most ridiculous thing I've ever heard," she says, passion coloring her voice and emotion making her French accent even more charming than ever.

Michael has a tiny, pleased smile listening to her.

"I was extremely busy with the business. And it also could involve you," she says, staring straight through the windshield in front of her.

"Me?"

"You."

"How?"

"We can't have a conversation with one-word sentences," she says, turning to him this time.

He looks at her too. "What have you got in mind?" he asks, but both instantly realize that that was the last thing they both had in mind, discussing business details right now.

"How about I take you out for dinner and we can touch base on it then? Besides, you look hungry," she says charmingly and the mischievous look in her eyes tells him another story.

"I'm starving for you," he says in a low voice. His corny statement sends shivers of pleasure down Stephanie's spine. She leans over and they kiss passionately again.

After a long kiss Stephanie starts panting lightly. Forcing herself away from him, she quickly brushes locks of hair from her forehead and placing the car in gear, drives away fast. "You will like this place," she says without looking at him, her face still flushed by strong emotions.

"It's been a long time," Michael says without looking at her.

"Yes. But it was good for us too, in a way," she says in a low voice.

"How?"

"I'll explain it to you over dinner and drinks."

"I like it already," Michael says with a small smile.

She places the car in gear and they drive away, fast and with precision, looking straight forward through the windshield, thinking. Michael does the same. There is a shared, pleasant and intense silence in the car, the only sound the roaring powerful and well-tuned engine in her sports car.

After a few maneuvers which show her familiarity with the city, she turns her car into a smaller, cobblestone street just off of the main avenue.

The building is old and beautiful. Large granite rockwork covers the front and a few steps leading to a large aged beech wood gate, giving the place a respectful and welcoming appearance.

Two valets in uniform stand by discreetly, waiting for patrons. The moment Stephanie pulls the car up to the curb they both approach her respectfully: a young boy and a young girl. After getting out of the car, Stephanie tosses the keys to the pretty young girl who catches it with a sure hand.

"*Grazie*," a valet says, politely standing aside and letting Stephanie and Michael, now also out of the car, pass.

They climb the six granite steps of the wide front, open the wooden door and step inside, led by Stephanie who feels comfortable here.

As soon as the door closes behind them, the artistic indirect lighting of the place soothes them with a welcoming hue. Michael looks around curiously and notices an elegant man impeccably dressed in a dark suit who is approaching them, smiling. His main focus is on Stephanie who casually waves at him.

The host is beside them now, delighted to see her. "What a wonderful surprise," he says and gives her a warm hug, quickly glancing in Michael's direction.

"You look good as always, Lorenzo," Stephanie replies and the host laughs, pleased.

"You are too kind," he says.

"We need a private booth," she says simply, but her words have a commanding impact on Lorenzo.

"No problem," he says. Please follow me."

They follow Lorenzo toward the back of the restaurant where there are three executive booths, all private; lush in appearance, all sporting a small tag on the table: *reserved*.

Stephanie and Michael take a seat and Lorenzo looks at the handsome couple with an expert eye.

"Enjoy this special night," he says in English with his Italian accent. "A waitress will be here shortly for your drinks and with the menus. Please take a moment and check my recommendations," he says in a low, modest voice.

"We'll do that. Thank you, Lorenzo," Stephanie says in flawless Italian. Lorenzo smiles pleased, removes the reserved tag from the table and disappears in the penumbra of the place.

The two lovers sit there in a shared silence and adjust to the new surroundings, trying to sort out their thoughts and powerful emotions. It is not working very well.

The cocktail waitress then shows up beside their table and her young fresh look and eagerness to please lightens up the atmosphere in an instant. They order drinks and finally lean forwards and look directly at one another.

"I'm happy you are here," Michael finally breaks the silence. Stephanie's eyelashes flatter but she leans forwards to begin to speak, the cocktail waitress shows up with the drinks.

Drinks served, they sip silently for a little while. Stephanie tries again.

"Like I said earlier," she starts slowly, looking for the right words this time to help her express better this avalanche of feelings in her heart. "The business is doing well but it's extremely demanding on my time."

"I understand," Michael says conciliatorily. "You are here now and that counts for a whole lot," he says looking at her.

"Do you mean that?" Stephanie asks in a small voice and Michael senses a gentle vulnerability in her; the way she twirls her hands watching him intently.

"Yes. When I met you over three years ago on that Black Sea beach I thought that it was no more than a summer love for you," he says in a small voice. "So much has happened since then. I thought it all was over," he finally says and it is visibly hard for him to utter the words.

Stephanie turns very pale, her large beautiful green eyes suddenly developing a dark hue, her fingers twisting the table napkin nervously and a small vein becoming visible on the side of her neck. "Is it?" she finally asks and looks at him with burning, piercing eyes which at this moment could cut diamonds with their genuine intensity.

Michael immediately resonates to her emotions and leaning back on his chair takes a few deep, slow breaths. He also realizes that the answer to Stephanie's short two-word question could and will forever alter the course of their lives. Closing his eyes he just sits there. The avalanche of powerful emotions are charging in as he vividly relives all the moments the two of them spent together in their sporadic three years of seeing each other.

His answer will change everything in one way or the other and his hearts strings are stretched now like violin chords when he finally looks at the beautiful young lady sitting in front of him, staring at him with intensity.

"No."

He looks at her - That simple short negative word never had a more powerful and positive effect than in that hot night on the warm shores of the Mediterranean Sea. Stephanie's eyes shine like live diamonds and she reaches her hand over the

161

table to finds Michael's, squeezing it hard and long. The intense flow of energy between the two of them is pure chemistry.

"I love you," she whispers, closing her eyes.

"I love you too," he echoes with meaning. They sit there for a minute holding hands and saying nothing.

The moment of bliss is interrupted by the waiter who brings them the food. While he is serving, Michael watches Stephanie in awe - he has never seen a more beautiful woman in his entire life; the young French lady is just glowing under the intensity of their shared love.

"You look beautiful," he whispers to her after the waiter leaves. She says nothing and sits in front of him quietly watching him.

"What are you doing to me?" she whispers back with thrilling excitement coloring her words.

"Just having dinner with a cute French chick I met a few years ago on the beach. A beach bum," he says and they both laugh, never taking their eyes off of each other.

"I have big plans for us," she finally says, sipping from her fresh drink. "Do you want to hear them?"

"Yes. Anything is good if it involves you and me," he says, watching her.

"Here it goes. Maybe now you will understand why I was away for so long last time," she says, picking at her food with a silver fork and collecting her words.

The night flies by too fast for them. Michael learns in passionate words that Stephanie actually set up a working division of her clothing company in Canada and she was sincerely hoping that Michael would like to get involved in her venture, so the two of them could always having the connection and keep on doing things... together.

But since both are very independent people, her plan includes long periods apart since she operates from France and Michael will be supporting her business from Canada.

The dining is excellent and after several drinks they leave Lorenzo's, Stephanie leaving a very generous tip to the staff.

She drives slowly this time and they made it safely to the luxurious hotel in the charming downtown.

They spent the whole night in each other's arms, both knowing too well that departures and lengthy separations are unavoidable and forthcoming.

***

When Stephanie drops him off at the main gate just after six o'clock in the morning, Eduardo is still on duty, saluting him with a smile as he walks by on his way to the Romanian quarters. Michael waves to him but does not feel like having a conversation this time - all he wants to do is goes to his bed, snuggle under the sheets, close his eyes and dream of himself and Stephanie.

His plans are instantly shattered the moment he steps in their dorm and Bastian immediately waves to hurry to him. Some of the boys are still sleeping so they keep their voices down. Michael approaches his bed.

"What?" he asks Bastian in a low, disgruntled voice.

"You seem to have had a great time out," Bastian says smiling. "You're glowing, what the heck?" Bastian says with a small smile.

"I spent the night with Stephanie and we're back on track again... sort of," Michael says. "What happened?"

"Sorry to burst your bubble, lover-boy, but we have a problem here," Bastian says and hands him a newspaper clipping showing one of their Polish friends lying dead on the pavement, covered with blood.

"Jesus!" whispers Michael sitting down on his cot, looking at Bastian. "What happened? This is *not* accidental death, this is murder. Looks like a personal vendetta to me." he says, looking at the clip.

"It is," Bastian answers. "He got involved with the wrong local gay crowd."

"Does the camp authority know anything about it?" Michael asks.

"I don't think so - not yet, anyway. The story just broke in the early edition," Bastian explains.

"How did you find out?" Michael asks him.

"Klava stopped by very early this morning. She was out last night with her new friends and they pointed it out to her," Bastian says.

"Right now it's not a good time to be murdered," Michael says with light sarcasm.

"Is there a *good* time to die?" asks Bastian rhetorically. "The news is gonna break to the camp authorities this morning, no doubt about it."

"Shit. There is not much we can do about it. We can't undo the facts," Michael says, looking at his friend. "I'd better break it to them myself this morning and try to sugar coat it a little bit," he says, thinking.

"Yeah. Something like that," Bastian agrees, getting up and preparing to leave. He answers Michael's mute question. "Going to work at a small bike shop. Come out sometime and ride the track with my Ducati. You'll love it," he says, heading for the door.

"I definitely will do that," Michael says. "Have a good day and I will talk to you tonight."

"*Ciao*," Bastian replies and leaves the dorm. A few moments later, Michael hears his friend's Ducati fire up and rumble away toward the main gate.

He reaches into his drawer and pulls out some camp policy documents. It looks like he has to do some work today despite his intended time off.

Michael changes his T-shirt into a fresh one, and grabbing his shoulder bag from his night stand drawer leaves the dorm.

Once outside, he lights up a cigarette and starts walking towards the administration building. It's still early, only minutes after seven o'clock in the morning and he figures nobody will be in the offices that early. He is wrong.

When he enters the main office he finds a young man dressed in a causal sports jacket, blue jeans and sneakers, white shirt and long hair, like his. He is sitting at one of the tables reading carefully through a thick case file. He looks up when Michael enters.

"Good morning," Michael salutes him in Italian.

"Good morning," replies the stranger giving a quick, analytical look to Michael, a typical cop-trained reflex of analysis and self-protection. Michael knows that look.

"I work in this office part time," he tells the young man. "Can I help you with something? I know how the filing system works in this office," he says.

"Thank you. My name is Giogardi Fetturi, police detective for the region of Lazio," he introduces himself in a self-assured voice.

"I imagine you are here to look up some info on a Polish person. Correct?"

"You mean a dead, murdered Polish person. Yes, that's correct."

"I figured that much. My name is Michael Agrafa, Romanian emigrant and part-time worker in this office," Michael says. "How can I help you?"

The Detective lowers his eye to the file in front of him. "Did you know this person?" he asks giving Michael a piercing look.

"I met him a few times and I partially worked on his case file, the very one you're holding in front of you," Michael says recognizing the file from Trieste. "The papers were almost complete for his flight to Australia," Michael says, watching him.

"Yes, indeed. You're very well informed, Michael. Did he have any enemies as far as you know? I mean here in Latina *or* back in Poland?" the Detective asks.

"Not exactly, as far as I know. I believe that the reporter of Latina's *Early Edition* was a little too eager to get his brownie points; doesn't make a very good impression on us or the city at large, for that matter. Reading the article I believe that he didn't have a clue what he was doing. It only provokes discord and a not-needed scandal in the city," Michael says angrily.

The Detective listens curiously while watching him with interest. "Aren't you the same person who had that television interview representing the refugees?" A moment later it dawns on him. "Of course, you *are* the same person. You did a good job for the camp," he admits.

"Thanks. But this is *not* good work for the camp," Michael replies.

"I am only investigating a brutal murder. The facts," the Detective says.

"He was in love with an Italian woman he met at the piazza a few weeks ago. She was married," Michael says. "That's all I know."

Detective Fetturi looks at him curiously. "You want me to make a statement to the public that this was a crime of passion?"

"I believe it was." Michael says. "Can I offer you a coffee?"

"Yes," the Detective says, "black with two sugars."

Michael nods and starts up the coffee machine, then walks to his office. "You might want to see this," he addresses the detective, offering him a small file resting on his desktop.

After a lengthy conversation with Detective Fetturi, Michael leaves the office. During all this time all he has been thinking about Stephanie and their last night spent together; the new dimensions he discovered in this beautiful French girl which had him thrilled for hours. The fragile possibility of seeing her again after his departure for Canada is also highly satisfying.

Right now, all he wants is to see her, to be with her.

Feeling restless and energetic, he walks down to the main gate and using the telephone calls the hotel asking for her room. He is almost ready to hang up at the tenth ring when suddenly Stephanie picks up the receiver, panting.

"*Allo*?" she asks in an emotional voice.

"It's me."

"I knew was you. I was in the shower when you called and I was so afraid I would miss - "

"I want to see you...now," he utters, surprised by the emergency in his tone.

"Me too. Give me a few minutes and I'll pick you up at the main gate," she says.

"I've got a better idea," Michael says, thinking fast. "How about I jump on Bastian's motorcycle and pick *you* up at the hotel and we can go for a little ride," he says, not sure of her response.

"I love it. I'll put on some pants then," she says with impatience in her voice, "and hurry."

"Yes," he says and hangs up the receiver heading back to the dorm. Reaching it he grabs two helmets and one fancy pair of riding gloves from Bastian's new Giga-Motto collection.

Outside, he pulls on his gloves, dons his helmet and fires up the engine with the key he found inside Bastian's main helmet. The fine-tuned Ducati comes alive, its engine purring like a wild cat. Michael loves the sound of that harnessed power and unleashed energy.

Mounting the bike he rides slowly to the main gate, and waving a small hello to the new police officer on duty he blazes down the street, thrilled by the rush of the wonderful freedom machine. He rides fast and skillfully, zigzagging through the downtown traffic with the ease of a leopard. When he finally pulls in from of the hotel, to his surprise he sees Stephanie standing at the curb, waiting for him. He stops beside her, lifting his visor.

"That was fast," he says looking her over. "You look wonderful," and he means it. Stephanie laughs, pleased, mostly that he is here for her. Michael removes his helmet and she comes over to him and kisses him on the lips, making the valets and by-passers look at them with wonder.

"Put on your helmet and hop on," he finally says, helping Stephanie stabilize her body behind him on the small seat of the sports bike.

Holding him by his narrow waist she pinches him. "I'm ready. Where are we going?" she asks.

"How about Gaeta Ariana Beach for starters," he says looking back to her.

"Sounds wonderful," she replies, squeezing him from behind. Michael nods and lowering his visor places the motorbike in gear rolling away on the sunny street.

They ride at a comfortable speed and Stephanie leans into the corner with him, making the bike glide smoothly through the twists and turns. This little detail gives Michael an additional dose of excitement. He occasionally turns his head and briefly looks at her and she counters his glance every time with smiling eyes.

They cruise along the seaside highway, the breeze brushing over their toned bodies, the sun bathing them in golden bliss.

After several minutes of enjoyable riding, Michael pulls the motorcycle into one of the Gaeta Ariana Beach parking lots. He helps Stephanie descend and then follows her, both of them removing their helmets and shaking their locks.

"This was a very nice ride," Stephanie says and coming closer gives him a tight hug. He responds quietly and the two lovers just stand there in the middle of the parking lot, clamped together for minutes.

Finally separating, Michael locks the motorcycle, securing the helmets onto the bike and, holding hands, they head towards the boardwalk.

The landscape is simply breathtaking; the colorful town of Gaeta looming ahead, built right on the very edge of the Mediterranean Sea, is basking in the morning sun.

Sun glasses on both of them, they reach the nearly-empty boardwalk. An occasional jogger runs past them, nodding and sweating. A few sailboats lazily drift across the blue waters of the gulf. An isolated seagull releases a caw whilst flying over their heads. The timeless sea washes the rocky shores in a relentless pursuit to conquer the beach but it has failed for millennia, extending the human lease one day at the time.

"I have grand plans for you and me," Stephanie says, her face and eyes full of sunshine and love.

"What's the rush?" Michael asks in his easy-going way. She squeezes him and wraps her arm around his as they walk on the path, watching the soothing sea. "Feels good to be together," he says in a low voice.

"Yes," Stephanie agrees with a sigh and they both instantly know that this togetherness won't last long. Not this time around. They walk silently for a long time, weaved into each other, listening to the moving sea and their relentless heartbeats.

"I'm a little hungry," Michael finally breaks their silence. "What about you?" he asks, stopping in the middle of the path and giving her an exaggerated dramatic hungry look.

She bursts into laughter. "That was very convincing, Mr. Homeless," she says.

"Because I truly am homeless for now. I'm borrowing time and borrowing space until I get to Canada," Michael says in a casual, even tone.

"About that. What have you planned for us for today?" she asks.

"Nothing too heavy-duty. Hang out a bit on the beach, chat... in the afternoon I am invited to join Bastian and his racer friend for a speed jamboree on the *Il Sagittario* race track - But I can cancel it," he adds quickly.

"Don't," she responds with conviction. "You love speed and where'll you find a better and safer place for some adrenaline then the *Sagittario*? Go for it."

"You sure? I would like you to come along," he says, uncertain of her reaction.

"I wouldn't miss it for the world." she answers, looking at him with bright eyes. He studies her for a moment.

"You mean that, don't you?"

"Yes. I want to take some pictures too," she says with enthusiasm.

He kisses her passionately and when they separate he takes her hand in his. "Why did we have to wait for this for almost two years?" he asks.

"You are ready when you are ready," she says simply and smiles at him. "That's my philosophy."

"I'll buy that."

"Come. I'll get breakfast... and I just love the town of Gaeta. It's so pretty and unpretentious."

They lock hands again and walk lazily towards the beachfront facilities just ahead of them.

The ancient small town perched on the shores of the Gaeta Gulf is breathing in the sun with all its pores. Colorful rooftops and building walls emanate a welcoming serenity. The narrow cobblestone paved streets intersect and wind up, down and sideways on the rocky shores of the Mediterranean Sea. Large arches and portals intersect with white stone decks and patios, private and commercial alike. Tiny boutiques and restaurants sprout everywhere, offering a wide variety of goods and services in a relaxed, typical laid-back Italian fashion.

Colorfully dressed people walk the streets, many of them tourists. The locals go about their daily business with open faces and bright eyes, used to the powerful Mediterranean sun.

"How do *you* like Gaeta?" Stephanie asks Michael, who is delighted by the sophisticated simplicity of the town and its people.

"It's beautiful," he says. "You've been here before, I can tell."

'Many times. I even did some business here, looking for a place for my store," Stephanie says.

"And?" Michael enquires curiously.

"I decided to open one in downtown Latina instead. It has more permanent traffic than the beach town," she says and her face suddenly lights up under the surge of a new thought. "Do you want to check it out after Il Sagittario? It will give you a feel of what business I'm doing and will offer a taste of the Montreal store," she says with hidden excitement.

"I'd love to do that," he replies and they both feel the electrical wires surging through their veins.

Led by Stephanie, they find a small eatery a few streets above the beach with an open view of the sea from a white patio. Coffees and croissants are served along with some Italian delicacies turning the breakfast into a new experience.

They take their time with the light meals, savor the coffees, and talk about a frail but promising future. They watch each other with new eyes every time they turn their heads. Since they finally connected again, something bordering on a miracle has happened to them both. The language of love has smashing down the solid barriers that both of them worked so hard for years to build.

The best part of this newly-rekindled relationship is the ease and smooth flow of words and ideas between the two of them. It has such a powerful and complete chemistry that it scares them with its focus and intensity. Yet, it all comes smoothly and effortlessly.

Stephanie takes another sip from her coffee and looking at Michael shakes her head. "I just don't know what has happened here in the last two days. I think I'm falling for you," she says in a small voice, in French.

"Me too," Michael says, sharing her feelings. "It's a bit scary."

"Very much so," she says in French again, and Michael smiles.

"Hello Stephanie," he calls and his voice sounds fresh and energized, excited, as if this was the first time they have met.

"*Allo* Michael." is all she can reply, but her whole body and soul resonate on the same wave. Her large, moist, beautiful green eyes tell him the entire story. He reaches a light hand over the table and Stephanie places her own delicate one into his.

"Nice meeting you."

"*Oui, aussi.*"

They finish their breakfast at a leisurely pace, Stephanie pays and Michael leaves the tip, both heading for a walk into the sun. Stephanie, who knows the town, takes them to the very tip of the peninsula to the *Torre d'Orlando* point from which they have a panoramic view of the Gaeta Gulf. Sitting on some driftwood they silently watch the sea for a while, often glancing at one another, finding their niche in this beautiful spring day.

After a while Michael gets up from the driftwood and picking up pebbles throws them into the sea. Stephanie watches his restlessness and knows that he's ready to go now.

"Let's go to the Sagittario. Do you need any special riding gear?" she asks him.

"I do, but I'll get it from the track. Bastian and his friend have some on display as they are distributing it," Michael says.

"Interesting," Stephanie replies, her business mind immediately connecting dots in her head. "Let's go."

Holding hands they return to the motorcycle and cruise back to the seaside highway *Via Flacca,* heading north back towards Latina. The sea is to their left, the town and colorful passing villages on their right; they have a fabulous time together. Stephanie often and Michael occasionally, wave back to the friendly locals as they ride, passing through their small villages.

After a few minutes Michael merges onto the *Via Pontina* highway which takes them away from the sea, heading in a northwesterly direction. The gentle hillside is populated with houses with green gardens and rocky yards sprinkled with flowery bushes. As the road advances through the more populated neighborhoods of Latina, Michael enters the *Strada Statale 148* which brings them towards the general area of the racetrack.

After a few miles of riding, the 'Il Sagittario' racetrack signs begin appearing on the highway. Michael follows them diligently and shortly afterwards they take the exit. A few streets follow with signs clearly indicating the track and the distance to it.

Within a few minutes they reach the main entrance which they find open. Since it is a week day, there are no races on the track, only racers and their friends and tuners testing their fast machines for the upcoming weekend race.

Riding slowly through the pit area where several groups have their machines and trailers parked on both sides, many of the young men wave smiling at the beautifully shaped passenger on Michael's motorcycle. She pretends she does not see any of them.

Within minutes, Michael spies Bastian standing in a small group of people, talking to a pretty Italian girl with long curly hair kept up in a tight pony tail. They are both wearing leather riding gears - jackets and pants and fine quality Giga-Motto boots. Bastian immediately recognizes his own motorcycle and enthusiastically waves Michael and Stephanie in.

Michael pulls up close, shuts down the engine and helps Stephanie dismount. He does the same and they both remove their helmets. "Fancy seeing you guys together again," Bastian welcomes, comes close and gives Stephanie a welcome hug. "You guys look great together," he says in French, close to her ears. Stephanie blushes and looks even prettier now.

"Thanks," she replies in English. Bastian turns to some arriving friends. "This is Viola; Viola, this is Stephanie, a long-lost friend... and Michael, my partner in crime."

"What's the status with the track?" Michael enquires, looking around the pit and beyond to the fast tarmac.

"It is clear for motorcycles in about ten minutes," he says checking his wrist watch. "You need some riding gear," and makes a discreet sign with his head - follow me.

They walk to Luigi's trailer which is parked just a few feet away. Bastian opens the door and the two friends step inside. The trailer sports several racks of fine Italian leathers for sports riding and motorcycle racing.

"Nice stuff," Michael says admiringly as he checks out the jackets, riding boots, gloves and many other accessories spread throughout.

"This is all Giga-Motto equipment. You like it?" Bastian asks him curiously. He has always valued Michael's opinion when it comes down to style and chic.

"I love it," Michael says picking up a couple of designer T-shirts with the company logo printed discreetly in small silk on the chest.

Bastian watches him curiously. "Thanks. She looks hot," he says watching him.

"Who? Stephanie? She's hot *and* fun," Michael says with passion this time.

"Just be careful there, Casanova. She has stomped on your heart a few times before," Bastian warns his friend.

"Only three times," Michael says, his tone leveled now. "This time is different."

"I've heard that before; don't get hurt."

And that's that. Bastian will never say another word about this. "Here," he says, handing Michael a red, black and gold leather jacket in the latest racing design. "This is your size."

Michael tries it on and it fits like a glove; loose enough for maneuvering the fast motorcycle, but smoothly following the rider's body with several cooling holes built into the leather.

"Try these as well." Bastian hands him a pair of riding leather pants in matching colors. "You'll have to try the boots on your own," he says and glances outside to notice Luigi talking amicably with Stephanie and Viola.

Within a few minutes, the two young men step out from the trailer and they look good, making a strong impression on the onlookers. Stephanie lets out a quick gasp when she sees Michael in the racing outfit.

The two friends are welcomed by Luigi who checks them over with pride. Bastian makes the introductions again. "Luigi, this is Michael," he says and the two men shake hands.

"I like your riding gear," Michael tells him. "This is very comfortable."

"I've heard good things about you. We shall try them out at the track," he says. "What are you riding?"

Michael points to Bastian's older Ducati. "Oldie," he says.

"In the right hands that Ducati could be a challenging machine," Luigi says smiling.

"I like it," Michael agrees.

The three guys are ready and eager to go out on the track. Michael keeps close to Stephanie who has never taken her eyes off him the whole time.

"You be careful out there, mister," she tells him in a low voice in French.

"We'll have some good fun for a few laps, that's all," Michael replies.

A minute later the three young men go to their machines and strapping their helmets on, fire up their engines. The sheer power of the three superbikes sends shivers down on Stephanie's spine. The atmosphere is electrifying.

With Luigi in lead, the three motorcycles coast toward the grid area and under the traffic's coordinator's green flag they enter the fast circuit.

For the first lap they ride at a moderate speed, warming up their tires and surveying the track surface for possible dangers such as cracks, small rocks or even oil spills.

When they have completed the first lap, Bastian leans on his machine and shoots forward at high speed. As if out of a reflex, Luigi and Michael do the same, sending their machines roaring after his own.

Bastian is in the lead now and despite the fact that they have closed the gap behind him, his exclusive racing skills keeps the other two machines in tow. It is only in a deep-angle hairpin turn where Luigi's more modern breaking system comes into effect managing to outbreak Bastian and instantly he takes the lead, with the other two only inches behind.

They blast by the main stand and pit area where Viola and Stephanie are watching thrilled, seeing the boys blast by at well over a hundred and forty miles per hour, disappearing a few seconds later into the next turn.

As their machines and tires warm up, so does their adrenaline and chiseled riding skills. For the next few laps they race each other at full speed, challenging the limits of their bikes - and their own skill - having a blast in the process.

When after several laps the three smoking motorcycles pull into the pit area and stop by Luigi's trailer, the three riders are drenched with sweat under their helmets. It might have looked easy to the onlookers, but riding at those high speeds and lean angles is hard work and it shows.

Stephanie comes close to Michael who wipes his sweaty face with a small towel Luigi has thrown at him.

'That was a wild ride there, mister,' she tells him in English, thrilled to have him here, beside her, in one piece. "It looked very dangerous."

"It was, but we had it under control," Michael says casually and pulls her closer to him. She shivers again in close proximity with his hard body.

"You guys were awesome," she says as Bastian approaches them.

"How did you like the old beast?" he addresses Michael, waving to Stephanie.

"Great power delivery and torque. It is a heavy bike so you really have to watch your breaking points," Michael says laughing.

"Yep. And *you* found them pretty quickly," Bastian says, looking at both of them.

"We're going into town for a drink. Do you wanna join us?" he asks them. Stephanie politely looks at Michael for an answer. *That's a change,* Bastian silently acknowledges.

"We've got plans for this afternoon, Bast. But thanks for the invite and the track time. It was fun," Michael says.

"No sweat," Bastian replies and goes to talk to Viola.

After a short time, Michael chats with Luigi about buying the riding suit from him at a discounted price, keeping the gear on. Stephanie comes close to him. He did not forget. "If you want, we can check out that store?" he addresses her.

"I *would* like you to see it. It's in Anzio, close to the harbor," she says, happy that he has remembered.

Climbing onto Bastian's older Ducati, he helps Stephanie mount and waving their goodbyes, rolls out from the track, heading once again toward the highway.

Their ride back to the city is a slow and leisurely one with both watching the pretty scenery and landscapes passing them by. Thirty minutes later Michael steers his bike into the downtown core and stops at the curb, lifting up his visor. Stephanie does the same. They are parked on the banked granite street in front of the Anzio Harbor and its historic center.

"This place is beautiful," Michael says taking in all the colorful boats in the harbor, the emerald green Mediterranean Sea, the elaborate rock buildings perched on the side of the water. "Where are we going?" he asks her.

Stephanie quickly looks around. "This is a perfect place to park the bike. I want you to walk with me downtown. It's all close to the water," she says, removing her helmet. Michael takes it from her and he locks them to the motorcycle.

"Come," she urges him, a little apprehensive, a little excited too. They walk close to each other, Michael absorbing all the colors; the stores and restaurants perched by the water. There are many people walking about, coming and going from numerous power and sail boats, strolling in the harbor for pleasure or shopping.

They advance a few hundred feet along the shore of the sea, blending in with the crowds. As they pass the food stands and restaurants they notice they are coming closer to the specialty boutiques of jewels, arts and crafts, ceramics and higher-end clothing. Michael follows Stephanie who is window shopping, checking out her competition.

After a short while she stops in front of a fairly large shop exhibiting trendy fashions for land and sea alike. "Neat stuff," Michael says, eyeing some of the men's fashions which he kind of likes.

"Let's check it out then," Stephanie says casually and leads the way into the classy store where everything is decorated with white bricks and beams and posts of aged polished wood. The floor is made of shiny red bricks, packed closely together almost like hardwood floors.

They start looking at the wares and Michael's attention is caught by a very flamboyant sailing jacket. He doesn't notice Stephanie talking to the store manager, both women occasionally glancing in Michael's direction. When he has finished checking out the jacket he approaches the counter where Stephanie is expecting him.

"How do you like it?" she asks him and she sees in his face that he loves the store and its style.

"I don't mean to be rude but this store is kind of neat," he says carefully.

"I'm glad you like it because *this* is my store," Stephanie replies laughing girlishly at his facial reaction.

"Nice!" he says a little shaken by the surprise. "Excellent location," he adds looking out through the window right to the open sea in front of them.

"Yes, we like it here too," she says in French this time.

Michael says hello to the manager who is a venerable looking lady in her fifties. It is now he notices at least three pretty young girls looking after clients throughout the store, wearing stylish uniforms and short dresses.

"Come. I'll show you behind the scenes," Stephanie says leading the way upstairs on a sweeping staircase of wrought-iron and wood. They reach the upstairs hallway and she unlocks a door as they both enter.

"This is my office, which is also used by Cassandra, my manager you met downstairs," Stephanie says comfortably, making her way around the desk and sitting in a leather chair with arm rests.

"Looks like you know what you're doing," Michael says looking at her.

"I know my business," she says, this time giving him that direct look which makes his heart miss a beat every time she does it. "The only risky link in this business is you," she says smiling mischievously.

"Thanks," he says neutrally.

"I'm falling in love with you, mister, and that's a dangerous business combination," she says smiling at him.

"It doesn't have to be," Michael says returning her intense look. "We can make it work. Don't forget that it takes two to tango," he says, watching her beautiful green eyes changing shade from light to dark and then light again under her emotional surge. "I love you," he says, reaching his hand across the desk towards her. She takes it and without losing it, gets up from the chair, walks around her desk and dives into his arms. They kiss passionately again until she separates and arranges her hair and posture.

"Not here," she says and is business-like again. "Let's go back to the store. I want to talk to my new girls a bit," she says and leads the way back from the office, down the hallway towards the store.

When they reach the main floor he looks at her. "I'll have a smoke outside. I'll see you when you are ready," he says.

"Okay. Thanks."

Michael gives her a small nod, and bowing to Cassandra walks outside, the sales girls stealing a quick and curious look at him as he leaves.

Once outside the store, Michael lights up a cigarette and walks across the sidewalk close to the docking side of the road. Sitting down on one of the vacant wooden benches fastened to the boardwalk he enjoys the afternoon beauty of the sea and port. He is not alone - there are several people walking also, taking pictures, talking and laughing. There is a cheerful atmosphere in the air and Michael's aching heart welcomes this ephemeral serenity.

Before he knows it, Stephanie shows up behind him and sits on the bench next to him.

"So how's business?" Michael asks her and she looks at him candidly.

"Very good; sales are up thirty-percent up for this month and I like that. By the way, the sales girls really like you," she says pinching his arm. He reacts.

"What did I do now?" he says laughing with her.

"It's that bad boy look of yours which got *me* hooked in too the first time we met."

"Nah," Michael says easily, not paying attention to the compliment. "What do you want to do next?" he asks her, in French this time.

"How about we walk along the beach a little here in Anzio, catch the sunset, then go back to my hotel and order drinks and something to snack on," she says, probing him.

"I like your plan," he replies.

Getting up from the public bench they walk side-by-side without physical contact until they leave the commercial area. When they reach the beach to the south, Stephanie grabs Michael's hand and they walk whilst holding hands and watching the restless sea.

"I see bright things coming up in the near future for us," Michael says, his dark eyes cast along the sea and beyond, listening to his intuition.

"You do... like you are my personal prophet? I hope it's all good," Stephanie says and wraps her arm around his narrow waist. He wraps his right arm around her shoulder as they walk slowly through the damp sand.

They catch the scarlet sunset and just before the sun disappears under the sea make their way back to the motorcycle and donning their helmets cruise at a leisurely pace back to Stephanie's hotel.

As when riding back towards the downtown core, Michael has a new and growing emotion that he is going to lose Stephanie again. He rejects and fights the thought and instead, reaching his left hand behind him, pinches her left thigh gently. She slaps his hand in good humor. Michael laughs.

They arrive at her hotel and this time he rides the motorcycle right into the multilevel parking garage. Removing their helmets they take the elevator to Stephanie's floor, eager to get to her suite. The room is classy and luxurious but the only thing Michael can see right now is a beautiful French girl he has fallen in love with... again. As soon as the door is locked she turns toward him and a moment later is in his strong arms, kissing him passionately.

"This time is different," she whispers in his ear, almost reading his mind.

"There are only so many times we can try until it breaks," Michael says, passion building up in his heart and soul. "Last time we came very close to the point of no return," he adds, pinching her chin lightly and aligning those mischievous green eyes with his.

"I know and I'm sorry for that," she whispers softly in French which pleases Michael; French being her native tongue, the words came out fresh, unprocessed by the analytical mind required for translation.

He kisses her passionately and lifting her up carries her in his arms to the king-size alcove bed.

Stephanie cries with excitement and anticipation. Her blood races almost faster than his when they quickly undress each other and jump under the fresh bed covers, holding each other tight. Stephanie's whole body shivers with his touch and for a while time freezes as the two of them immerse in the powerful and dangerous act of love.

***

The morning finds them still clutched together, Stephanie's long and curly locks resting on Michael's face, tickling his nostrils. He reaches his hand to his face and the gesture awakens him. Leaning over, he kisses Stephanie's delicate neck. She smiles in her sleep and waking up, rises onto an elbow, kissing him gently.

"Good morning, pretty girl," Michael says and slips out from the bed, beginning to dress.

"Good morning," she whispers, eyeing his firm bum.

"Do you want something to eat?" she asks him.

"Just coffee, please," Michael says; Stephanie reaches for the telephone and orders for them.

She lazily gets up from the bed and taking some clothes with her, disappears into the bathroom.

Michael, dressed, walks out onto the small balcony and taking in the beautiful morning lights up a cigarette, gazing at the city and the sea below them.

There is a knock at the door and when Michael realizes that Stephanie is still in the bathroom he walks over to the door and opens it. A young male waiter comes in and places a carafe of coffee along with various accessories on the small coffee table. Michael gives him two-thousand Italian liras.

"*Grazie*," says the young boy and noiselessly leaves the room.

Michael pours coffee into the two cups and fixes Stephanie's just the way she likes it - one sugar with two creams.

When she finally steps out from the bathroom she looks like a movie star - new fresh clothes from her own company's collection give her an airy, fresh and feminine making look - even more beautiful if that is possible. Michael watches her with great pleasure.

"Oui, *tres jolie*," he says.

She comes over, sits on the couch and they sip the coffee, she lighting up a cigarette.

"When do you have to go back to the camp?" she asks in Italian.

"Any time before ten-ish," he replies. I have to see some people in the morning and I am working in the office in the afternoon. "I've got the bike so you don't have to drop me off this time. When do I see you again?"

"About that..."

Michael feels the sudden pressure in his chest and his earlier premonition comes racing back to him.

"Yes." he acknowledges her words.

"I'm leaving this morning for Torino," she says, not without difficulty. "It is a fashion-related engagement I made two months ago with a clothing manufacturer and I can't cancel it now. It's too late," she protests with a nostalgic tone but her mind is made up. Michael realizes that and understands.

"When are you leaving for Canada?" she asks him, seriously concerned but also interested.

"Not sure. It is safe to say within two weeks. I'll find out more about that this afternoon in the office."

"You have all my numbers to find or message me on, and I will call you back wherever you are," she says and taps her hand on the empty seat beside her. Michael gets up from the lounger facing her and walks around the coffee table, dropping in beside her. She leans over and kisses him with passion and affection.

"You smell like the sea," she says.

"And you smell like lavender, *mon cher*," he says. "Do I see you before I leave to Canada?"

She gives a deep sigh which places tiny creases around the base of her fine nose. She's planning her busy schedule inside her head and Michael waits patiently.

"Probably not, but I will try to change some plans - which won't be too easy. I really want to spend more time together. The Canadian division is also coming to its final setup stages with the Montreal Chamber of Commerce so... one way or the other, we will be back together as soon as possible," she says, looking at him and holding his right hand with both of her own.

"If not, I will call from Toronto once I have found a place, as well as my bearings in the city," Michael says looking at her.

He stands and pulls her up with him. She happily follows and they embrace and kiss passionately for a long time.

Michael again has a nudge of a feeling that things won't be easy but they will survive it somehow.

When they separate and look at each other, she senses his new premonition. They are so fine-tuned with one another that it is almost eerie. "What was the premonition this time, my personal prophet?" she asks.

"I see challenges and a bumpy road ahead but we'll make it through somehow," he says, laughing and kissing the tip of her nose. "I'd better go, Stephanie."

They kiss lightly again and Michael runs his fingers through his hair, grabs his riding jacket and looks at her.

"I'll walk you to the door," she says in a small, emotional voice which is unlike her. She is falling for him again.

"Have a safe trip to Torino. You're driving?" he asks.

"Yes. Driving keeps my eyes on the road and my mind occupied; it's good for me," she says and this time her eyes are moist. He kisses her forehead. It is a tender gesture:

"We are young. We've got the energy and we'll deal with it. See you in Montreal," he says and a moment later walks out of the door, gently closing it behind him. Stephanie makes a couple of quick steps towards it before stopping, and releasing a sigh she walks out on the small balcony, looking at the beautiful view, waiting for him to appear on his motorcycle.

A few minutes later he does and she is wondering if he will look up in the room's direction. He does, and seeing her there gives a small wave, his motorcycle blending into the city traffic a moment later.

Stephanie sighs once again, and returning to her suite, begins to pack.

Chapter 11

The sun is burning hot onto the rooftops of the international refugee camp when Michael rides through the main gate and waves a small hello to the officer on duty. The cop waves back, recognizing Bastian's motorcycle.

Michael cruises slowly through the aisles until he reaches the Romanian dormitory. He parks the bike on the concrete pad beside the main entrance and removing his helmet walks into the building.

As he walks through dark hallway, visions and vivid images of him and Stephanie begin to play on his mind with raw intensity.

When Michael enters the dorm he walks to his corner and drops onto the bed, staring into the ceiling. He quickly looks around; there is nobody else in the room at this hour. He releases an unrestricted deep sigh. He misses Stephanie already.

Slowly and gradually he starts collecting his wits, letting the emotion subside. He has a ton of things to do, typical for him. Being bored has never been an option for Michael, starting at a very young age when lack of input made his rich imagination engage and invent his own games, toys and entertainment. Throughout all his school years he was a leader not a follower, people coming to *him* for adrenaline kicks and excitement.

"I just have to keep myself busy," are the words he releases out loud, a minute later grabbing his hygiene bag and a towel, heading for the showers.

When he returns, he is fresh and full of energy. To his surprise he finds Bastian in the room.

"Fancy seeing you again," Michael welcomes his lifelong friend.

"Good morning, Casanova," Bastian replies.

"Don't call me that. I love that French chick," Michael says.

"I know you do. How goes it... I mean with you and her?"

"We had a great time together. She left this morning for Torino."

"When are we leaving this camp?" Bastian asks.

"Good question. It's been on my mind too. Since I'm working in the office this afternoon, I'll find out for us," Michael replies.

"That would be very educational and informative for us both," Bastian says and notices the colorful riding leather jacket on Michael's bed. "How do you like the Giga-Motto stuff?"

"Very nice. I think you will do fine distributing it," Michael says. "I will definitely buy some gear for myself."

"Good. We'll give you a deal," Bastian says.

"Do you guys carry this fancy stuff for women too?" he asks his friend, an idea developing in his mind.

"There are not that many female riders out there yet," Bastian says. "The product is definitely available though."

"Good. I'll get back to you on this; I've got an idea."

"Do that."

"What's on your agenda for today?" Michael asks him.

"Day off; just hanging out. Since the Ducati's back I might go for a ride later."

Michael nods. "Why don't we take the Ducati and goes somewhere together? Have a coffee and chat a bit. We haven't done that for a while, and besides, I need your opinion on something," Michael says, looking at his friend.

"Sounds like a plan," Bastian agrees. "Let's do it now, then."

They both get up, Michael taking his riding jacket, Bastian also. Grabbing their helmets they leave the room.

This time it is Bastian who drives, with Michael hanging on behind, wearing the same stylish Giga-Motto jackets.

They progress slowly this time enjoying the sunshine. They ride down on the seaside highway, past Anzio and end up in a small fishing village with a café perched right at the edge of the sea.

"If this patio was any closer to the Mediterranean we'd have to wear swimwear!" Michael comments as the two walk onto the patio and find an empty table.

They order two large cappuccinos from the mustachioed waiter with the name Paolo; mid-forties, jovial and confident, probably the owner of the small café. Once the coffees arrive they sip some and then, stretching, take in the sea for a few minutes. Sailboats and fishing boats are strewn across the harbor and the light breeze makes the spectacle quiet beautiful. "How are things with Tatiana?" Michael asks his friend.

"Not too good. I miss her but I think I have to let her go. She changed her destination lately; she re-applied for New Zealand instead of the USA and she wants me to go with her," Bastian says not too happy with the situation.

"New Zeeland is awfully far away but it's a beautiful country with great people," Michael says.

"I know that but I'm not willing to go there. Not now, anyway," he says. "I really want to give this Giga-Motto line a go in Canada, and maybe later in the US. Imagine the market potential. I have already started the process with Luigi."

Michael lights up a cigarette and looks at him. "How serious are you about this girl?" he asks him.

"Back there in Trieste I thought I fell in love with her," Bastian says.

"You sure as hell looked *molto inamorato* to me back there," Michael says laughing. "You and I... we always fall in love with the wrong women," Michael says with a slight touch of sadness in his voice.

"What is really going on with you and Stephanie?" Bastian asks carefully, knowing that there is a lot of history to this relationship and his question could touch a raw nerve.

"I don't really know. That's the thing, Bast. Every time we are together the whole world just clicks and everything works like clockwork - no shit," he says looking at his friend.

"You guys have got great chemistry, you always had, and that's why you are still seeing each other." He sips from his coffee, checking out a couple of pretty girls in mini-skirts who have just arrived at the patio, and then turns back to his friend. "You are both very independent thinkers, strong headed ... If you learn the fine technique of accepting the other's priorities before your own, you guys might get somewhere," Bastian says laughing, realizing that he has touched the right button in his bud's heart.

"Since when are you such an expert in matters of the heart?" Michael asks in a soft voice.

"I'm *not* good with them... I always get burnt, but I know *you* quite well and I know Stephanie too to an extent. This is just a viewer's observation. And *that* is a field I'm strong at, buddy boy," he says, laughing and waving at the two pretty girls who have taken a table across from them. They wave back to him.

Michael sips quietly from his cappuccino, thinking about Bastian's words. Bastian in the meantime gestures to the girls and a moment later walks over and sits down at their table. The three of them start talking, the girls relaxing in Bastian's easygoing, non-intrusive company.

Michael watches him for a moment, shakes his head slightly and pays for the coffees, turning his gaze back to the sea. A short while later, Bastian returns, the girls gone.

"They are from Switzerland and they would like to hang out with us tonight if you're interested?"

"I have to work shortly, mister," Michael says.

"I know that. I meant *after* work, of course."

"I just left Stephanie a few hours ago. I still can smell her perfume," Michael says shaking his head.

"Okay, I got it, lover-boy. Have it your way - but if you change your mind, let me know later so I know how to handle this," Bastian says seriously and Michael starts laughing: "Take me back so I won't be late for work," he says.

The ride back is fast and furious, Bastian cranking up the speed a notch or two. They both enjoy the trip, making the dash back to the camp in record time.

"Here we are," reports Bastian, pulling the motorbike up in front of their dorm and removing his helmet.

"I would've freaked out on the ride if I didn't know you, remember that," Michael says and punches his friend in the shoulder: "Later." He removes his riding jacket and gives it to Bastian: "Drop it on my cot if you don't mind. I have to stop somewhere first before I head for the office," he says. Bastian takes the jacket with a nod.

Michael says 'bye' and starts walking toward the indoor gym building and supplies room. His steps accelerate after he glances at his wrist watch. Taking a corner he finds himself in the middle of a soccer game taking place right between the buildings. It's a mix of men and women including some teenagers. Michael carefully walks around them and passing the game, approaches a smaller residential business set far back from the alley connecting the regular buildings.

There is a tiny white picket fence around the front of the freshly painted white house. Michael reaches the front door and knocks lightly. He hears some shuffling slippers inside and a few moments later the squeaking door opens; an old woman in her seventies with grey hair, wearing a very old-fashioned dress looks at him from her curved posture.

"*Bongiorno*, Senora Fiorentina. Is Giancarlo at home yet?" Michael asks the elderly in Italian woman, who finally seems to recognize him.

"My eyes are not very good any more. *Vieni, Vieni...* come inside," she invites him. "Giancarlo is taking a quick shower. He will be out any minute," she says, showing him a chair to sit on.

"He was waiting for you," Fiorentina addresses him.

"I'm sorry, *Senora*. I got a little tied up and I want to tell him that if he is home tonight after my office hours, at eight, I'm happy to come back," he says.

"Sure, sure," Giancarlo's mother says. "He will be at home for sure."

"Thank you then and sorry for the mishap," Michael says and backs out toward the door. "I will come back a few minutes after eight o'clock, tonight," he says and she agrees with him.

"*Bene, bene...*"

Michael leaves the house and hurries towards the Administration office, blaming himself out loud for forgetting his commitment with Giancarlo, to continue the English lessons he has been teaching him for a few weeks now. The janitor and his wife are dreaming of taking a trip to California and he wants to speak the local lingo.

The Administration office is busier than usual today - people are bustling around carrying files, speaking on the telephone, interviewing new arrivals, typing documents. When Michael steps into the office and heads for his desk, Veronica, one of the senior clerks, approaches him and requests he come to her office. He follows her inside and sits in front of the desk, leaving the door open.

"I have a case file which is overdue and I would like you to look into it - and perhaps wrap it up for me," she says, handing over Michael a folder with an older gentleman's picture on it. "He is Hungarian," Veronica explains watching Michael look at the picture. "You speak the language and you can read and translate his hand-written statement. He barely speaks any English."

"I can do that," Michael says looking at Veronica. "I have a question for you," he says and she nods. "Any indication of my approximate departure time to Canada?" he asks her.

"I checked the advanced cases like yours this morning. There were some delays in the process and you will be leaving two weeks tomorrow for Toronto. And yes, your friend Bastian is departing a week later to Vancouver."

Michael smiles at her gratefully. "Thank you."

Taking the case file he leaves Veronica's office and reaching his own desk, immediately starts working on the case.

When he finally finishes typing in the documents, the translated statements and Hungarian official papers, it is almost eight o'clock in the evening. Being the only one left in the office at this time of the night he takes the case file over to Veronica's office and leaves it on her desk, shortly afterwards leaving the building.

Saying goodnight to the police officer who is locking up, he heads down the aisles toward Giancarlo and Fiorentina's little house.

***

6:00am and there is a positive energy flowing through the Romanian dorm as the men and boys scurry around with the new day's planned activities. Bastian is all dressed in his mechanic coveralls and shakes Michael awake.

"Wake up," he calls. Michael finally opens his hazy eyes and rolls out of the bed.

"What time is it?" he asks, putting on his jeans.

"Just past six o'clock and you've got to go to the furniture factory, remember?"

"I do, but they don't start until eight. Right, I need a ride down there."

"Hello... good morning!" Bastian teases him, handing over a clean t-shirt from under his bed. "I start at six-thirty," Bastian adds. "What time do you want me to pick you up?"

"Six is fine, just come through the back yard. I'll be working in the gluing section," Michael explains.

"No problem."

Other men walk by them saying 'good morning'. Michael and Bastian grab their helmets and follow the group out of the building.

Bastian fires up the old Ducati and they are almost ready to go.

"How's the *new* Ducati coming along?" Michael asks him.

"I should wrap it up today, as a matter of fact. If everything turns out okay with the final settings you can ride this beast until you leave. I'll try to sell it before I go."

"You're the man," Michael says, cheerfully getting ready to mount the bike.

A minute later they leave the compound, Bastian riding skillfully through the wide streets until they reach the furniture factory. Michael dismounts and punches Bastian's shoulder. "Six o'clock," Bastian says and an instant later raises the fast bike on the rear wheel, riding off on it alone, making all the arriving workers stop and stare at his departure.

"Show off," says Michael, laughing and heads towards the main entrance, chatting with some of the workers he already knows.

He works hard and fast. Michael has never trained in carpentry but has always been a fast learner. They only had to show him the process once and he has picked it up, improving over time. He remembers a few years back when he started racing fast and dangerous motorcycles across Romania when an older racer, a veteran in the sport at that time had told him: "You have to get good before you get fast. That goes for everything you do."

Michael has taken that simple motto to heart and applied it to everything ever since.

The gluing and assembly of furniture he was doing today followed the same motto and it worked.

When five-thirty in the afternoon rolled around, he has made his quota and is chatting casually with some Italian colleagues. Cleaning up and changing into his street clothes he walks outside to the yard, waiting for his friend.

Michael is having a cigarette, sitting on a stack of veneer wood when a fancy, colorful superbike rolls by him heading toward the other entrance. Michael watches it curiously and to his surprise he thinks for a moment that he recognizes something. A minute later the fast bike pulls in front of him and the rider removes his helmet.

"So what do you reckon?" Bastian asks him, referring to his newly-finished motorcycle.

"Looks like a million bucks," Michael says, jumping off the veneer stack and walking around the motorcycle, checking the technical details of the machine with knowing eyes.

"Nice work," he concludes. "You should get a pretty penny for it before you leave," Michael says with admiration.

"I hope so," Bastian replies. "I need some seed money for the distribution line. Let's go." Michael jumps onto the back seat and Bastian rides away, slowly and responsively this time. They arrive at the small auto-service shop Sandro's, where Bastian works for now. The old Ducati is parked in front outside.

Michael really feels the fever to ride a motorcycle, for him, one of the best ways to blow off frustration and a bad day. There are still no signs from Stephanie and time is running out.

"Let's go for a run with both bikes," Michael says.

"Yes, let's do that," Bastian agrees. Michael takes the key from his friend and fires up the other motorcycle. Mounting it, he looks at Bastian who gives him the thumbs-up and a second later pulls out from the curb in a storm with Michael right behind him.

They ride fast and furious, coming close to the edge of danger several times but that is okay - it is in these moments that the adrenaline runs high and the spirit feels free.

They ride away from the city, jumping on the seaside highway, passing Anzio again, heading toward Rome. They ride fast along the coastal highway, passing cars and slower bikes until satisfied, they pull in at a sea lookout lot and turn the engines off, slapping a loud hi-five.

"That was fun," Bastian says, excitement still glittering in his eyes.

"I needed a good dose of this too," Michael agrees, lighting up a cigarette and gazing at the open sea.

"Any word from Stephanie yet?" Bastian asks him, suspecting the source of his friend's poorly concealed bitterness. Michael shakes his head.

"I miss her," he admits.

"I know you do," Bastian says knowingly.

"And you?" Michael asks, hinting at Tatiana.

"Me, on the other hand... I had a brief chat with Tatiana on the telephone yesterday. Her mind is set on New Zeeland."

"And you?"

"We broke it off. I wished her all the best and that's it," Bastian says, his jovial open smile gone.

"You'll get over it," Michael says.

"I always do, but still..." Bastian says with a little sigh. "None of this mushy stuff. Let's head back; I have to meet Viola at nine," he continues and Michael laughs - yes, he's friend will be over his old heartthrob soon. The two men are very different. They mount their bikes and with a nod start riding back to the camp.

When they arrive the sun is setting on the Mediterranean Sea, sending long shadows on the building and the people strolling on the aisles between buildings. As they dismount, Bastian looks at his friend. "You can keep the key until you leave. I'd like this new Ducati for a while."

"You said that; you're the man, Bast. Thanks," Michael says happily. His transportation independence is solved for the remainder of his time here. "I need to take a ride downtown to get something. You have fun with Viola," he says placing on his helmet again.

"No worries ... Stay out of trouble," says Bastian and walks up the stairs of the barracks.

Michael fires up the engine and rides away. He rides lazily, enjoying the abilities of the powerful motorcycle. As if driven by a subconscious feeling, he can't help but turn towards the direction of Anzio and before he knows it, the Ducati stops in front of Stephanie's boutique.

Being a romantic at heart, he knows quite well that he should not be here but ignores the thought because his vivid imagination helps him relive the moments spent here with Stephanie, down to her perfume flaring his nostrils. Removing his helmet, he walks across the road and takes the same bench he took last time, and like last time also, he lights up a cigarette and gazes over the gulf, his mind full with images of Stephanie.

A few minutes later a female voice coming from behind him, startles him, "She called here today, and told me that she really misses you," the older lady says; words which makes him swivel rapidly to face the person saying them. Cassandra is standing there erect and elegant, wearing the store's designer clothes, looking at him with sympathetic eyes.

"It's so weird... I don't even know why I'm here," Michael mumbles, lost for words.

"You must love her just as much as she loves you," Cassandra replies with deep understanding. "She is still in Torino and she will be very busy for the next few days."

"Well, if you talk to her again, tell her that I am leaving for Canada in just under two weeks. Nice to talk to you, Cassandra... and thank you for the message. Bye now," Michael says, crossing the road with Cassandra, heading for his motorcycle.

"Good luck with everything," she says in Italian.

"Thank you. Same to you."

He dons his helmet as Cassandra walks into the store. Two sales girls are watching him curiously through its windows. Michael starts the engine, waves a brief hello towards them and rides away, heading back to Latina.

Why had he come to Anzio just out of the blue like that, he is wondering as he rides back. Then he remembers Cassandra's words and figures that somehow he knew that she had a message for him in the store. The thought of her thinking about him cheers him right up. "I must be in love with her or something," he mumbles to himself, suddenly in a good mood.

***

The following days fly by as Michael and Bastian alike are busy tying up their loose ends in Latina, at the same time preparing for the new beginning procedures and protocols expected of them in Canada.

Bastian finally cuts loose with Tatiana and 'adjusts' his relationship with Viola, sets up the details for Giga-Motto distribution with Luigi and sells both Ducatis to rookie racers on the Sagittario racetrack.

The departure day is rapidly approaching and Michael still hasn't heard a word from Stephanie, making him nervous and restless again.

"She will call," reassures Bastian a number of times, noticing his friend's stressed state of mind.

It is around eight o'clock on Friday, the night prior to their flight when the speakers throughout the camp call for Michael to report to the security office for a telephone call. Michael and Bastian are sitting on their beds in the dorm, discussing details of their arrival to Canada when they hear the announcement.

"You'd better hurry. It must be Stephanie," Bastian tells him at once - but by this time Michael is halfway across the dorm and heading for the door. He arrives at the police booth to see Eduardo watching him panting. Catching his breath, Michael looks at the policeman inquiringly. He shrugs and smiles, pointing to a telephone receiver on the other desk.

Michael is trying to compose himself but it is difficult - he snatches the receiver and places it at his ear:

"Hello?"

A moment later and his whole composure has changed. He is suddenly standing tall, the worrisome wrinkles around his eyes gone. "I'm leaving tomorrow morning for Toronto," Michael says in a soft voice into the receiver.

"Sorry I couldn't call you earlier, business is nuts right now. I'm calling you from Brussels, Belgium. I miss you like crazy!"

"I miss you too," Michael answers, his voice choked with emotion.

They chat for a while and the conversation ends with Michael promising to contact her when he has a permanent phone number in Toronto.

***

The early morning finds Michael all dressed up and shaved, ready for the big day. He has an average-sized suitcase on his cot and packs in his meager belongings: a few shirts, some jeans, clean socks, underwear, and a book. He also packs his Giga-Motto riding jacket and gloves, his bag of hygiene stuff and a helmet. He looks around for objects he might have forgotten. He cannot see any.

Putting on his light sports jacket with brown leather elbow patches, he sits down on the cot and meditates for a few minutes. Not long afterwards, Bastian returns from the showers and seeing Michael all ready to go, comes over and extends his hand. Michael shakes it rigorously.

"You call me when you're ready, in Vancouver," Michael says. "Use the numbers I gave you. Stephanie's store will be a safe way to connect."

"I've got it all here," Bastian says, patting his leather shoulder bag. "Good luck with everything," he says - and he really means it.

"Same goes for you - I will spread the word on the Giga-Motto goodies," Michael replies.

"Thanks."

Michael picks up his bag, grabs his suitcase and walking to the door, exits the dorm, never to return.

And that is that. A simple yet powerful goodbye.

Chapter 12

Toronto, Canada
May 1980

The red and white painted streetcar barrels down Queen Street with severe determination. The conductor, an Iranian fellow in his sixties, holds the jumpy control levers with an iron grip. He cranks the steering lever strongly to the right to follow the steep radius of the tracks, pushing the heavy electrical public transport vehicle against the inner steel of the rail, making it squeak like a banshee from hell.

Worried passengers look at each other in alarm. A moment later, the massive streetcar stabilizes and in his heavy accent the Iranian conductor announces the next stop: "Old City Hall."

Michael is one of the passengers who gets off, his leather jacket zipped up to his chin, the imitation fur collar up, a long scarf wrapped around his neck. He balances his bag on his right shoulder as he heads toward Young Street in downtown Toronto.

He landed in Toronto nearly two weeks ago and immediately went through all the registration procedures which took days. Emigration Canada provided him with an apartment downtown along with a little money to spend on food and hygiene. The money he saved back in Italy has also come in handy. Despite missing Stephanie like crazy, he has not called her yet. He has had to get his basic setup accomplished first, get a feel of his new life which does not account for much for the time being.

On one of the first days of his arrival, while he was staying at one of the government subsided hotels after a full day at the Emigration Offices Canada, he came down in the evening to the small piano bar where a black musician played the blues like a virtuoso. They got to know each other. Gerard was a

University student at Ryerson University, just a few blocks away from the hotel. He was taking film and dramatic studies which instantly built affinities with Michael's stage directing experiences from *his* days at University, just before the 'big escape.'

Over the next few weeks a strong bond had developed between the two young men. Gerard took Michael with him to several of his college parties where Michael met many exciting people, all students with high passion and dynamic drive. Michael began to get more comfortable with his new life direction. Gerard had a second job as a Waiter at the Royal Canadian Yachting Club on the island across the harbor. He took Michael along one day and got a job as a bartender-trainee at the club's well-assorted lounge-bar.

His dedication and attention to detail made him receive generous tips from the well-heeled patrons of the bar, helping him adapt. Michael knew that this was only a short, transitional experience but he enjoyed it fully nevertheless. Learning the pulse of the city and its various styles and people only flared his vivid imagination to dizzying heights.

He occasionally also talked to Bastian in Vancouver. His friend, also a survivor, was doing the same - learning the system, the new country and the people. His jovial and easy going nature and his open smile made him a likeable person opening many doors for him. He worked as a Mechanic in a car service center for the present as he was building up a small network for his Giga-Motto line of products.

Still not ready to call Stephanie but missing her like crazy.

***

One blustery night at the Yacht Club where there are nearly no patrons due to the nasty weather, Gerard and Michael meet Hillary, a pretty girl, also a Ryerson University student. She and her boyfriend have just brainstormed a new live performance drama show and are looking for talent to complete the team.

Michael eagerly reads the script and falls in love with the dynamics of the play. "I can help you direct it," he tells Hillary who immediately becomes interested once she learns about Michael's live stage experience and background.

***

Michael, Gerard, Hillary and Francis meet at a pub downtown and over a few drinks Gerard and Michael get acquainted with their friends' vision and approach for artistic execution. Michael immediately comes up with a couple of audio-visual angles which instantly hook Hillary and Francis. Gerard, who also is a trained and talented dancer, shows the group his rendition of the stage dynamics and dance. His friends are flabbergasted by his new and unorthodox approach.

"I really think we've got something here," Francis raises a toast for this new meeting of minds. They all join in cheerfully.

By the end of the night the four of them have an action plan in place. They all decide to meet as soon as their schedules permit. Gerard will have the nights off from the hotel in two days, on a Wednesday. Hillary and Francis finish school at about four in the afternoon. Michael does not have a schedule yet. They all decide to meet Wednesday night at seven at the old Metropolitan United Church on Queen Street, where Francis has obtained the large basement hall with a built-in stage for rehearsals. Before they part, Michael asks Hillary for a copy of the script which she happily provides to him.

"I'll bring it back on Wednesday," Michael assures her.

"No sweat. Just to let you know... both of you," Hillary says glancing at Francis, "on Wednesday we will bring in some people who, we hope, will be part of the cast - if they are good enough."

"Can they dance?" Gerard asks curiously.

"Yes, they can. Some of them are supposed to be quite good, although we'll find out Wednesday," she says laughing.

"In that case I will sketch out a few moves we might try out with them. Do we have a sound track made up yet?" he asks Hillary and Francis.

"We have worked on that for a while now, Hillary and I," Francis says. "We'll bring the cassette Wednesday and put it in the firing line," he adds.

"Cool. In that case maybe I should take a copy of the script too," Gerard says and Francis reaches into his large gym bag and gives Gerard a copy of stapled and typed pages of the script.

The group finally splits and Michael, alone now, hurries for his small apartment, new ideas and creative thoughts starting to germinate in his active mind.

When the elevator cab reaches his level on the ninth floor, Michael's creative wave suddenly fades away, instantly replaced by an intense gut feeling which is almost painful. He knows it well by now because over the years he learnt to pay attention and heed to those not so subtle warnings or *alerts* as he calls them. He rushes down the hallway to his pad and when he barges inside the messy place he instantly notices his cheap, garage-sale-special answering machine flashing a red light.

He relaxes somewhat now. It's only a message and just a very few people knows his new telephone number - he can count them on one hand. He starts tidying up the place a little. Placing his loose clothes in the closet he picks up some take-out wrappers and plastic utensils and chucks them in the garbage can. When he is all done, without hurry he takes off his sneakers and putting his feet up on the scratched coffee table he picked up from the curb, he finally reaches for the answering machine.

He presses the *replay* button and in a quick whirl the tape starts playing. Michael jumps so high and so fast that he hits his elbow on the wall and his back against the stand-alone lamp, knocking it over. The lamp shade rolls away and stops in the middle of the small living room.

The answering machine's recorded voice is talking directly to him: it is Stephanie -

"Michael. I finally found you, thanks goodness! It's me and I'm calling from Paris. We need to talk; I miss you like crazy! Call me as soon as you get this message. Ciao and call me *subito*"

Michael sits down on the edge of the coffee table and thinks about him and Stephanie. A couple of minutes later he presses the replay button and listens to her voice again... and again.

He quickly glances at his wrist watch - ten in the evening. He calculates the European time zone, four o'clock in the morning... He hesitates for a moment then releasing a deep sigh takes out a slip of paper from his wallet and starts dialing a long string of digits.

"Allo?" answers a sleepy voice after three and a half rings.

"It's me..."

There is a long silence on the other end of the line and Michael can hear panting breath which matches his own. "It's Michael," he repeats in a soft voice.

"Why didn't you call me earlier?" she asks him, her tone happy to hear from him.

"Wasn't ready." he answers quickly telling the truth. "How are things?"

"Business wise, very good. The Montreal store is almost finished. Personally... not so good," she says in a girlish voice.

"What do you mean? Are you alright, Stephanie?"

She feels the genuine concern in his voice and feels better already. "I'm fine," she says in French, hesitant.

"I love you," he says with great difficulty but that's all she wants to hear. Her tone has changed now; strong, confident, happy. "I love you. Have you found your way in Canada yet?" she asks.

"Getting there. I like it here," he says. "I'll tell you more about it when I see you."

"Talking about that, *mon cher*, I'm flying to Montreal to finalize the store details next week. I would like to meet you there when it's all finished," she says with both business savvy and personal passion mixed in her voice.

"You have my number. Just call or leave a message when you're ready and I'll drive down there," Michael says, feeling a massive weight lifting from his heart. It is so good even just to talk to her, to hear her voice, her uneven breathing.

"I will call you in about a week," she says. "I need to go back to sleep now, mon cher. Can't wait to see you," she adds and Michael senses the sleepiness in her voice.

"Likewise," he says in French. "I'll be waiting for your call."

"*Au revoir* for now and thank you for the call... Ciao..."

"Ciao." he says and hesitantly hangs up the receiver, his fingers still gripped around the cradle after the line goes dead.

"Oh, boy," he sighs at the visions he sees in his mind about the time when he is going to meet Stephanie in Montreal. Smiling, he slowly reaches for the performance script resting on the coffee table and starts reading it.

***

It is late at night and Michael is still sitting at his dining room table writing and sketching images on a virtual stage he has drawn on his legal pad. Francis and Hillary's script is resting in front of him, opened at page twenty-nine. He picks up the pad and holds it at arm's length, picturing himself from a spectator's perspective looking down at the stage. He changes a few lines on his sketch, adds some boxes, dresses the stage some more.

Getting up from the table he walks over to the window. Looking down in the back alley of Shelburne Street he lights up a cigarette, opening the window and gazing over the lights and structures of the neighborhood. His flared-up imagination sees a large theatre hall where a dynamic performance is in full progress. He senses the pulse of the stage and the sweating dancers' and actors' sharp focus as they deliver their parts, locking the live audience in their immediate and powerful spell.

The following morning he sleeps in, takes an invigorating shower and dressing in his jeans, white t-shirt and sneakers slips into his fine Giga-Motto leather jacket and leaves the apartment.

The Emigration Office gives him a large bundle of reading information and various government-issue guides for getting a job along with a small allowance money-draft under the international political refugee status act, to help him survive this beginning stage.

Buying himself a large cup of coffee, Michael sits on a bench in the small George Hislop Park between Charles St. East and Isabella Street, and leafs through the mound of information at hand. He is working tonight again at the Toronto Yachting Club and has some time to kill. A fast sports motorcycle cruises by on Isabella Street sending sudden shivers down Michael's spine. "I need... no, I *want* a bike again," he tells himself, but right now is hardly the time or place for a motorcycle.

Back in his apartment, he diligently spends a few hours on the job front and watching television, listens to the way people talk, behave and interact in this world. *Learning how to be a Canadian.*

Exhausting his resources for the time being, he eagerly returns to his script and sketches, sinking into them, making notes and corrections, until it is time for him to walk down to the Toronto Lake shore and take the ferry across to the Yacht Club.

The club is in full swing tonight. The moment he arrives at the bar, the manager places a large order of drinks in his hand:

"We have a birthday party here today," he says.

"On a Tuesday?" Michael asks.

"Yes. She and her husband are leaving for Antigua tomorrow. Get those drinks and if you need help, just ask me," the manager says and walks over to the head waiter giving him directions about the dinner servings. Michael sees Gerard serving at one of the tables and that makes him really happy. Turning to his bar, he rolls up his sleeves and starts mixing drinks.

Once the party's immediate needs are satisfied and the other patrons are attended too, Gerard shows up at Michael's bar.

"Looks like it's gonna be a busy one," he addresses him.

"Hey. Good to see you. It's busy, but not that bad. Are you coming Wednesday to the Church?"

"About that..." Gerard starts, a tinge of excitement in his voice. "Have you read the script?"

"Yes, I did. I liked it. The way they wrote it leaves lots of leverage for dance scenes and the directing," Michael says, equally enthusiastic.

"Exactly; I like that a lot," he agrees and pauses for a moment, thinking. "I did some dance sketches I would like you to take a look at," he says.

"That would be my pleasure. I did some sketches myself, about the stage placement and dramatic angles and stuff," Michael says.

"That's great. We have to work together anyway," agrees Gerard.

"Stop by here at coffee time, if you're not too busy and we can bounce some ideas around," Michael says and Gerard likes that thought a lot.

"Done deal. See you then," he says and hurries away as the manager shows up at the bar with another drinks list for Michael.

The night gets busier than expected and the two friends never have a chance to sit down and go through their notes and exchange ideas. It is nearing the end of their shift, close to midnight when Gerard swings over with a tray full of deserts. "Are those all for me?" Michael asks him jokingly.

"Sure!" says Gerard. "Listen... do you want to have a drink somewhere after work and check out these sketches?" he asks.

"Why not," Michael immediately agrees. "The night is young."

"Good. I'll see you after work then," he says. "These deserts are getting heavy."

"All those calories weigh a ton," Michael jokes and raises a cheer with one of the tall glasses he is working on. Gerard just shakes his head and moves toward the birthday party.

***

It is after midnight when Michael and Gerard finally manage to get away from the club and catch the last ferry to the mainland. They are both a tad tired but the passion for the play keeps them bright and alert.

"There is a quiet bar and sandwich shop on Church street, if you want to check it out," Gerard says as they walk off of the ferry.

"Sure," Michael says simple. "It doesn't matter."

Zefir's Bistro is quiet at this time of the night. There is one young couple sitting in a corner, going through some projects on paper, much like them; university students, most likely.

The boys settle at a table and order coffee. "How you like the play, so far?" Gerard asks Michael across the table.

"I like the dynamics of their vision; lots of energy. The trick is how to capture it and spill it onto the stage," Michael says looking at Gerard.

"I agree. I also believe that radical body movements synchronized properly with the theme and the music would make an impact."

Michael becomes a little excited. Those are his thoughts exactly. "Show me what you've got," he says pointing at Gerard's folder resting on the table.

"Okay."

***

The Metropolitan United Church on Queen Street in downtown Toronto is quiet at this hour. The time is a few minutes past seven o'clock in the evening. There are three cars parked at the rear entrance of the church where a door leads to a large and spacious basement complete with a full size stage.

Michael has walked by the church a few times before admiring its architecture but this time when he approaches the back door he feels jitters of excitement and nervousness. Walking the wide hallway he listens for sounds; a few voices can be heard coming from the other side. He opens the door nearby and looks inside.

He immediately recognizes Hillary and Francis who are surrounded by about a dozen young people, guys and gals alike, listening to Francis. He stops when he sees Michael and waves to him, making the whole gathering turn their heads and check out the new arrival.

Michael waves a small hello as he approaches the group.

Francis introduces him, "Hey guys. This is Michael, our tentative artistic director."

"Hi," Michael says, more relaxed now. "Try to give it a shot," he continues, looking around the place. "Gerard not here yet?"

"He called earlier. He has an exam this afternoon and will be a little late," Hillary explains. Michael nods in acknowledgement and reaches for his shoulder bag, extracting the folder with his notes. The group accepts him and turns their attention back to Hillary and Francis, with the exception of Rebecca, a beautiful brunette with long curly hair tied into a ponytail, black dancing tights and vivid eyes staring at Michael.

He does not know that he has instantly become the main interest of somebody he has not even properly acknowledged or met yet.

Hillary turns to the stage where a young man with long hair and a flamboyant sweater is setting up the sound system.

"Since most of you have read the script by now, I assume, we're gonna play some tracks so you can get a feeling for the concept. Let me know what you think," Francis says. He glances at Hillary who immediately addresses the sound tech.

"Chuck. Could you play out the first scenes for us?" Hillary asks. Chuck gives her the thumb-up and activates some buttons on his console.

They all turn to the stage that is currently empty, but they know that whatever they might do later it will take place up there. Spatial orientation, Michael calls that. Chuck dims the lights on the stage by activating his switches.

In the penumbra of the theatre, the crystal-clear running of mountain brook water is heard; a sound effect which gradually turns into a storm of sounds, increasing in intensity. His eyes closed, Michael works on matching the pure sound with the images staged by him earlier in his notebook. Rebecca is watching him intently.

The music intensifies still further as some of the light effects click on the stage, setting up a somber mood. Michael's closed eyes twitch for a moment. Rebecca is moving a step closer to him. As the music builds to a crescendo, a slight crack of light penetrates the hall for a brief moment. Gerard walks into the hall and immediately stops, watching the empty stage and listening to the music. Like Michael, he is instantly transported by the sound and his vivid imagination engages his own vision of the opening scene.

The music suddenly stops.

"It has good depth to it," Gerard comments as he approaches the group, who this time is watching him.

"Everybody, this is Gerard, our tentative choreographer," Hillary says and Gerard waves a small hello. The youngsters offer him their unbiased welcome.

"How did the drama exam go?" Francis asks him as he gets closer.

"Very dramatic as expected, but I think I did okay!" laughs Gerard. "Looks like we've got something to work with," he says meaning the group and the music alike.

Francis steps into the middle of the circle and raises his hands calling for everybody's attention.

"Ladies and gentlemen, since we are in this together, allow me to introduce everybody to everybody else. My name is Francis and my partner here is Hillary. We wrote the piece together and we put the ad-hoc sound system together too. We both are open for try-outs and suggestions as we get deeper into the play development. Here we go... Michael: artistic director; Gerard: choreographer; Rebecca: lead dancer; Josh: lead dancer; Patrick..."

This is the first time Michael makes eye contact with Rebecca and instantly feels her biased intensity when she looks at him. His eyelashes flutter in surprise for a passing moment.

Francis continues the introductions for everybody while Hillary climbs on the stage and talks to Chuck about the next scene.

The atmosphere is warming up now as people relax and tune into this new concept, all eager to sink their teeth into it and show their best performance ever. Michael is no exception. While Francis is gathering the dancers, Michael and Gerard connect on the side of the stage and verify their earlier agreements regarding their scenes.

"I think you should take Rebecca and Josh and do your planned intro for a test. I want to see how they fill the stage and if they mesh... call it a warm up if you wish, and then we can do the group dance immediately following. What do you figure?" Michael asks his friend.

"I like it. Let me warm up my key dancers then we can both work the stage together for the second scene," Gerard agrees and the two look at each other with excitement.

"Let's have some fun while we are at it," Michael says.

"Yeah... I like that," Gerard says and looks at Francis and Hillary who are waiting for them. "Here goes," he concludes and walks over to the two creators, relaying his intentions to them. Hillary and Francis nod and briefly glance at Michael who at the moment is busy going through his notes.

Francis picks up a wireless mic from Chuck's control booth and calls the dancers who are warming their legs on and off the stage to attention. They all gather round as he explains the next step to them. Rebecca and Josh get closer to Gerard while the rest resume their warm-up.

"I assume you guys have read the script already," Gerard addresses the two dancers. They both confirm this. "Good. This is what I have in mind..."

Using dance jargon he explains his intentions and stage movements to them. The dancers like it and immediately make some moves from his plan. Gerard nods and the two take more space on the stage and do a few routines under Gerard and Michael's close vigil. When the two are warmed up, Gerard calls them close to him:

"This is only a preliminary. You two relax, we just wanna see how it looks and feels with the music. Ready?" They both nod quickly, Rebecca taking a last glance at Michael before they move into position. Gerard walks over to Chuck under Hillary and Francis's curious scrutiny. The music fades in as everybody clears the stage for the two dancers.

Josh is assuming a curved, dramatic posture on center-stage as Rebecca, a wild and fearless creature of the night, starts circling him with smooth and agile dance moves which reveal her fluid and toned body. Her curiosity apexes when Josh suddenly throws his arms in the air and jumping aside start chasing her.

The stage becomes a whirlwind of kinetic energy all smoothly synchronized with their body movements. He catches up with her and now, together, they fill the stage with their dynamic performance. As the two bodies blend their motions as if getting acquainted and accepting one another, the music fades gradually making them slow their motion accordingly.

The music stops. So are the dancers, holding together.

"Something like that," Gerard calls out with enthusiasm. Hillary and Francis exchange a quick glance. They are both grinning. Francis moves to center stage and approaches the sweating dancers.

"I think we've got something here," he says with an open face.

"We're still learning the script," adds Josh... and Rebecca agrees.

"I think the story's great," she says.

"We definitely have something to work with. Good job, guys," Francis says.

"Thanks."

"Since you are already warmed up, I believe Michael has something to contribute to the scenes, too?" Francis says as they all look to the second row center where Gerard and Michael are discussing details of a scene, using their hands and arms for emphasis.

"You guys have something to share with us?" Francis asks them through the mic. The two young men climb on the stage and Michael gathers all the dancers around him.

"Since you all read the script, I'll jump right into the second scene dynamics. Gerard and I came up with a little workshop, to see how it looks," he explains.

He takes three dancers and places them in certain locations on the stage. He returns to the group and addresses Rebecca. It is now the first time that the two make direct eye contact and he, for a passing moment feels the intensity of those black eyes focused on him. He does not think twice about it, walking with Rebecca toward center-stage, explaining to her the dramatic charge of the scene.

"Gerard will address the body motion and the moves in a minute," he tells her.

"Okay," she says in a cold tone which doesn't escape Michael who looks at her directly:

"Everything okay?" he asks genuinely. She finally smiles and nods. She just wants to be *noticed* by him.

Michael walks over to Josh and works with him on the scene dynamics. The other dancers follow and a little while later they are all in place. It is Gerard's turn now to get the kinetics of the movements. Since his thoughts are meshed with Michael's, the dancers have a good grip of the two men's efforts and they all love the dynamics.

When Chuck turns the tracks on and Francis nods the green-light, the bare stage of the church comes alive. The young dancers led by Rebecca and Josh breathe life into the script. The powerful, synthesized sound effects support the dance moves as if they belonged together. And they do.

There are a few hesitations, a missed step here and there, but the whole assembly of the performance is wonderful, almost fluid.

Michael, Gerard, Hillary and Francis watch the dancers in awe as the young volunteers deliver this performance on a string of instruction never executed before.

When the music finally fades, the group, shining with excitement, surrounds Rebecca and Josh in a live cordon of protection. Michael and Francis release sharp whistles of approval while Gerard and Hillary applaud enthusiastically.

When the excitement simmers somewhat, Francis makes a few steps toward the crew. "I think we've got something good here," he addresses the dancers. "Not bad for a first-time impro." He turns toward Gerard and Michael and says, "That goes for you guys too."

Michael gives him the thumb-up. "Not bad," agrees Gerard.

During this cool-down session Rebecca wipes her face with a towel and approaches Michael from behind. He is standing alone, taking in the group of people he has decided to dedicate some time to in the near future. "We can do better," Rebecca says and when Michael turns around she is glistening with sweat and excitement. She looks beautiful and makes an impression on Michael.

"Rebecca," he says in a calm voice. "You startled me a little. Nice work," he says, his eyes involuntarily brushing over her tight and shapely body.

She notices it, pleased. "Maybe one day we could catch a cup of coffee and talk about the play?" she says coyly.

"Maybe," is all he says and before he walks back to Francis and Hillary, their eyes connect and hold for a brief moment. There is a silent string of information passing at high speed between them. He nods and walks back to his friends.

Chapter 13

The week has flown by quickly since Michael committed to assist the Street Cry Theater in helping to develop this new and exciting show. His old directing skills, unused for almost two years, come back to him naturally.

He really enjoys the work and that simple fact makes things go better as they all have fun in the process too. It is now the end of the third rehearsal and Hillary, Francis, Gerard and Michael have eliminated almost all of the bugs from their development process. They have changed or rather re-written several track sections making the show tighter, more intense. Hillary is both composer and sound technician when Chuck is not present for whatever reason. She is also a driving force, a talented and wonderful filmmaker in the making.

Michael spends several hours with Francis, talking him his own approach to stage delivery and presentation of Francis's original content. Together they have worked out a very dynamic scenario which had made Gerard scratch his head for a while, trying to match his own insight with his choreographical abilities. The dancers have had their share of fun and excitement, giving them the unique chance to show and develop their own dancing abilities.

Rebecca, as a lead dancer, excels in her imaginative and smooth body motions. She's so smooth on the stage, her movements are almost fluid.

Michael enjoys this enormously and when Rebecca makes some very discreet advances toward him, he starts thinking about Stephanie even more. He misses her so much, hence he is not responding to Rebecca's hints. *It is a passing crush - if even that - and it will pass*, Michael thinks about the beautiful and talented dancer, a university student majoring in modern and contemporary dance.

***

It is late night in the city when Michael returns from the yacht club alone; he has a tightness in his stomach warning him of some sort of development. He attempts to trace the source of his anxiety and finds several. Too many, he decides, and gives them all up. Lighting up a cigarette he heads for his apartment, thinking about the play - and as an integral part of the development, of Rebecca too.

When he enters his bachelor suite he immediately notices the flashing red light on his answering machine. He picks up the receiver; there is only one message.

"Hey handsome, I'm in Montreal now. Call me asap! This is my Canadian number: 877..."

"Holy Jesus!" Michael shouts with excitement and reaches for a piece of paper, jotting down her number. Reaching for the receiver he dials it immediately. Stephanie picks it up on the fourth ring:

"Allo?"

"It's me." he says softly.

"Michael! How you doing?" calls a happy tone.

"Good. I have been thinking about you a lot. You alright?" he asks.

"I'm fine now. Are you coming over?" she enquires with a hint of longing in her voice.

"Give me the address and I will be there tomorrow afternoon. I have to talk to some people before I leave Toronto. I missed you," he adds in a small voice.

"I missed you more, mister. C'mon up, we have so much to catch up on."

"How is the store coming along?" he asks her.

"Great. It's finished and the grand opening will be next Sunday. I hope you'll be here for it," she says.

"I'll try to be. I will call you from Montreal tomorrow night," he says, his mind thinking fast.

"Good. Here is the information; you got a pen handy?"

He quickly writes down the address and her new telephone number.

"Got it. See you tomorrow."

"Oui. Au revoir," she says and they hang up.

Her chiming voice is still ringing in his ears when he goes to sleep after his nightly hygiene routine.

The Next morning Michael jumps out of bed before seven o'clock, shaves and showers, dresses causally and heads out from his suite. The brief conversation with Stephanie has totally energized him - as always. Finding a swagger back in his step, he walks to a small café on the block.

As soon as he drops his weight on a chair, a fresh cup of cappuccino arrives from the owner.

"Thank you, Kosta. How are you this morning?" Michael asks.

"Very good, Michael. Open for business, as usual. How is the play coming along?"

"Nice development. I've got some really good dancers; it's a lot of fun," Michael says, looking at the Greek's wide open and friendly face. "I need to use your telephone for a few local calls, if that's alright?" Michael says.

"Anytime. Any breakfast today?"

"The usual, please."

"Coming right up," Kosta says and walks away into his kitchen.

Michael sips from his coffee and starts scribbling into a pocket notebook.

Once he finishes his breakfast, he makes a few calls, including one to Francis and another to the emigration office, informing them that he will be out of town for a few days.

Walking back to his building, he calls his Romanian friend, George, who lives in the same apartment complex. He meets with him in the underground garage and George gives Michael basic instructions for his rusty but super-fast Mach-I sportster.

Michael pays attention and pays George some cash for the rental. "Remember, it's still for sale," his friend tells him. "This is a good trip to test it out. If you like it when you come back, we can talk about it."

"That sounds good. I'll call you as soon as I get back... and thanks," Michael says.

"No sweat. Have fun, but be careful with the gas pedal - she's fast," George says laughing.

"Okay."

Michael gets into the car and starting it up, gradually rolls it out from the garage for a test spin around the block. He then returns to the apartment building, parking the car in front of it. He quickly packs a sport bag with basic hygiene stuff and a few fresh clothes and rushes out back into the car.

Once the tank is refilled, oil level checked and windows cleaned up, Michael places his shades on and puts the car in gear, heading for Montreal.

Chapter 14

Michael drives slowly at first, getting the feel of the old muscle car. Just before turning onto Gardener Express Way, still in Toronto, he punches the gas pedal. To his surprise - and almost panic - the car shoots forward so fast that the front wheels turn, in an instant making a three hundred and sixty degree black donut in the middle of the intersection.

Michael quickly gets it under control and a moment later he burns the tires onto the Express way, laughing out loud. He rides fast now, enjoying the machine's powerful engine and good, sporty handling on the road.

Playing the eight-track to its fullest he blazes along, occasionally glancing behind for police cars. Shortly after he merges onto Don Valley Parkway and heads North-East toward the city of lights, beautiful Montreal.

He drives steadily for around two hours, totally enjoying the beautiful scenery and the spring revival energy of nature. He switches highways and merges onto the 401.

The driving map stretched open on the passenger seat tells him that he will be shortly approaching the city of Kingston, Ontario, Gerard's home town. "I wish you were here with me, buddy," he says out loud thinking about his dear new friend and the great talented group he has become part of. He laughs in good spirit for three reasons. One: speaking to Francis and Hillary, and having left them with his direction sketches for the next two scenes, they are fine without him for a few days. Two: he is about to meet and hold the beautiful girl he loves so much in spite of the fact that she has broken his heart more than once in the past. Three: the energy of the day and the beauty of the changing landscape which he is now blazing through.

He slows down his car and watches the signs on the highway - he is getting closer to Kingston now. A couple of miles further down the road and he exits the highway, looking for a place to eat and refuel.

He drives a couple of blocks in the old city and finds a small diner besides a gas station. He decides to get the gas first. Opening the hood he checks both the windshield washer fluid and oil levels, and fills up the tank with the highest-octane gasoline.

In the store he decides to grab a drink and a sandwich to eat as he drives. He pays with cash and a minute later he drives away looking for the entry ramp for the highway. He finds it by following the street signs.

Driving at legal speed, munching on his sandwich and listening to the eight-track, Michael feels at ease now. A sudden feeling of warmth encompasses him all over when he thinks about Stephanie. His foot automatically increases the pressure on the gas pedal, making the fast car shoot forward. He suddenly forgets about food and stays focused on his driving, his mind miles ahead of him, already in Montreal in the company of that French girl who has somehow made a lasting mark in his restless heart.

A highway sign indicating 1000 Islands Parkway flashes by him and shortly after he takes it, continuing his drive through the breathtaking lake and cottage country.

***

It is late afternoon when the first highway signs start indicating the city of Montreal is within reach. Michael is rested but anxious, driving with focus, when the first towns neighboring the large city flash by him, making him slow his drive. Not long afterwards he enters the outskirts of the city, and knowing Stephanie and her style, aims for downtown Montreal, following the well-marked signs.

Half an hour later he pulls his Mach-I up to the curb on St. Paul Street, only blocks away from the large harbor. Getting out from the car he looks for a public telephone booth. He sees three of them. Heading for the nearest on his side of the sidewalk, he inserts the coins and dials the number Stephanie gave him. She picks up on the second ring:

"Allo?"

"It's me. I'm in downtown Montreal right now-"

"Michael!" she cuts in excitedly. "Whereabouts?"

"I'm on Rue Saint Gabriel and Rue Saint Terese, downtown," he says looking at the street signs.

"You're just north of Rue Saint Paul, running across below you," Stephanie says with excitement. "You're only a few short blocks away from me. Listen, I'm staying at the Hotel Du Vieux Port on Rue de la Commune and Rue Saint Pierre, facing the harbor just around the block. Come to the hotel. Room four hundred and eight."

"Got it. I'll be there shortly. I love you... and I need a stiff drink!" he says in great mood.

"Granted," she laughs. "C'mon up, I'm waiting for you," she says, her voice charged with chimes of expectation.

"See you soon," he says and hangs up.

Getting back into his car, he drives down onto Rue Saint Gabriel and turns left on Rue de la Commune, built on the edge of the harbor. Michael smiles knowingly about Stephanie. His assumption was right.

Within minutes he is pulling into the guests' parking lot of the newly-refurbished granite façade of Auberge Du Vieux-Port.

"Nice," he says to himself, walking across the lot toward the main stylish entrance.

He climbs the entrance steps and enters the cozy lobby of the hotel. Walking to the elevator he pushes the *up* button and waits. The large carriage arrives, spilling out an old elegant couple and two young ladies sporting charming smiles. Entering alone, he presses the fourth floor button looking at the pictures on the walls.

When the carriage opens its door with a soft clink, Michael looks out at a wide, luxuriously carpeted hallway. He steps out and traces the aged brass room number attached to the doors. He finds Stephanie's and stops for a minute to collect himself and rest his pounding heart.

The door suddenly swings open and Stephanie, more beautiful than ever in her silk housecoat, jumps into his arms, kissing him passionately.

He responds to her kiss and lifting her in his strong arms, carries her into the suite, closing the door with his heel.

The modern room is breathtaking, with giant windows looking over the Saint Laurence River. Michael gently carries Stephanie in his arms to the large alcove bed in the middle of the room

"It's been too long," she whispers, wrapping her arms around his neck and pulling him closer. He kisses her voluptuous lips as they start undressing each other, driven by their passion and hunger for one another.

When they finish making love, they hold one another tight, snuggled under the satin covers. Michael, his arm wrapped around Stephanie's shoulder, looks around the place: stone and brick walls, brass beds and exposed beams reflect the hardwood floor in an intimate and stylish décor. He kisses Stephanie's heated forehead.

"It is so good to be together again," she says, in English this time, her French accent coming through strongly. Michael just loves it. He kisses her forehead again in acknowledgement.

"How have you been?" he asks her softly.

"Very busy. Business is booming; it almost feels like it has a life on its own," she says in French this time, her words sharp and focused. "I have a good team of top managers around me and that makes it a little bit easier," she continues, looking up at his face: "And you?"

"Not bad. I've got a good feel of Canada now, with more to come. My legal processes are all finished now so it's time for the real action to begin again."

"Excellent," she says. "I just might have something for you, if interested."

"What? The Montreal store?"

She nods. "Since it's the first one in Canada I need a strong hand on the reins, somebody I can trust," she says looking at him seriously this time. And that is the reason her business is so successful - she keeps a sharp eye on markets and trends, a keen sense of time and place and has especially good people skills.

"You can show me the details," he says, interested but not forcing the subject.

"In due time," she replies and turning around kisses him again.

The passion ignites anew in both of them and the early morning sun finds them clutched to one another, Stephanie with an angelic smile on her face, Michael relaxed, his eyes twitching under the rays penetrating the bright room.

It is morning now. Opening his eyes he sees and feels Stephanie glued to him, breathing lightly, her right arm resting across his chest. He kisses her gently on her silky hair and she awakens, turning to look up at him. "Bonjour," she says in a sleepy voice.

"Bonjour," he replies and caresses her naked back. She slowly awakens and slipping out from under his arm turns to him. "I'll take a shower to freshen up," she says.

Michael nods and gets up himself, looking for his scattered belongings. "You did a number on my clothes last night," he says. "I can't find half of them."

"Half of them is good enough for me," she says laughing and walks into the bathroom. Michael collects the last of his garments and walking over to the suite's kitchenette, prepares some fresh coffees. While the percolator growls along he walks to the window and opening the sliding door steps out onto the small granite balcony looking at the busy Harbor. His hungry eyes dig into the fresh Montreal morning, his eyes cast across the water, following visions from their future unfolding in front of him. "Oh, boy," he releases with a small sigh. 'Better fasten your seatbelt," he tells himself and comes back into the suite.

As he prepares two coffee cups, Stephanie walks out from the bathroom fresh and pretty as a daisy. She's dressed barefoot in a pair of stylish khakis and a white flowery white shirt with huge pockets and an embroidered outlandish collar.

Michael whispers with admiration. She laughs and coming closer to his, wraps her arm around his waist smelling the coffee.

"Yum," she says helping him out with the saucers, cream and tea spoons.

"It's all for you," he says looking at her with great pleasure.

"There is a really good place for breakfast right here in the hotel - Narcisse - you want to check it out later?" she asks him.

"We could do that. Remember, I'm just visiting. You are in charge," he says easily.

"Good... I like you already," she says and Michael rolls his eyes, offering her a cup.

They get ready at a leisurely pace and descend to the main floor where they have a delightful breakfast at the hotel's own breakfast nook.

"That was outstanding," Michael says as they leave the place with the Manager's greeting.

"They do a good job here," Stephanie says with a casual voice cemented by experience and know-how.

They exit the hotel and Stephanie wraps her arm around Michael's as they take in the rich tradition and style of the Old Port Montreal. Stephanie is the one leading their casual walk which is carefully planned by her detailed mind.

They check out shops and boutiques along the few short blocks between boulevard St-Laurent and chemin de la Côte-Sainte-Catherine, which sell high-end fashions, home furnishings, decorative items, artwork, books, kitchenware, toys and children's items, and gourmet food. There are plenty of restaurants, bars, and cafés in the area in which to rest your feet and check your purchases.

As they walk back down to the port area, they reach yet another string of select boutiques on the popular strip. One of them, placed in one of the century old red brick and beams building sports a familiar name: *"Stephanie's."* Michael looks at his friend inquiringly. She laughs heartily at his stunned look - the place is terrific.

"How many Stephanie's do *you* know?" she asks him.

He plays along - he stops, put his index finger against his temple, deep in thought: "Let's see now... there is this gorgeous chic from Lyon I met a few years - "

Stephanie punches him lightly into the ribs: "That's the only one you allowed to remember; there are no other!" she says charmingly and leads the way toward the main entrance.

"My manager's name is Cristina, and she's very good for her young age; finished top of her class at the School of Design and Fashion. She's French, too," Stephanie says as they enter the store. "Fluent in English also, of course," she adds.

The store is as classy and good in taste as Stephanie herself and all her other stores. The building once again has white walls with aged beams crossing the ceiling and supporting the large loft which looks down onto the St. Laurence River.

The fashionable designs are arranged with gusto throughout the store, and this time there are several beautiful mannequins throughout in dynamic and challenging postures.

"Wow!" Michael says, taking it all in as Cristina, an elegant young woman in a very stylish outfit comes toward them smiling. The girls have a brief hug and the casualty of their gesture reveals to the observant eye a long and deep-rooted friendship. Stephanie makes the introductions and Michael is pleased with the manager's professional manners and charisma.

"Pleased to meet you," Michael says, and looking at both of them he addresses Cristina, "I have a feeling that you two have known each other for a long time."

The two ladies exchange a brief look which Michael notices. He knows that he has surely scored a few casual brownie points.

"Allow me to show you around a little," Cristina says, and making a hand gesture to one of her employees leads the way through the store, explaining a little to Michael about the trends and manufacturers and the designers behind them.

Michael learns quickly that Stephanie has a very complex and well-tuned international operation he under-appreciated before. Besides his love for her, a new respect for her talents and business acumen is also blooming in his heart.

The three of them spend several hours in the store and in Cristina's office upstairs, the ladies teaching Michael the workings and details of this competitive business.

"I don't know about you guys, but I'm starving," Stephanie says and they all agree with her. They stop the business work and walk out from the store, led this time by Cristina who knows the neighborhood as if it were her own.

They enter a small moms-and-pops restaurant where Cristina is addressing the owners by their first names. The service and food are excellent indeed. During lunch, Michael learns more about Cristina and her long-lasting friendship with Stephanie, which goes back to their elementary school in Lyon, France.

It is important for Michael to know this information because if everything goes well, he and Cristina will have to trust one another in conducting the business of managing the store. At this point Michael does not quite know what his future position might be, but observing the girls' talk and Cristina's silent respect toward him, he figures top management.

After lunch, more relaxed now, they return to the boutique where Stephanie and Cristina introduce Michael to all of the sales people, five to be exact. He is presented by Stephanie to her staff as the Canadian Representative for the chain.

Later in the afternoon, tired but energized by the day's developments, Stephanie and Michael say goodbye to Cristina and after leaving the store explore some of the attractions and delights that Old Port Montreal has to offer.

Tired and happy, the two young people enter one of the waterfront café's for a latte. They order and settle into one of the small booths looking over the water.

Michael can't keep his eyes off of his beautiful French girl.

"I know that look," Stephanie says with a mischievous smile. "That old 'bad boy' boyfriend of mine," she says. Michael flashes an innocent, almost angelic look:

"I have absolutely no idea what are you talking about," he says, with a deadly serious voice.

Stephanie can't help it and bursts into a crystalline laughter. Michael joins in. "Not bad for a rookie Canadian Representative of my company," she says, and reaching over takes his hand, holding it in hers. They look at one another for a long time.

"I need a drink," Michael finally breaks their connected silence.

"Sounds excellent," Stephanie agrees and they flag the waitress, ordering some fine cognac to seal their deal and heart-throbbing renewed relationship.

"Only with a French girl," Michael cheers to some obscure annotations racing through his mind, but somehow she clearly understands and perceives them, toasting with him.

"Oui; bien sûr *mon cher*," she laughs.

They don't know it yet but they have a powerful, almost unbreakable chemistry. Time will have to prove that.

"So what do you think about this whole Stephanie's Co. stuff so far?" she asks with a keen eye on him.

"Very impressive indeed," Michael says and he means it. "I feel lucky to be part of it, Steph," and gives her a direct look.

She sighs: "Yeah. Me too. I just hope it's going to work out well," she says in a melancholy tone which takes Michael aback for a second.

"You mean-" he tries.

"That's exactly what I mean," she says abruptly interrupting him, reading his same page: "I mean between you and I. Business details are easy to iron out; people's emotional psyche not so," she adds in a fragile voice.

"Are you are talking about me or you?" Michael asks looking at her.

"Me."

And that was all she says for the remainder of their time at the bistro.

Michael breaks the heavy silence, "Let's go back to the "Vieux Du Port," and she looks at him with gratifying eyes. They get up from the table and he leaves some cash to cover their bill and includes a tip on top. On their way back to the hotel she wraps both her arms around his waist, squeezing him hard. "I want you," she whispers in his ear.

"*Je tu veux plus*," he responds and squeezes her soft shoulder.

The trip to the hotel is fast and direct, charged with longing and fearful desire.

***

The drive back from Montreal to Toronto is different from the previous ride. Michael is driving fast his Mustang charger not paying much attention to the road and the traffic. And this is not a good thing. He nearly has a head-on collision with a transport truck from Quebec. He swirls the steering wheel in the nick of time to save his life and avoid a horrific crash.

Snapping back to reality he starts paying attention to the road and traffic but his mind is still flashing back to Stephanie and her perfume, still lingering in his nostrils.

Following a few close calls he somehow manages to reach his downtown bachelor pad without injuring himself or anybody else. Taking a hot shower he cuddles himself under the blankets and reliving vivid images of him and Stephanie together, falls asleep with a smile on his face. Nevertheless, in spite of his resistance, the next scenes of the play are starting to develop in his subconscious mind.

The telephone starts ringing in the bachelor suite making Michael wakes up. He waddles over to the dining room table where the telephone is rattling.

"Hello?"

He scratches his scalp, listening; it's Gerard, happy to hear that he is back in town.

"That's fine, Gerard. How's the crew progressing... that's great."

"Rebecca was asking me about you," Gerard says in a lower voice.

"That's cute; I'll see them all tonight. So, what time shall we hook up... you and me?"

"It's my day off from school today; teachers' conference of some sort. How about my place in half an hour? Just enough room to swing a cat - or a dancer - around," he jokes.

"Fine. Shoot me the address; I've got some wheels now," Michael says and writes down the details on a notepad from the tabletop. "You're just a few blocks away from me. See you in half an hour or so," he says and hangs up the receiver.

Stepping in to a cold shower, he wakes himself up in a hurry. Getting out just as fast, Michael dries out and dresses, rubbing his long hair with a fresh towel.

Clean shaven now and wearing a pair of worn jeans, sneakers, a white T-shirt and his Giga-Motto leather riding jacket, he fires up the Mach-I and drives away into the beautiful sunny Toronto morning.

He only has to check on his map once before he turns onto Gerard's street, a cluster of old character warehouse buildings. Michael likes it already. His artistic eye catches the light filtering between the buildings, casting colorful slivers onto the ancient walls.

He parks the Mustang in front of the main entrance hoping to find it undamaged on his return. To his delight, he remembers his friend telling him that the car has a working alarm system. He sits back in and starts to figure the system out. Once he has, he alarms it and exiting the car locks the door. There is no visual or audible acknowledgement that the alarm has been set. Shrugging his shoulders in disbelief, he enters the large brick building.

The lobby looks like a warehouse reception office - which once it in fact was, in the heyday of Toronto mercantile. He approaches one of the two industrial elevators with open iron grills staring into an artificial abyss. He pushes the *UP* button which lights up right away in an ugly, glowing amber.

There is a sudden rattling, a cranking and grinding sound of heavy metal gears as the large cab sets in motion on heavy steel cables. When the cab arrives in front of Michael, he is staring at a steel grilled cage; he does not know what to do. As he studies the mechanism of the warehouse elevator though, he instantly understands it, seeing the mechanical workings. He casually leans forward and grabbing the steel grill doors with both hands, he pulls them apart and steps into the cage. He pushes button five on the console and the heavy cab starts ascending with a rattle of chains and mechanical couplings. After a few long seconds he reaches the fifth floor and the large steel cab stops, remaining motionless.

Pulling the iron gates open, Michael steps into the wide hallway, looking around curiously.

The naked lamp hanging crookedly from the ceiling on bare wires light up some numbers on the large heavy doors set far apart from each other. He finds unit #6 and pushes the doorbell button, waiting. He hears movement on the other side of the door which a moment later slides open with a rattle. Gerard is standing in the sudden light coming from the windows behind him. "Good to see ya," he says and makes room for Michael to step inside.

"Likewise," Michael replies, looking around the large open space which has a big loft at the other end. "Fabulous place you've got here," he says following his friend.

"Yeah, it suits me fine," Gerard says, laughing. "How was Montreal?"

"Just awesome; very good times," Michael responds, smiling at fond and recent memories. He turns his gaze to the apartment. Large industrial windows from floor to ceiling allow plenty of natural light into the studio space. There is a shower partition on one side, with two bicycles leaned against the wall, a coffee table and various leather couches and lounge chairs spread randomly throughout. A big colorful rug is resting under the table. Large art work hanging from the walls gives the place an intimate, artistic feel.

Michael leans over and touches the charred-looking old hardwood floor. "This is still good for dancing on?" he asks looking up at Gerard.

"You betcha it is. We use it all the time, including today - it's great for warm-ups and small scenes."

"Talking about scenes, maestro, how far did you get with the play?" he asks his friend.

"We did quite well. I think we are about a third into it. This is the time for you to take a look at it and make sure we haven't run aloof. We all missed you," he says.

"I missed you guys too... our old big family, nice to come back to," Michael says - and he means it.

"Listen, here's a copy of the script with some of my highlights in it. I want you to go over it and tell me what you think," Gerard says and hands him over the manuscript.

"Glad to do so; I need to get back into it anyway," he says and without further ado starts reading the modified script. He smiles and frowns now and again, make some notes of his own on the edge of the copy, reading on with focus.

"This looks pretty good... on paper. I really want to see it on stage, in flesh and blood, sweating it out," he says looking at his friend. "What I figure is for tonight, let's start with a quick demo of what you guys have done so far, then if needs correcting we can take care of that, and move to the next scene in the script - which is a tricky one," Michael says.

"Glad you said that; I agree. We need to put our heads together very carefully with that one," Gerard says, reading over the scene in the copy he holds in his hand.

There is a knock and Gerard walks over and opens the squeaking industrial door.

Josh and Patrick, the top male dancers of the play walk into the place and seeing Michael cheer him happily, slapping hi-fives.

"Good to see ya back," Patrick says.

"Good to be back!" Michael replies. "I see you guys made some nice progress while I was gone," he says.

"Yeah, we tried to keep it afloat and get our legs moving and warm," Josh says.

"Hillary and Francis are a little anxious about the deadline," Gerard says. "Michael, since these two guys are already here, we can look at some of those fight scenes coming up for tonight."

"That's an idea," Michael agrees and turns back to that scene in the script. "Since it's a very dramatic scene, I picture something like this..." He jumps up from his seat and takes advantage of the large floor space available. "We start from the center with Josh and Rebecca. As the music builds, we have Patrick, Joanna..."

He runs through his vision twice with the guys, listening to their input, making corrections, changing some moves for Josh and Patrick. The scene begins to shape up under Gerard's supervision. "I thing we've got something workable for tonight," Michael concludes nearly two hours later. The four friends agree and the dancers leave the place.

Alone now, Gerard and Michael sit down and look at one another.

"It's good to have you back," Gerard says.

"It's good to be back, Gerard."

"Talking about that fabulous city of Montreal, I might be dancing with their Ballet Jazz of Montreal group," he says.

"Get out of here," Michael says excitedly. "They are one of the best in the country, to my knowledge."

"They are," Gerard says humbly. "That's another ballgame all together."

"Congrats."

"Thanks"

The two friends put work aside and Gerard makes some coffee. The two have a good chat about present and future projects until Michael gets up, and apologizing to Gerard, leaves his place.

"I'll see you tonight," says Gerard at the steel door.

"Yes. The church will be smoking tonight - with new energy," Michael says laughing. "Later."

Back in his old roadster, Michael is bursting with energy himself. His creative mind fired by new ideas and dance dynamics, he can barely contains himself. He needs to do something and he suddenly remembers what. Driving quickly back to his bachelor pad, he grabs his swimming shorts, some shampoo and a towel and throwing it all in a gym bag he leaves the place in a hurry.

The community pool is not very busy at this hour of the day so he dives in and swims furiously for several laps until he feels his heart adjusting to a normal rhythm. He keeps on going for several more laps.

By the time he has showered he feels purged, streamlined and focused for the tonight's rehearsal. Driving at the speed limit he returns to his apartment and dropping on his back on the sofa, immediately thinks about his matters of the heart - Stephanie.

For most people, the short respite between now and the approaching rehearsal would hardly be the right time for affairs of the heart. For Michael however, it is a little different. Stephanie and his passion for the stage both were deep seated love affairs in his heart. In a bizarre way they converged; with one's well-being helping the other and vice versa.

His mind quickly rehashes the approaching rehearsal process then shifts effortlessly to his time spent with Stephanie in Montreal and the implication of the possible business opportunity she spoke of.

The business of fashion he could skip if push came to shove, but the other two elements remain as solid and durable as a construction of the Roman Empire. He releases a sigh and a moment later is sound asleep.

He is up again when the telephone starts rattling loudly on his dining room table. Waking up with a start, he picks up the receiver, glancing at his wrist watch: 6:12 pm.

"Hello?"

"Michael?" Relief. "It's me, Francis. We were a little worried about you," Francis says.

"A *little*? Just kidding, Francis. I spent time with Gerard this afternoon and we will both be at the rehearsal tonight. We've got some new stuff for you and Hillary to check out," Michael says casually.

"That sounds just great. Sorry to bother you... I'll see you guys tonight, then."

"Yes, see you tonight," Michael says and gently hangs up the receiver.

"I thought you were somebody else," Michael says out loud and walking into the bathroom, washes his face with cold water, waking up fast.

In the living room the telephone rings again. He quickly runs for it, as if his life was on the line: "Hello?"

"It's me..."

Michael's heart skips a beat - but he is happy now; it is Stephanie. He rolls his eyes with relief. How bizarre.

"I was just thinking about you," he says and that is the truth.

"How are you?"

Her emotional tone of voice sets the mood for a short and intense conversation only privy to the two lovers...

When Michael reluctantly hangs up the receiver, there is a wild gleam of excitement in his eyes. Putting on his Racer leather jacket and his pilot shades, he grabs his shoulder bag and slamming the door descends the stairs this time, burning some of the excess energy built up inside him.

The roadster starts at the first attempt and Michael drives away, stopping at a gas station to get some fuel. When he goes inside to pay, he grabs himself a large cup of coffee and returns to his car.

When he pulls into the Church's parking lot, several cars are already parked there. He recognizes Francis and Hillary's, and Gerard's camouflage Jeep but that's about it. Walking inside the Church he is instantly familiar with the soundtrack playing on the sound system. When he gets closer, he sees Hillary on the stage with Chuck, the sound tech, while Francis is glancing over his copy of the script. Rebecca, wearing a black sweater and leg-warmers gives him a quick, eager look.

"Michael! Good to see you back!" Francis welcomes as the gathering looks his way.

He waves a brief hello addressing them all, "It's good to be back; that Montreal is a nightmare," he jokes with a broad smile which says quite the opposite, maybe a little *too* much to Rebecca's observant eyes and sharp female instincts. "I could use a briefing," he says and Francis waves him over.

"He's making a phone call from the office," Francis answers Michael's searching eyes, "He'll be here in a minute."

"I need him; we discussed and hashed out some scenes that I can't start without him," Michael explains, his intense eyes checking the stage where a few new props have been installed. "Those are props for part two," Michael says pointing to some of the light structures on the stage.

"We are not there yet but we would like to be," Hillary answers through the mic from the stage. "Welcome back," she says and Michael waves and blows her a kiss. She comes off the stage to join them at the same time as Gerard, who is returning from the clerical office. Michael and Gerard punch knuckles and exchange a quick glance - they are in tune with each other.

"Let's do this," Gerard says addressing the whole gathering. They all come closer to Gerard and Michael. "Michael and I had a brainstorm earlier today and we have some sketches with the moves in scenes eight and nine which we will try to cover tonight."

He distributes copies of the moves to the dancers and Francis and Hillary alike. Michael looks at the stage and asks Hillary for the mic.

"Chuck! Please dim the stage and play the track for beginning of scene eight," he calls to the sound tech through the mic. Chuck gives him the thumb-up as the stage starts dimming and the dramatic sounds of the working scene fades in.

"It helps to visualize the moves," he says to his crew. They agree. "Gerard, take over for now," he addresses his friend. There is a quick nod from Gerard.

"Listen, everybody. For starters, how do you feel about the sketch-to-mind-to-soundtrack-to-soul combo so far?" he asks and receives various nods, shakes and mumbles. "It will come to you; as you have seen in the script, we have two positives and a bad negative - that's Patrick, the bad boy." Gerard says seriously and they all talk theatre. "Josh and Rebecca, the goodie two-shoes, have a real issue with Patrick and we have to show that in dance. Let's get on the stage," he says and everybody moves up, Michael handing him the mic.

"The sound will help us get into the mood. Get in position," Gerard addresses them. The dancers rush into their role positions across the stage. "Rebecca, Josh: you guys have to set the mood - powerful emotions: fear, love, loss, young passion..."

Rebecca blushes in the penumbra of the stage and nobody notices her reaction to Gerard's words. *It's only a play.*

At the next highlight of the sound track, Josh and Rebecca start their dramatic ritual dance of passion and fluid motion which flows in perfect synchronicity with the dynamic sound. The support dance characters join in, and as the scene comes closer to its climax, the dancers really begin to feel the heat of the play, the emotional turmoil erupting everywhere on the stage and in the ether of the theatre, generated by calculated young blood and creative minds.

There is something magical happening on the stage at this very moment; all the dancers are so tuned in to the scene that they are already spilling into the next scene of the script. Michael, who watches the performance very closely, waves at Chuck who catches his quick gyrating hand. Michael's index finger twirling above his head tells him the message - keep on rolling into scene nine. Chucks nods in acknowledgement.

The play and the music start blending into the dancers' soul and there is no written script anymore. Driven by powerful forces unleashed by their professional skills and abilities, they flow on, driven by creative instincts at their best, creating a live show in front of Michael, Gerard, Hillary and Francis's delighted eyes.

When the soundtrack reaches the last bars of scene ten, Michael looks at Chuck who has been watching him all along. Michael makes a gradual sweeping motion with his hand telling him to fade the scene out slowly, gradually. Chuck nods and scene ten smoothly decreases in intensity and volume, fading into a deep, palpable silence.

The dancers, sweating and exhausted, slowly stop their motions and catch their breath. They look at each other and then turn towards the four people sitting in the second row watching them with astonished looks. Michael leans over to Gerard on his left: "Tell them something. You've got the mic."

Gerard comes out of his own revelry and speaks, "One word - OUTSTANDING!" He passes the mic to Michael.

"The man said it; outstanding! Great job!"

There are a few seconds of whilst Hillary and Francis collect their thoughts - it is their show after all. Michael passes the mic to Francis who takes it and stands up.

"We've got something very good here. No, we've got something *great* here." He becomes a little emotional.

The dancers put on their leg warmers and sweaters and join them in the rows. Michael cannot help but notice that Rebecca is glowing with an inner beauty he has never noticed before. When she gives him a direct look, he nods with admiration.

After the dancers rest a little, Gerard and Michael make some adjustments to the scenes and they play it again twice more. It is almost eleven o'clock at night when they finally wrap up the rehearsal, all fired up and excited by their accomplishment.

"I'm buying a round of drinks if anybody's interested," Francis offers, looking at his crew.

"I'm in," Gerard says.

Rebecca catches a look at Michael who meets her eyes.

"Okay," Michael decides.

"Me too," echoes Rebecca.

Josh and a few more dancers all agree on a drink. Some others have to study or have other plans for the night.

The Irish pub is a short block away from the Church and is called *The Nasty Leprechaun*. The group walks over and when they enter the old single-story granite building they are pleasantly surprised by its rich and elegant wood décor. Posts and beams support daring wooden arches and there are two different levels inside.

They find an empty booth and the six of them order drinks, looking curiously around the merry pub where waiters and waitresses wear green hats and sport funny shoes.

The drinks arrive shortly and Francis makes a toast to the group, "To our successful opening show." They all cheer and drink to that. After a little while they settle their thoughts and busy bodies, starting to relax. Small conversations open up between the people at the booth about the school, the play and their group efforts. Michael sits silently watching his friends having a good time which he also shares.

"You are rather quiet for such a dynamic evening," says Rebecca, who is sitting next to him.

"Just taking it easy. I'm a good listener," Michael responds and clinks his glass with hers. "Cheers."

"Cheers," she says and blushes charmingly; Michael notices.

"Good moves back there on the stage. Like a pro," he says.

"Thanks. You and Gerard put an exciting scenario together."

"It's not difficult when you have a good script to work with," Michael says, staring in front of him.

"What you two did was to take a script and turn it into live magic," she says with enthusiasm.

"You guys did that on the stage. It was a great team effort. And good fun too, I hope?" he says.

"Yes, for sure. We love to dance," she says and looks at him. "What about you? I haven't seen you around before this play came along?"

"I haven't been here long. I just moved to Toronto from Europe a few weeks ago."

"That explains a few things," she says looking at him.

"All bad, I imagine," he says.

"Not at all; to the contrary," she says and blushes again like a teenager.

Gerard turns to him from his right, "Francis wants to talk to you," he says. Michael leans forward and looks at Francis.

"Hillary and I gotta go now. Call me sometime tomorrow. I wanna run something by you," he says across the table.

"I'll do that, Francis," Michael says and waves goodbye to the leaving couple. He turns toward Rebecca: "Care for another drink?"

"I should be going too, but thanks for the offer."

"I'll walk with you back to the Church," Michael says and she enjoys that.

"Okay."

They say their own goodbyes to Josh and Natalie, another of their dancers, and leave the place.

Out in the cool evening they walk side-by-side for a while, nobody saying anything. Michael lights up a cigarette and so does Rebecca. They walk and smoke silently for a little while.

"How was your trip to Montreal?" Rebecca breaks the silence.

Michael reacts to her question, his mind instantly flashing back to Stephanie. Rebecca's sharp instincts are on target. "Was she happy to see you?"

Michael reacts to her words and she does not miss a beat. "Yes." That all he says - Nothing too fancy, not too much, not too little.

"Is it serious... I mean, between you two?" she asks in a small voice without looking at him. He feels her face burning beside him.

"That's a tough question you just threw at me," he says looking at her pretty face.

"Well, is it?" she says nervously.

"She stomped on my heart more than once before," he says cautiously.

"And you returned for more," she concludes. They walk silently for a while. "You're still in love with her," she says in a sure tone, knowing that her instincts are right. Michael looks at her curiously and does not answer.

By now they are entering the Church's parking lot where their vehicles are parked. She turns her pretty face toward him:

"It is a pleasure working with you on this project," she says with only slightly concealed emotion in her tone.

Michael sustains her look. "Likewise, and I really mean that," he says.

"Good night. I'll see you next Wednesday," she says heading for a hot red sports car parked a few stalls away from his roadster.

"It's a great pleasure having you on the team, Rebecca," he calls after her. She waves an acknowledgement and enters her car. A moment later, she places the powerful vehicle in gear and takes off, burning tires until the end of the parking lot. Michael watches her with a sigh, smiling from ear-to-ear. She is his kind of a girl - and a great dancer too.

Chapter 15

The days and weeks fly by furiously. There is literally no time to be bored or lay back idling for Michael, but that's okay - this is the way he likes it, the way his biorhythms function at their best.

There have been several rehearsals of the show, which has intensified in its development as the deadline comes closer. It demands a large chunk of Michael's time and he is loving every minute of it - the dance, the creative fever, the music and the camaraderie. It's all good.

It is not only the live performance taking its toll on Michael. Stephanie and her generous business proposal are also a big part of his thoughts. He has managed to drive down to Montreal two times in the last month, signing legal documents, getting to know the ins-and-outs of a foreign franchise and - the best part - spending quality time with Stephanie; just the two of them.

He quits his bartender job at the yacht club, much too busy with the play's development in Toronto, the business in Montreal, and flirting with Stephanie.

The opening night of the drama is fast approaching in two weeks, and though Hillary and Francis's creative initiatives the buzz in the city is growing fast and spreading, placing even more pressure on Michael and Gerard's shoulders. It is the kind of pressure they easily can handle.

The last few upcoming rehearsals are taking place in partial costumes and almost full stage décor at the Premiere Dance Theatre on Harbor Front, downtown Toronto; the theatre where the gala opening of the play will take place. Chuck's innovative sound designs make a great added impact to some of the scenes and the performing crew, and Gerard and Michael alike are pleased with the changes. Hillary and Francis smile modestly in the shadows - it was their idea and suggestion.

Ten days before the gala opening of the dance show, Michael receives an urgent call from Stephanie, who is in Belgium. Cristina has had a very serious car accident in Montreal. She is in critical condition and she asks Michael to immediately take over the reins of the store.

"I'm flying up there in two days, three at the very most, straight from Brussels. How are you doing?"

"Okay; it's complicated. I can drive up today. What do you want me to do?"

"I know that is very short notice, *mon cher*, but I have nobody else to turn to," she says, her voice filled with regret and longing. "I have things set up there for you. This is what you do..."

She explains to him using precise words and descriptive images what to do until she gets there from Belgium.

"I miss you," she concludes.

"Ditto," he says.

"How is the play coming along?" she asks, genuinely interested.

"The premiere is in ten days," he says.

"I wanna come to the opening," she says excitedly.

"I'd love that. We can work out the details when I see you in Montreal," he says.

"That's a good plan. I'll see you there," she says and they hang up.

There is so much to do and so little time.

He walks over to his small balcony, takes a long look at the city landscape and, returning to the dining table, starts making phone calls.

***

He makes it to Montreal just before four o'clock in the morning. This time he goes straight to Saint Mary's Hospital where he immediately enquires about Cristina's condition. Learning that she is in a more stable condition now, he writes a 'get well' note to her and leaves the hospital, heading to the downtown hotel Stephanie has already booked for him.

Taking a quick shower, he drops into bed and is dead to the world a moment later. The hotel's service call wakes him up five hours later and he heads for the clothing store, grabbing a butter croissant and a cup of coffee on his way to the Old Port.

Here, at the shop, he is expected by the staff and is brought up to speed by the interim manager, Maxinne, a thirty-something bright eyed elegant lady assigned by Stephanie to take over the store until he arrives.

The staff are devastated about Cristina's accident and are alert and eager to help Michael. For starters, Michael requires private time with Maxinne in the manager's office where they go through the numbers and the balance sheet. The numbers look fine and the store is making a handsome profit to date. Also, there are no liability issues or tax mishaps.

Out in the store, Michael swaps some merchandise from the back to front of the store, twists a couple of mannequins around, adding some more 'attitude' to the inert statues of elegant young ladies. He spends a few hours in the store, talking to the staff, watching them deal with the public, getting into the groove of the fashion business.

By the time closing time comes at almost seven o'clock at night, he is exhausted. Saying goodbye to the staff, he returns to the hotel where he has a light dinner and goes into his room, making phone calls to Toronto, following the play's progress and last minute changes. His last call is to Belgium where he catches Stephanie and the two have a good yet brief chat, allowing Stephanie to go back to sleep due to their time zone difference.

The morning sun finds Michael awake and alert already, making sketches for the last few scenes of the play, writing notes to himself. The telephone rings and Michael checks his wrist watch: 6:24 in the morning. *Who could that be* he wonders walking over to the receiver.

"Hello?"

It is Gerard and he is nervous and agitated, speaking fast, swallowing syllables, unusual for him. Michael learns in abrupt and angular words that Hillary and Francis's promo campaign is producing even more buzz in the city, building up high expectations and making Gerard very nervous.

"I wish you were here," he tells Michael.

"Me too. I'll be there shortly, as soon as I wrap up my end of the business over here. I might bring Stephanie along too," he tells Gerard.

"Oh, my! We'd better be prepared with a sophisticated critic like her in the audience," he says, half-jokingly.

"She's tough but she's also biased this time; we should be okay," Michael laughs and helps Gerard relax a tad. "Just keep the spirits high. I'll be back in Toronto in a day or two," Michael reassures him as they terminate the conversation.

Walking down to the hotel's restaurant, Michael has a wholesome breakfast with coffee, preparing himself for the upcoming day. Once finished, he tanks his Mach-I and heads for the Old Port. He and one sales person will attend the store while the rest of the staff visit Cristina in the hospital.

***

It is late in the afternoon in the store and Michael is talking to a young couple above some of the garments available. He notices that the young man feels more comfortable talking to him about some of the sailing gear he is interested in. He makes a point of that in his mind, helping his customer try out some recommended items. He never notices that while doing this, a very elegant and beautiful young woman has walked into the store and is watching him curiously from the counter. It is only when he comes to the till with his client when he notices the beautiful brunette watching him intently

It is Stephanie, smiling candidly at him. He nods and finishes his transaction with the client, asking one of the sales girls to place the purchases in a box. He sounds professional, competent and relaxed in doing this.

The couple leaves and he turns his full attention to Stephanie. She looks magnificent as always. Her long hair is done up in a new-attitude style, and she's wearing trendy clothes and garments which tell you with just a single glance that shopping at Stephanie's is a good thing. He catches his breath and walking over kisses her on the cheek, sparing the sales personnel from a passionate emotional display. She does the same but the look in her eyes holds the promise he was hoping for.

"Thank you for coming down at such a short notice," she says to him.

"Not a problem. I went to see Cristina and she's recuperating nicely," he says.

"We will go back again and see her together," Stephanie says and he immediately agrees. She looks at Maxinne: "Carry on as usual. Michael and I have a lot of catching up to do on the business," she says. Maxinne knows exactly what is going on.

"Of course. The girls and I are taking care of the store. Go," Maxinne says and they all turn their attention to the main entrance where just then, a group of four teenage girls have just walked into the store. Maxinne heads in their direction while Stephanie and Michael go upstairs to the manager's office.

Needless to say, that the moment the two step out from the store area and close the door behind, they immediately clutch into a long, passionate kiss.

"I needed this," Stephanie says, panting and coming up for air.

"I missed you. How are things in Europe?" Michael asks her.

"Very good right now, thanks for asking." She looks at him directly: "I need juicy details about that dance extravaganza you're working on," she says. He pinches her chin lightly.

"In due time, *bellissima*."

They walk into the office and Michael, all business now, shows her the standings of the operations and the positive cash flow of the store.

They spend a few intense hours doing business, with Michael learning more from Stephanie, who is an expert in sales and marketing campaigns. Michael mentions his experience with the male customer to her and figures the store needs a man in sales as well, to make the male customers more comfortable with the products sold to them. She gives it some thought and agrees with him.

"I'll contact some of the placement agencies I know here and you can do the interviewing yourself for the right guy - after the dance show premiere, of course," she says looking at him.

"I can do that," he replies.

They have another lovely dinner in the city, at a different restaurant this time but the service is exquisite and the ambience is more than welcoming. Over dinner and drinks Michael gives Stephanie a lowdown on his directing efforts with the young group of talent he has hooked up with. She is delighted by his enterprising spirit while he admires her so much for so many things, too many to mention.

The night following is full of promised and fulfilled desires; the passion flies high and the spirit soars.

***

Michael arrives in Toronto the following night after visiting and spending time with Cristina. Stephanie decides to stay in Montreal for the remainder of the time before the premiere, taking care of her new franchise, driving down to Toronto on the day of the gala opening.

The first thing next morning, Michael meets with a relieved Gerard and the two iron out some of the production's wrinkles, preparing for tonight's full dress rehearsal, only two days before the big night.

It has barely passed six o'clock in the evening when Michael pulls his 1971 Mustang Mach-I into the Premiere Dance Theatre's parking lot. There are a few other vehicles parked there but he does not recognize any of them. Shoulder bag strung on his shoulder, he walks to the back door of the theatre which is strictly for artistic personnel only.

When he gets inside, Michael has a shiver of excitement running down his spine. The old building is beautiful. Not so much pretty, but laden with a patina of characters and artists passing through its arched hallways for nearly a century, giving it a silent and potent charm.

Finding his way around, he sees various people walking the hallways, exiting and entering doors. As he advances, he sees a large door which reads in bold, *STAGE - Keep Quiet.* He gently opens the door and enters to the backstage area. He immediately notices Chuck, their sound tech on the side of the stage, working on his numerous buttons, switches and sliders for light and audio alike. He notices Michael at the same time.

"Over here," he waves to Michael. "Good to see you back," he welcomes.

"Good to be here. How is it going?" Michael asks him, looking around curiously at the large stage with all the props in place. "How do you like this place?"

"It's nice and big and the A-V system is the cat's ass," he says proudly.

"How have you found the acoustics of the hall?" Michael asks very concerned about the sound quality.

"Pretty good, you will love it," Chuck says and sets up some buttons on his dual console. "Listen," he calls Michael.

A moment later he activates one of the more dynamic sound tracks from the script and the music erupts into the theatre hall with the power of an unleashed avalanche, so intense that it makes Michael shrink his shoulders, almost overwhelmed.

"Wow!" he exclaims, pleased. "This is 'cat's ass,' as you call it. Great acoustics."

He starts walking on the stage, checking the sets and the locations, looking at the dynamics of motion available with the current settings.

"How do you like it so far?" a friendly voice comes from behind. Michael turns around and sees Gerard standing there with his usual sketch book. They shake hands, happy to see each other.

"I like it. How about our crew? Do they like it?" Michael asks.

"They love it now. We had to modify a few props to allow them the freedom of motion they required. They were right too. What do you figure?"

"Looks good 'cold' but we need some hot bodies here to warm it up," he says and Gerard agrees with his words: *Breathe some life into the stage.*

"The acoustics are great here; we should take advantage of that," he tells Gerard. "We gotta synchronize the lighting to the sound to the dancers and the narration and we've got a pretty decent package here," Michael says, his eyes half-closed, visualizing the live performance and the sound and lights to complement it.

"They should pay you more for this job," Gerard compliments him, his creative eyes immediately seeing Michael's approach.

"Yeah, right," Michael laughs. "How are the dancers doing lately?" he enquires.

"Just excellent. As the premiere approaches they are literally on fire ; you'll see for yourself tonight," Gerard says as they both turn their heads toward the squeaking side door to see three of the dancers walk in, followed by Hillary and Francis. One of the dancers is Rebecca, Michael notices with a pleasant smile.

Chuck starts up the sound track of the show and plays it low, as advised earlier by Michael. The volume is so low that is almost subliminal, touching most of the ears present, slowly getting them into the mood of the powerful play-dance.

Hillary and Francis are brought up to speed with Michael and Gerard's action plan for tonight. Francis adds some suggestions which they all discuss and when all settled and agreed upon, they turn to the performers, getting ready for the scene rehearsals.

"We will do a no-costume," Gerard speaks. "Warm-up for a scene or two then we take five and do the full nine yards in costumes. Look at it as if this could be the actual premiere night; it helps chill the bugs a bit," he says then turns to his notes as Michael exchanges a quick look with Rebecca who comes over and looks directly into his face:

"How was Montreal?" she asks squarely.

"Not bad, considering. One of our friends got injured in a car accident. She's much better now though. And how are you doing?" he asks.

"That's bad to hear, Michael. I'm okay. Doing this thing and getting ready for my exams starting next week," she says.

"Busy schedule! Let's stay with this show for the next few days and we can relax somewhat following the premiere," Michael says.

"Yeah. Let's do that. I gotta go back to the gang. We're almost ready for warm-up," she says and he nods with a friendly smile.

In the next few minutes, Gerard, assisted by Michael, brings the team up to speed with their plan. The dancers, as one, get into position and the audio-visual system kicks in, setting them in motion.

Michael, watching them from the sidelines, is very pleased with the dynamics of the scene, the dancers making the stage finally come alive.

At the end of two difficult, physically demanding scenes, Gerard and Michael look at one another and their silent connection say that they are on target to say the least. Francis also nods at the two - *we're getting close.*

After their ten minute break and costume time the dancers come back with new vigor and passion, making the theatre vibrate under their intense live performance.

***

The next three nights before the premiere are going just as well but by the last day the tension is almost palpable among all members of the group, including Michael. The performance is clock-work but everybody is nervous almost to the point of breakdown.

In the morning hours of the big day, Michael receives a telephone call from Stephanie. She is calling from Toronto, as she has just driven into the downtown core. Michael who has been expecting her eagerly drives down in his Mustang and meets her at a café he has chosen. The reunion is exciting as always when two lovers get together after a few days of separation.

Michael learns from Stephanie that Cristina is recuperating fast and she is eager to come back to work.

"That is out of the question though right now," Stephanie says. "I spoke with her doctor and she said that she needs a few more weeks to heal and regain her strength, along with some physiotherapy."

"You want me go up there whilst she recovers?" Michael asks her and she smiles, pleased by his offer.

"That's very sweet of you. We will discuss the options maybe after your big opening night. How is it going?" she asks, genuinely interested.

"We all are nervous as hell but on the other hand I think we are prepared for this," he says and she loves his nervous boyish looks.

"I'm definitely looking forward to tonight," she says, taking his hand in hers and squeezing it. "There is a good buzz in the city about it."

"Thanks," he says softly. "What's happening in Belgium?" he asks her.

"I'm glad you asked. One of my designer clothes manufacturing outlets is there. I just came from it. We renewed our contract for another year," she says and looks at him, pretty proud of her accomplishment.

Michael just looks at her and his heart misses a beat.

"What?" Stephanie asks, sensing his emotions toward her.

"Oh, nothing... I just missed you," he says with fake casualness.

"Me too," she admits. "So, what you want to do for the rest of the day, mister director?" she asks in a way which is filled with desire he does not miss.

"How about we go back to the hotel and I show you my stamp collection," he throws in the classical cliché. She laughs delightedly.

"Wow," she coos. "That sounds so exciting... let's do it."

They finish their coffees, leave a generous tip on the table and exit the café.

"Follow me," he says simply and she nods whilst lighting up a cigarette and getting into her red sports car.

The rest of the morning they spend in bed, making love, cuddling, enjoying each other's company like never before. The tension of the upcoming premiere and the following new stage in both of their lives makes the day intense with anxiety, excitement and anticipation.

After they shower and leisure around the suite in hotel propriety housecoats, Stephanie notices that Michael does not have anything decent to wear for the gala opening.

"What are you wearing tonight?" she enquires.

"Oh, that. I was thinking about running out this afternoon and buy a sports jacket," Michael says casually.

"I don't think so, mister," Stephanie says, reacting with a cringe. "We'd better get dressed so we can step out and get you something decent to wear. C'mon," she says, suddenly excited with the prospect.

"Okay," Michael grumbles reluctantly and begins to dress.

Within minutes, under some gentle persuasion from Stephanie, the two of them are dressed casually and leave the hotel taking Stephanie's car, with her driving. As they drive she looks attentively at the neighborhood, her keen and versed eyes spotted out clothing stores for men. They drive for a while until she parks the car in front of a boutique store. Michael looks at her alarmed.

"I can't afford to shop here," he says.

"But I can," she says laughing.

"You sure of this?" he asks half-heartedly.

"Very sure."

They enter the store and are immediately approached by an older, very classy gentleman who offers them assistance. Stephanie and the gentleman step aside and start talking in small French voices, occasionally glancing at Michael. After a short while the gentleman addresses Michael.

"This way, please."

Michael follows the store manager and Stephanie to a section of fine dress shirts, ties and suits. The two of them go through a couple of racks, occasionally glimpsing at Michael who just stands there. After a few checks they pick a couple of suits and a couple of shirts for Michael to try out.

He takes the garments and wordlessly goes into a cloak booth, closing the door behind him. When he comes out a few minutes later, the store manager and Stephanie drop their jaws at his appearance. The suit is elegant and falls causally but perfectly on his well-built physique.

The shirt with a fine tie loosely tied into a knot complements the new shoes.

"How's this?" he asks, unconcerned.

"I think we should stop right here," says the manager watching him with expert eyes.

"I agree," Stephanie says. "Make sure he likes it too, though," she says and pulls Michael by his hand in front of a full body mirror. "What you think?"

"Good enough for me," he says once he briefly glances over the mirror image.

"I think you look a million bucks," she says happily. The manager nods in agreement.

"So be it then," Michael concludes, shrugging his shoulders and while Stephanie takes care of the billing process, he returns to the changing booth and removes the suit.

Stephanie pays for the outfit while the Manager places it in a box.

"You didn't have to do this," he tells her once they are on the street.

"I didn't, but I love to do it," she says. You are now also representing a chic fashion clothing chain, don't forget. Image is everything, remember?"

"I expect some feedback from you on the images you'll see tonight at the show," he says smiling.

"Don't you worry about that, mister... what now?"

"We can go down to the lake and catch some fresh air at the lakeside," he proposes.

"Sounds good," she says as they both get into the car and she drives them to the lake promenade.

Walking the boardwalk hand-in-hand has a feeling of magic in it. They both realize this when several young people crossing their path smile in their direction. It's so good to be together again and it shows.

They go for a long walk, chat about the play, detail some business for Montreal and eventually return to Stephanie's car and drive back to the hotel, fresh and alert.

Time flies when they are together, as always. They have lunch in the room, make love and sit on the small balcony watching the city and sip coffees for a long time - just hanging out - and it feels wonderful, since neither one of them is used to this type of idle time. When the early evening comes upon them, Stephanie starts doing her hair in the bathroom.

"You get dressed, mister director... show me what you got! Add some attitude while you are at it," she says watching him.

"That always comes with the package," he jokes and slowly starts gathering his garments. "What kind of attitude would you like for tonight, miss?" he asks her.

"How about a bad-boy/avant-garde director Attitude?"

"That's easy... that always comes naturally," he says, smiling and starting to get dressed. Stephanie smiles to herself and steals a look at him. She really has a powerful on-again, off-again, on this guy he met more than three years ago on the wild shores of the Black Sea and barely seen him since. They met a few odd times during these years and they broke it off more than once with powerful emotions all over the map, just to seek out each other again with yet more passion and driving desires. She gave up trying to figure out this strange phenomenon which only happens with her and Michael, and decided to let her instincts guide her when it came up the subject of this, wildish, charismatic and unpredictable guy.

When she finishes her last touches with her makeup and steps out from the bathroom she stops at the door pleasantly shocked by what she sees. Michael stands there, his back turned to her, talking on the phone. He is fully dressed for the gala opening and he looks excellent. She comes behind him and rising up on her tiptoes, kisses him behind his ear. Michael shivers vehemently and nearly drops the telephone receiver.

"It's Stephanie... she molested me again!" he tells Gerard who laughs in the receiver. "That's fine, I'll see you in the booth in about an hour," he hangs up the receiver and turning around and without any warning kisses Stephanie on the mouth. She responds feverishly and they wrap their arms around each other and after parting their lips hold each other tight for a long moment. When Stephanie gently pushes him away he is watching her with lover's eyes.

"I like that look, mister director, but I have to get dressed for the gala," she says, stepping away from him and starting to pick her fresh clothes from her suitcase. Michael sits down on one of the loungers and watches her with great pleasure.

"You make me nervous," she says, glancing at him but she does not mean it.

"Sorry, but you see, I take great pleasure in watching those nice curves of yours," he says and she blushes a little, pleased.

She finishes dressing and turns toward him: "How do I look?" she asks, watching him carefully for a true statement.

"You look beautiful, *mon cher*," he says and she is indeed plain stunning - her carefully picked designer clothes are simple but sophisticated and at the same time easy-wear but dressy, nothing short of the fashion and trend setter outfitter which she really is.

"Thank you." She looks at him. "Shall we?" He takes a step toward her and kisses her on her forehead.

"We shall," he says and they leave the hotel suite.

When the elevator reaches the lobby level and the two step out from the car and walk toward the exit, many guests and personnel alike stop and watch them in awe because they look awesome together. The young good looks are one thing, but the invisible power of love coming through tenfold and making them glow is another.

Acknowledging the onlookers politely, they walk outside and take Stephanie's car which she didn't bother to take to the garage, leaving it parked on the street.

"I'm a nervous wreck," Michael says after they get in.

"That's understandable. You have worked so hard for so long to make this show perfect, but from this point on it is totally out of your control, right?" Michael nods. "Now the play has a life of its own with the people you directed to execute it. It is their time to shine now," she says looking at him.

"My words exactly. How come you're so perceptive about matters of the theatre?" he says smiling, looking at her.

"I've been around live drama and theatre too, earlier in my life," she says casually as they drive toward the theatre. "I still love it," she adds. Michael watches her perfect profile and feels like rushing over and kissing her again. He refrains, as she is driving in busy traffic.

After a few more blocks they enter the Harbor Front area and find a spot up front on the packed parking lot with a small plaque marked *ARTISTIC DIRECTOR* beside another one title *CHOREOGRAPHER*. "You deserve it," she says, taking his spot as the two exit the car and head for the main entrance this time.

The place is packed in spite of the fact that is still relatively early. Various people from the live theatre and dancing circles are all present, dressed for a gala opening show. Most of men wear tuxedos and dark suits whilst the women each make their own individual statements with the latest trends. There is a cheerful atmosphere in the theatre. It's a dance/play show to watch and enjoy and maybe to praise or criticize. The pressure is on for the creators, Michael included.

Nevertheless, when Stephanie and Michael enter the theatre hall there is an instant buzz. People are watching with pleased smiles, others with squinted, jealous eyes and others yet just pleasuring their sight with the couple's presence. First they run into Gerard and his pretty girlfriend and introductions are made.

"He talks a lot about you and now I can see why," Gerard says to Stephanie.

"Really?" Stephanie asks. "I didn't think he would do that."

"I didn't," Michael says casually. "He's making it all up."

"I believe we meet the real creators of this night's gala," Michael says and waves to Francis and Hillary who walk towards their group, saluting many people they know, on the way. The introductions are made and more and more people are staring at Stephanie and Michael - but they are not even aware of it, Michael too nervous right now and Stephanie too busy helping ease his anxiety.

The six of them, Francis and Hillary, Gerard and Tracy, his girlfriend, and Michael and Stephanie, walk upstairs and take their gala center booth dedicated for the creators of the shows. Since the theatre hall is lit up a lot of people are looking up and watching them, the key people of the show.

"This had better go well tonight," Francis says, twisting in his central and visible seat. "A lot of people are staring at us. What might we have done wrong?" he says half-jokingly.

"It the performance goes as planned, there will be no need for us to dodge bullets or rotten tomatoes," Hillary responds laughing.

"That's the spirit," Gerard says, as nervous as one can be, never moving his eyes from the closed curtains of the stage.

In the next few minutes the hall lights dim out and a spot light appears on the stage, in front of the curtains. As the hall immediately falls silent to the point that we can hear a pin drop, an elegant gentleman in an impeccable tux and long gray hair, approaches the center stage from the side. He steps into the spot light where a microphone is instantly lowering from the ceiling, in front of him.

He looks at the great audience and without further ado leans into the microphone:

"Good evening, ladies and gentlemen. My name is John Cee and I represent the Performing Arts Society of Toronto. I would like to take the time to introduce to you this brand new artistic development accomplished by filmmakers, dancers, live drama and writing students from the Ryerson University."

There is polite applause and then John Cee addresses his audience again briefly. "Without further ado, please welcome to out show... Gilgamesh."

The spot light dims and follows John Cee as he exits the stage. The moment he disappears backstage, the lights starts dancing in provocative colors, almost fluid, as the dramatic sound effects fade in, building a somber and captivating mood in the audience. Even Stephanie and Gerard bite their fingernails in expectation... or something they can't quite define - it is a powerful emotion without a shape or name, but dominant and almost overwhelming.

And that is exactly how Michael wanted it to be when he designed it and rehearsed with Chuck two nights before the opening gala. As the audience tenses up under the power of the music and visual effects, he gives a little smile - it has worked.

When the tension reaches its carefully designed climax and the audience, including his friends, sit in their seats on the edge of their comfort, the lighting and the music alike, suddenly changes. The stage is invaded by light and bright, warm colors as the music transforms in the rhythm of the lighting throwing the audience into a realm of delight and ease - it is now that the curtains raise fast and the dancing group in their best costumes conquer the moment and their vibrant energy of motion locks their eyes into a carousel which shakes the soul.

It is now that Stephanie, her face flushed, looks at Michael and silently places her hand into his palm. He squeezes it lightly without moving his eyes from the stage. Everything he worked for so hard with his friends, is happening right here, right now, in front of his eyes. The scenes develop in dramatic crescendo, from one to the next, stealing the audience from their seats and transporting them in a world so different, so dynamic and bizarre but so wonderful at the same time that they start to relax and ride with the main flow, so carefully designed by Michael, Gerard, Hillary and Francis.

When the music is finally decreasing in intensity, trickling down to a whisper, the dancers, in character, taper off their intensity and gradually freeze on center stage. It is the end of a fast, first act.

There is a deep silence.

A moment later the audience explodes in applause, several people offering fervent, standing ovations. Michael wipes off some sweat from his heated forehead and looks at Stephanie. Her passionate look tells him that they have done something right so far with this show.

The second act starts slowly and builds up its momentum with high power dance and narration which takes the audience through a whole rainbow of emotions, but the end result is a cleansing emotion, almost like a catharsis.

The whole show and the performance is a success and Michael himself is nearly in tears because he knows that this show will pave the road for many of these young talented dancers along with Gerard, Hillary and Francis. At this glorious moment he does not even remember that he has also been a key part of it, but that is okay too.

Chapter 16

The warm summer of 1980 in Toronto, Ontario makes, yet again, significant changes in Michael's life. The Gala Night has been a great success for the young team of creators and performers.

When the morning newspapers publish daring critiques and accolades about the Gilgamesh show at the Harbor Front, Michael knows that his young team of friends have carved a path for a challenging and successful future. In spite of his deep passion for the theatre he keeps his promise and a week later, returns to Montreal to take the reins of the boutique shop in the Old Port.

He will continue to drive back and forth between Toronto and Montreal, attending the clothing business in Quebec and continuing his passion for the performing arts in Ontario. He enjoys both, especially when Stephanie decides to stay longer and longer periods of time with him on every one of her numerous trips to Canada.

Epilogue

Toronto, Canada
Eighteen Years Later

It's a sunny afternoon in the trendy business district of downtown Toronto, Yorkville Street. Michael is sitting at a table in one of the sidewalk cafes talking on his mobile phone: "But of course. I fully agree with that, Bast. I can't wait to see them... tomorrow at seven pm is just fine. I'll meet you at that little bar on Terminal 3, the name escapes me-"

"*The Three O'Douls*," corrects Bastian from the other end.

"That's the one. I'll be there tomorrow and then we can come to my cottage in the Muskoka, catch up a little."

"How are you doing? Haven't seen you in years."

"*Four* years."

"Right. It feels like a long time; I'll see you tomorrow."

"Yeah... tomorrow."

He terminates his call and takes a sip from his coffee and Brandy, turning his focus to a bunch of pages in a folder in front of him... but right now his mind is somewhere else. Removing his spectacles, he stares across the concrete downtown jungle.

***

A large four-by-four followed by a trendy BMW enter the long, winding driveway leading to Michael's cottage, a spacious post-and-beam house on the lake in Muskoka cottage country, about a hundred miles north of Toronto.

Michael drives his SUV towards a large log cabin on the shore of Lake Muskoka.

He stops in front of the cottage and turns to the BMW following him where four people are getting out looking around curiously.

"Welcome to the Muskoka woods," he says, happy to see his friends. Bastian, Jee-Jee, Klava and a handsome boy of about ten look at him from the BMW. They ascend the large stairs leading to the main entrance and enter the cottage, following Michael.

The place is large and spacious with cathedral ceilings supported by large raw-looking beams. Floor-to-ceiling windows look at the pretty lake outside the cottage. The place is not luxurious but earthy, cozy and comfortable.

"This is beautiful," Klava says, looking around and noticing a large framed photograph showing a beautiful woman and a teenage boy.

The young boy on her side, Damian, her son, walks to the large windows and stares at the lake.

"I like your lake," he says.

Michael smiles, "It's not only mine but tomorrow, if you'd like, we can go on a boat ride. It's a pretty fast boat."

The young boy is excited. "That would be *so* great."

"That sounds so dangerous," Klava says "I don't know, Michael..." She stops and looks at her friends.

"Right... this coming from a young girl who survived that tanker ride?" Michael says empathetically. "Don't worry, *mom*. We'll go for a ride and we'll be safe and have some fun too," he says.

"Sorry, Michael," Klava says. "Ever since Peter is gone I have acted way over-protectively with Damian. I'm so afraid for him. He's the only one I've got."

The friends all fall silent for a few long moments in the memory of Peter, their old friend from the Refugee Camp.

After a while Michael breaks the silence. "What happened?"

Klava sighs, "As you know from the camp, he was a top notch architect, specializing in heavy structures and military installations. To make it brief, the Canadian Armed Forces asked him to fly down to Iraq and fix some bridges for them. He died under an insurgent attack on their compound."

"We all miss him," Michael says.

His friends nod silently.

"What about you, Jee-Jee? It's been about seven years since I've seen you last," Michael says, looking at his elegant and stylish friend.

Jee-Jee blushes like a girl. "My, my, my... I became a successful corporate Lawyer, much-hated by certain groups, and in my spare time I'm a high-class "call-girl," he quickly looks at his friends, "Just for kicks!" His friends laugh. "I'm filthy rich," Jee-Jee continues. "I do the 'call' thing just for fun. I love to cross-dress."

Bastian laughs, "I know that. You borrowed many of my outfits to modify them into unrecognizable objects which looked great on you only," he says.

"Many of my clothes too," adds Michael. The Lawyer/ hooker Jee-Jee laughs delightedly.

"C'mon guys, make yourselves at home. Anything to drink, eat?" Michael asks, good host that he is. They shake their heads for now. "Klava, tells us more about you. It's been a long time. How's life in England?"

"Damian and I live in Lancaster now, but we spend a lot of time all over Europe. We still live like gypsies and we love it," she says. "Damian has many competitions, including this one coming up in Toronto. He loves chess and is very good at it."

"Peter and you both played it very well," Bastian says.

"He learnt most of it from his father. He had a real passion for chess.... just like Damian," Klava says. She becomes emotional, "It's so good to see you guys. I just want to let you know that I crossed paths in Europe with many people from the camp in the last few years and they all have fond memories."

"It definitely was an eventful transition in our lives," adds Bastian. "But how about turning to the present and future; the next generation," he says.

"Speaking of which, Bastian, where is Matthew?" Klava asks him.

"He's at school. Taking criminal science at UBC in Vancouver," Bastian explains.

Klava turns to Michael. "What about Christopher?"

"Oh. He's in Paris with Stephanie for a few weeks. He met a girl there he really likes. He's eighteen and pretty wild," Michael says.

Klava smiles at old memories: "Not nearly as wild as his father at his age, I'm sure," she says.

Michael shakes his head and sighs at the same memories, "It's great to have you here. I'll make some coffee and something for Damian in a minute," he says. He gets up from the lounger. "Come. I want to show you something," he notes and they stand up, following him to the lower floor where there is an audio-visual home theatre, all set up with sound and large seats in front of a giant screen.

"Make yourselves comfortable," he says as they all sit in the deep seats, looking around curiously. Once they are all seated and comfortable, he dims the lights and activates some buttons on his remote control.

A whirling, stirring sounds effect fades in, instantly getting his friends' attention. An aerial shot of the campo di profughi, Trieste, Italy fades in.

"No way!" exclaims Bastian.

"Way... just watch it," says Michael with a small smile.

CPSIA information can be obtained at www.ICGtesting.com
Printed in the USA
LVOW13s0009020514

384116LV00001B/3/P